A Heavenly Interception

Book Two in the Anarchy of Angels Trilogy

Eddie Georgonicas

Credits

Cover Artist: Gemini Judson
Editor: Kitty Carlisle

Printed in the United States of America

Dedication

A big thank you to Carla Beer. And for their endless support on my writing journey, love to my daughters Lucinda and Elisha. Also to and in memory to a wonderful and loving grandmother, Pandora Georgonicas

CHAPTER ONE
The Contest

Like an excited child asking his teacher for permission, the referee's hand flew up. "Ippon!" he said crisply. The point brought the fight to an abrupt stop.

Johnny had been awarded the full point, with a front kick to Tony's midsection. After feinting with a right punch, Johnny had deftly raised his right knee and thrust out his right foot. The ball of his foot had caught Tony in the lower ribs, delivering the scoring blow.

They were fighting in the National Karate Tournament. Tony stood taller than Johnny. Height ran in Tony's family and, at an impressive six foot and two inches, Tony used his height and slender build to his fighting advantage—mostly. Johnny was stockier and of average height, which put him a few inches shorter than his friend and current opponent.

His flexibility and speed, in this instance, conquered Tony's height.

Tony didn't know what was worse, the blow to his ribs or the seconds he had left to try and recover the score. They had been tied at three half points each, but the full point, the Ippon, had taken Johnny into a clear lead. The score now sat at five and a half points to three.

One more point against Tony would take Johnny's score to six, giving him full match point and victory. Tony knew he had to fight adventurously to try and recover the Ippon in a very short space of time. The corner adjudicator had already shouted a warning for thirty seconds left. His only hope now was a draw.

Tony had to push aside the pain throbbing from his lower rib cage. This was not a time to think about the bruising, it was a time to muster up every bit of energy he had left.

The referee lined the young fighters up.

"Hajimei." Immediately upon the referee's command to start, Tony leapt into the attack.

Only seconds had passed. "Yamai!" shouted the corner adjudicator. The fighters stopped instantly.

"You've got to be kidding!" exclaimed Tony to no one in particular. Among the sound and commotion of the tournament, the only people to hear him were Johnny and the man scoring the fight.

The referee approached the two young contenders. "Well done, boys. That was an exhilarating fight."

He then turned to Tony. "Regardless of the outcome, son, you fought well."

He stood with one contender on each side, waiting several seconds as a few words were spoken over the microphone. It was the typical winner's announcement, bathing the contender in short-lived glory.

The referee raised Johnny's hand and a congratulatory cheer rose up from the crowd. It was then that it truly sank in; Tony had been defeated by his opponent, long-time friend and neighbor, Johnny Black.

George, their instructor, was saddened.

He had entered himself and his two favorite students into the tournament. As luck would have it, the boys had been drawn to fight each other in the second round; an elimination round. It was evident to all that one of George's most prized students would not be going on to potentially represent Australia in the Internationals.

But a decision had been reached and George's younger brother, Johnny, had been the victor today—a bittersweet victory at best.

As Tony left the fighting mat, George intercepted him at the edge of the fighting arena. "I don't know what to say. You fought well," said George.

"Thank you, Sensei," said Tony, respecting the traditions of Karate and his Sensei instructor.

"That was a tough fight," said Johnny, trying to lift the spirits of his young friend.

"I'll be okay. It just sucks we had to meet in the second round."

Tony was competitive by nature, which accounted for the 'dark cloud' hanging over his head. But his friends and fellow Karate students realized his emotional state would be short lived.

But before it was, there was a bit more to be said.

"To be eliminated so soon—it's unfortunate, but it's the luck of the draw, I'm afraid," said George, who now had to concentrate on his own fighting efforts.

He had won his second-round fight. Three more wins had him a guaranteed place on the International Team. There was still about half an hour before Johnny would go up against his next opponent and closer to an hour before George would fight his.

These events never ran on time.

George kept his eyes on the back wall of the stadium. The display board was enormous. It gave a great visual from every corner of this huge gymnasium, which was big enough to hold four basketball courts and plenty of spectators.

They were now announcing the fighting agendas through to the finals.

"Jesus!" exclaimed George, his seriousness quickly turning to jest.

"What?" asked Johnny.

"It's you and me, little bro. Fourth round!"

The random draw had not served the South Australian team well. It potentially meant only one South Australian fighter could go on to represent the team of six, which would be sent to Munich,

Germany, to fight at the International Karate Championships.

The clock ticked by ever so slowly. In the scorching heat, the next thirty minutes seemed to take an age. But it wouldn't be long before the moment of truth arrived.

"Stretch out," instructed George.

Tony went with his friend to one corner and helped with his warm-ups.

Soon the announcement was made and the time to fight had come.

Johnny lined up with a fighter from interstate, an opponent from country Western Australia. Johnny stared across the mat, focused on his opponent's mid-section. He slowly ran his eyes up his opponent, stopping when he got to about six feet and four inches. He was very skinny, quite tall and had no issues with demonstrating his speed and flexibility into the open air of the fighting arena. This didn't faze Johnny; height and build meant nothing, but fighting spirit was everything.

"Watch your distance," said George.

"Close in quick, use your hands," added Tony.

The strategies were being fired upon Johnny one after the other, but Johnny had to focus on his fight, concentrate on relaxing and releasing the tension. It was only then that he would be able to strike with the speed of speeds.

Standing on the outer edge of the ring, Johnny stood with feet together and hands down by his side; straight and upright, like a soldier at attention. He then bowed from the waist. Tilting his upper body forward slightly, he paused for the briefest of moments and then returned to attention. This was considered courteous and was used as a sign of respect before the fight.

He then walked over to the middle of the ring, shook his opponent's hand and took up his position on the fighting mat.

Johnny's opponent bounced around on the spot, little jumps and hops back and forth and side to side. As the fight had not yet begun, he was not allowed to move off the marked starting point.

Maybe it was nerves or maybe it was his way of loosening up before the start. Either way, Johnny chose to do the opposite and remained in his fighting stance, feet planted solidly on the ground. His right foot was slightly ahead of his left, his right fist out in front, his left a fist's length away from his belly button. Johnny remained calm and focused on his tall opponent as he watched every bounce.

"Hajime," said the referee. The fighter from Western Australia continued to dance around, only now more vigorously. Trying to look for the scoring opportunity, he moved from side to side with great agility.

Johnny remained solidly planted, trying to entice an attack. He had to close the distance. His opponent was agile and flexible. Combined with his above-average height, he was a formidable opponent.

Suddenly, the Western Australian threw a deceptive move. He aimed his roundhouse kick to the body, but then redirected it to the head. Johnny fell for it.

"Ippon!" shouted the referee. The execution was a clean strike to an open and unguarded face, unopposed and with mild contact.

The cocky young fighter from the west bounced around like he had won a gold medal in the Olympics.

"C'mon, Johnny, you can get it back!" shouted Tony from the sidelines.

Johnny had taken the point personally, losing sight of the ultimate objective. It must have been very obvious because his brother's words had got to him.

"Let it go, Johnny. Focus on the fight," demanded George.

The referee lined up the two fighters. Once again, one danced while the other had his feet planted solid. The fighting styles had now been differentiated and set. The referee swung down his arm. "Hajime."

Soon the cocky opponent had dropped to one knee. He put his guard up and, by crouching and covering up, made his body and head area as small and as guarded as possible. Johnny stepped back, confused by the tactic.

"Fight, fight!" demanded Johnny.

The Western Australian knew exactly what his unethical tactic meant to his opponent. Simply put, he had shut down Johnny's opportunities to technically score a point.

Johnny showed off well-executed technique after well-executed technique.

His attacks were timed to just touch the body and head striking areas, as per the rules of the tournament. No excessive power strikes to the head were allowed, while a bit more force was permitted for body strikes.

Johnny maintained his integrity, keeping his techniques well controlled and beautifully executed. Finding the opening and making contact earned a half point, a full point if the attack was undefended. However, Johnny could simply not score a point.

"C'mon, ref!" shouted Tony, frustrated.

The crowd did not take well to the unsportsmanlike tactics and began to boo the fight. Johnny didn't know what to do; he could keep throwing out kick after kick until the end of the round, but it would serve little purpose.

Even the referee didn't know what to do and allowed the fight to continue.

The boos got louder, as shouts of disappointment came in from the spectators.

Technically, the cocky Western Australian had not done anything wrong other than exploit the rules of the competition.

Johnny's patience was turning into anger. His calmness festered into the beginnings of rage, bubbling up like a volcano ready to spit out its lava.

It had all got a bit too much for him.

He stepped back just enough to throw his strongest

roundhouse kick. There was no holding back this time, as he followed through with all of his speed and might.

The roundhouse smashed through the opponent's guard, smacking him square on the lower jaw. The cocky fighter went down for the count.

Johnny knew what this meant for his chances to get into the finals. He wasn't too fussed and was more engrossed in the cheers of the crowd, lapping up every moment. He smiled back at the crowd, acknowledging their cheers of approval. His hands went up a little and he did his own little dance in his own precious little spot on the fighting mat.

The referee stopped the fight. He pulled Johnny to his corner and called the medic to the mat.

The cocky young fighter was holding his jaw in extreme pain.

As tradition dictated, Johnny kneeled on the mat facing away from his opponent, looking directly into the eyes of his brother, who shook his head in disbelief. George didn't have to say a word; his eyes said it all.

It didn't look too good for the drowsy and concussed Western Australian, who stood up, nursing his dislocated jaw. The medic went to have a quiet word with the referee. After a short exchange, the referee called off the fight. Johnny was about to learn defeat did not necessarily equate to winning.

Johnny was immediately disqualified. His opponent had won the fight, but could not go on to the next round.

Johnny bowed and walked off, refusing to acknowledge his unsporting opponent.

"Bloody referee! He should never have allowed that!" said Johnny.

"You threw it all away, and for what?" said George disapprovingly.

"What did you want me to do—dance around for three minutes while pretty boy sits there and does nothing?" Johnny was growing impatient. Deep down, he knew what he had thrown away, but, unfortunately, he had got caught up in the moment and had done something he would come to regret.

"C'mon, guys, let's get a drink." Tony tried to mediate the small feud between the brothers.

As the trio walked off, the crowd was still cheering. Johnny stopped, turned and smiled back, giving the cheering crowd a wave.

It was still a half hour before George was due to fight. Johnny hoped George would not spend the time on a lecture about sportsmanship.

Back in the tournament, the excitable crowd and sweaty participants contributed to the stale air that filled the large stadium. There were several fighting arenas set up; more than enough fighting entertainment for the fans and friends of the competition.

The finals were drawing near and the pressure to perform was high. George's time was fast approaching. By the third round, there were only two states which still had teams: the host state of Victoria and South Australia. There was only one fighter left representing South Australia, and George couldn't be prouder of his efforts to represent his home city of Adelaide.

George's next fight went like clockwork; a clean and fair fight with an array of fighting techniques thrown by both opponents. George had clearly out skilled his opponent, obtaining an easy win of five half points to one.

The next round for George was an instant win. The young cocky fighter from Western Australia had been incapacitated. The forfeit, thanks to his younger brother, saw George go straight into the final round.

This gave George the opportunity to watch the fight that decided his next opponent. George watched intensely, trying to ascertain weaknesses, strengths and potential opportunities.

Both were good fighters, but fought completely differently. One opponent moved a lot, danced and pranced, bobbing in and out looking for the opening. The other preferred to mix it up a bit.

He settled, then stepped side to side unpredictably, and then simply held his stance, like a cheetah waiting to pounce. When he moved, he moved with speed and ferocity.

The battle was long and intense, but the eventual victor was the dancer.

Final fights were being fought and Australian representatives were being decided on. Australia was sending a team of six fighters and, so far, five had been chosen.

This was George's moment and, as tradition dictated, George bowed and entered the fighting arena. Before commencing, the two fighters faced off briefly. When the fight began, George's opponent danced and pranced around as he had done in his previous fight, with his home city of Melbourne supporters cheering him on.

This Karate practitioner was well known and well respected throughout his home state. "Gino! Gino! Gino," echoed around the stadium.

Many had left their stadium seats to surround the center mat. The last fight of the day and the ultimate decision maker.

George had to block this from his mind and focus on the task at hand. George switched his fighting style, never settling, trying to remain as unpredictable as possible.

He was steady and stationary for a little while and then pranced and danced, switched and changed, and never allowed his opponent to anticipate what might come next.

The fight was very much a face off, with very few techniques being thrown.

Neither participant wanted to over expose himself. Whilst there was intense concentration on the fighting mat, the crowds were starting to lose interest in a fight which appeared to drag on and on.

It remained a battle of minds, until George saw an opportunity arise.

Without hesitation, he stepped forward slightly and twisted, executing a back kick. The heel of his foot went straight out and caught the light-footed fighter square in the ribs.

The opponent staggered back, trying to catch the wind that had been knocked out of his body. The strike was fair and within competition regulations. George was awarded the full point.

"Nursing his ribs a bit, isn't he?" Johnny said loudly to Tony.

Some cheeky laughter followed between the two friends, who were sitting right by the fighting arena. The fight may have been boring, but these two young friends were excited for their instructor and mentor.

The winded opponent fought cautiously for the rest of the round. George had not only knocked the wind out of him, but also his fighting spirit.

He continued to move with grace and speed, but seldom attacked. George tried to score, but found it hard to land a scoring point.

The fight ended.

Not the most exciting of fights, but a most exciting outcome for the three South Australians.

George was jumping in the air as Tony and Johnny jumped all over him, cheering for their sensei's victory. A victory that would have him represent his country in the sport to which he had dedicated his life.

George's victory was their victory.

CHAPTER TWO
Why Can't I Settle in Heaven?

A former wife, mother and grandmother walked the open plains with her eyes fixed on the distant horizon.

Why won't I settle in Heaven? I am not sure I like playing nurse to wounded souls, Angels or spirits. It seems like the attacks come more frequently now. I sometimes feel like I am back in war-torn Greece, a place I left a long time ago. But the memories of war never leave.

Damn you, Devil!

The Devil has all of Heaven worried. His attacks on Heavenly ground were few and far between, but now—now it seems like it happens every other day.

We're holding our own, but we pay the price of war. And so it seems, death exists even in Heaven. Figure that out!

There are rules here, too; the rules of Heaven. But why should I go through it? The Angels have that part rehearsed to a tee. And I need to stick around for this. These newly arrived souls are about to be lectured by the Angels and then it's up to me to play counselor.

That I don't mind so much. It gives me a sense of motherly purpose.

Pam stood on the outer edge of a gathering of freshly arrived souls, whose formal introduction to Heaven was about to be had. She knew what she had to do and she was good at it. However, this particular part of the process was not for her. For now, she did not interfere and remained an outside observer.

"When an earthly soul enters the spiritual plane, by default it will enter the Kingdom of Heaven. Angels and loved ones that have already crossed over will then try and nurture the newly arrived soul," said the Angel Raphael.

"It can be a difficult transition for some," added the Archangel Gabriel.

Like Olympic athletes, the Angels stood tall and toned. Their chiseled faces and handsome features would have put them in line for any male modeling position, but their morals and egos were above that.

Angels stood for the greater good and lived for the Heavenly cause. Above all, they were the protectors of Heaven and those who walked in its loving presence.

Being rewarded for good looks and muscular physique was not high on the angelic agenda. What was, however, was fighting the evil that lurked beyond the Transitional Border, a sinister presence that lived deep within a land of fire and brimstone.

"Lucifer is always on the lookout for newly arrived souls. Souls he can perhaps nurture in a different way, an evil way," said the Angel Raphael.

The Angels were advising a few young adults who had tragically lost their lives in a boating accident. Their death had been quick and painless, but their transition into Heaven was taking a bit more time.

The youngsters had been given some time to themselves to reflect on their lives and come to terms with the realization they had now crossed over.

They now had to move on.

The initial period alone helped prepare them for what was to come, and understanding some of the fundamental laws of Heaven could sometimes help those who had died in sudden circumstances.

It still took time to heal a soul whose death had been tragic and unfortunate, but time was something Heaven had plenty of.

"When the life lived has been good and worthy of a

Heavenly place, then the counseling, the mentoring and the transition from an existence on Earth to an existence in Heaven is of no consequence. The soul quickly learns to adapt to his or her new existence and is willing to help out in the Heavenly matters and the way of our God almighty," said the Archangel Gabriel.

"Now, in your new existence as a member of Heaven's family and in our true form of Heavenly light and pure energy, should this be damaged, should this energy force dissipate and therefore, for a better term, die, then it will, by default, re-enter Heaven. And yes, death exists in Heaven," instructed the Angel Raphael.

"But there is much counseling involved," added the Archangel Michael.

"Heavenly souls can rarely comprehend dying. There is a lot of time and energy spent in dealing with this type of Heavenly phenomenon.

"Lucifer knows this and is always on the lookout to exploit such confusion, always trying to tempt the soul into leading an existence of temptation and evil; taking the soul to live a life in the depths of brimstone and sulfur—a place we call Hell," continued Michael.

This conversation was perfectly executed, each Angel knowing his cue, when to come in and what to say. A speech they, with no doubt, had delivered before many newly arrived spirits over the course of the existence of man.

Archangel Michael went on. "Now, there is choice in the matter. Do we, as a heavenly entity, counsel the confused spirit with the help of loved ones who have crossed over? Or do we send the soul down to live its next incarnation as man or woman? And should we decide to re-incarnate and send the soul down to live its next existence, then it is mostly done with the help and guidance of Heaven.

"As Angels and spirits who serve the way of the Holy Trinity, the Father, the Son and the Holy Spirit, we try and direct this man or woman to live a life of good and righteousness.

"This will make their next transition into the heavenly plane a much, much easier task."

The young new arrivals to Heaven listened intently as they were being lectured. They sat in awe, mesmerized by the beauty and presence of the three Angels.

There was little difference between the Archangels Michael and Gabriel and the Angel Raphael. They all stood impressively tall, with athletic builds and handsome features.

However, the Archangels Michael and Gabriel were of a sturdier build than Raphael, as they were the warrior-class Angels; the fighters and protectors of Heaven.

Their heavenly beauty was strengthened by the awesome, white swan-like wings poised on their shoulder blades. As the Angels spoke, their angelic wings were fully extended, close to four meters in total wingspan, perfectly trimmed with not a feather out of place. They added visual grace to the delivery of a heavenly lecture.

The young new arrivals continued to listen as the Angels progressed with their heavenly lesson.

There was empathy in their voices. The Angels, however, were not sympathetic. Sympathy suggested the angelic hierarchy shared in the grief or emotion of loss. This was not the case; they simply identified with the emotion of crossing over. It was Earth which provided the preparation for a lifetime in Heaven.

The Angels knew Heaven was the better place and Earth was the afterlife. Their lecture was always delivered from that viewpoint. It was in Heaven that they would all find their place and purpose in life.

The Angels continued their instructive talk. "It does not always go to plan, my young friends," said Raphael. "Sometimes the spirit is so disturbed that when it starts to live its new life on Earth, it lives it filled with cruelty, anger, destruction and all things bad and evil. Our efforts sometimes fail. The soul can re-enter Heaven in a state which is far worse than when we last saw it. This is when Lucifer will pounce. He is almost guaranteed to take the soul into the depths of Hades," said Raphael.

"We try and protect these souls, offering much of Heaven's resources and time. We try very hard to change and nurture the soul back into an existence of good. We take much effort in hiding these souls from the prying eyes of Lucifer himself," said the Archangel Michael.

"What about Angels dying? I thought you said you couldn't live life as man or woman?" asked an inquisitive young man who had only recently walked the Earth and now had to come to grips with an existence in Heaven.

"This is right. Everything discussed applies to an Angel, only the possibility of sending an Angel to Earth is no longer an option. But the anguish experienced by an Angel dying is as severe. I know, I have been through this many a time," said Michael, "as has Gabriel," he added.

Gabriel looked at the boys, nodding his head slowly and subtlety.

"The Holy Trinity will personally see to the counseling and rehabilitation of a fallen Angel, for if Lucifer gets hold of an Angel who has re-entered Heaven from a heavenly death, then it will be tortured for many years. The longer the torture, the worse the anguish."

"What is worse for Heaven is the transition of an Angel from good to evil," said the Angel Raphael. "Lucifer will personally see to the torment of an Angel. The Angel is tortured in the depths of Hades, away from the light of good, the godly light of Heaven, for decades. Eventually, the heavenly skin of an Angel will turn to a darkened and toughened hide. The skull will harden and toughen. The eyes will grow bigger and darker, adapting to the dim and black depths of Hell. The feathery wings will be singed and burnt. The transition from Angel to Dark Angel will eventuate, given enough time. Then Lucifer has one more warrior in his evil army."

"So, Dark Angels don't fly?" asked one of the young new arrivals.

"On the contrary, my young friend, they grow wings; blackened and leathery old things. They are not as graceful in flight as angelic wings, but they can achieve great heights and speeds," replied Archangel Gabriel.

"I get it!" said the young inquisitive man in the front. His voice was proud and joyous, like he had won a door prize at the local Saturday night dance.

"The Devil wouldn't want the Angel to die because the Angel would re-enter Heaven."

"Yes, my friend. I have had my share of Lucifer and we have met in battle and in torture many a time. Try as he may, I have withstood his many attempts to convert me. I came back to Heaven before I had any chance of becoming a permanent resident of Hell," replied the Archangel Michael.

"As have I," added Archangel Gabriel.

"And I," added the Angel Raphael.

Pam had not moved from the outer edge of this gathering. She was close enough to hear, but far enough to not get in anyone's way.

Pam had heard this conversation many times before, and so she paid little attention to the procedure, other than knowing when to take over.

The Angels continued with their discussions, but Pam had, for the moment, reverted to her thoughts and feelings. She couldn't get her mind off her own family and how they coped without her, especially her grandson, Tony.

Her stomach would have been churning with the raw emotion, if it could; as if it were being strangled from the inside. A set of invisible hands would have twisted and stretched out the organ whose responsibility lay with providing its body with nutrition and sustenance. But that sort of human emotion was long gone. Nerves, stomach, digestive systems and human anatomy were all things of the past.

However, worry and tension existed.

Feelings existed.

These sorts of emotions had been elevated to a different dimension, but, nevertheless, they existed.

I feel so sorry for these young people, but sorrier for their families. At least they've had their time in Heaven, had the time to adjust. But any way you look at it, if you have had a child of your own, you already know; if you don't, then you can't possibly understand. They are so young, so innocent. This one reminds me of my grandson; his inquisitive nature, so much like my Tony.

It has been twelve years since I saw my grandson.

Time! Now that's a new adventure. Twelve years on Earth can be like yesterday in Heaven. I still can't quite get the hang of that, but there is something about the way time travels on Earth and in Heaven. The two are not connected. Drives you nuts sometimes, trying to keep up with it all. But try telling them that.

Anyway, I know it happens, I know people die young.

It's not this.

I've gotten over that. It doesn't bother me like it used to.

Yet, my grandson and his mum, my daughter. It's young people's deaths which bring back some unbearable memories for me.

I adore him so, I miss him incredibly. I never got a chance to say goodbye to him on Earth, but I did in Heaven. My passing was all too quick. At least, that's what they tell me.

I can't remember.

One day I am walking and talking, the next I am in Heaven contemplating whether I'm really dead.

It wasn't until I ran into my daughter and her husband that I knew the truth. I knew it because I had had to bury them a few years earlier. I will never forget the day the police came to my house and broke the news. How does one break the news of a death to a parent? It must have been hard for them. I wish I could thank them for their sincerity. The policewoman especially—she was so understanding. The accident killed my son-in-law instantly but my daughter lived on.

She suffered so. It broke my heart to see her all stitched up and bruised, the morphine dripping in to soothe the pain of her massive spinal injuries. But death hit her soon after and well before me.

I wish it had been the other way around.

I'll give Heaven a rule! How about a parent never has to experience the burial of her child? That rule would have made my life a lot nicer. So much nicer.

No sooner do I get to Heaven and meet up with my Mary and her Charlie then they're off on some angelic mission back to Earth. Reborn!

Reborn to whom?

I don't even know where or who they are. It's all been a bit secretive.

Then, of all things, my Tony ventures up here. And this bit still amazes me.

It defies everything I know of Earth and of Heaven, yet symbolizes the endless glory and power of my God.

My Tony, he didn't die. He came up with an angelic interest. He and his friend, Johnny taken for the sole purpose of accomplishing what the Angels couldn't. And once they accomplished their task, they were sent back to Earth with no memory of what they had done here in Heaven.

But he left his mark, my Tony. He made all of the Angels so proud. Him and his young friend, Johnny. God, they've known each other since they were born and nothing could prove their loyalty to one another more than venturing deep into the darkness of Hell. An angelic mission to lay a heavenly light that will burn forever. A heavenly disturbance in Hell. The dark creatures can't adjust to the heavenly light. That I know for sure.

But things were so rushed that my one and only grandson couldn't say goodbye to his parents. I had to fill in the gaps for my Tony, tell him why his dead parents were not available to talk to him in Heaven. Tell him why they couldn't take the time to meet up with their one and only child.

He was sent back to Earth so quickly—in a flash. And I didn't have a chance to say everything I wanted to say. He wouldn't have remembered any of it, but it would have been nice to have done so anyway.

I know I shouldn't be annoyed, but I am. Each and every time someone young dies, I cannot help but think of the lives which have been affected.

Because, much like the lives of the families of these young people, I had to say goodbye to my grandson. I had to bury him with a twist—bury him in Heaven; a funeral in reverse. I had to give him a funeral so he could go back and live his natural life on Earth.

He fulfilled his heavenly mission with Johnny by his side. He and Johnny now lived life once again, on Earth, unaware of how they have made Heaven proud. How proud they have made me.

I love my new home and I understand my new existence serves a greater purpose, but, oh, my Mary, my sweet, precious daughter—how you suffered. It's not fair. I buried her on Earth and I buried her—well, perhaps fareweled her—in Heaven.

Still! No one, and I mean no one, should have to bury their loved ones twice over.

CHAPTER THREE
Traditional Family

The two young friends sat side by side. "Will you come with me?" asked Johnny. "George has gone to train with the Institute of Sport for two months, all expenses paid, including his trip to Germany. He was going to go to Germany whether he won the contest or not."

Johnny hesitated for a moment before speaking his next words. He felt guilty about the circumstances that had surrounded his opportunity to travel abroad. He knew it could not have been easy for Tony.

Johnny's throat was all dried up, like coarse sandpaper. The built-up tension made it difficult to swallow. But it had to be said and there was no point hanging onto the inevitable.

"So he's handed over his airfare to me. I just need to come up with the spending money."

Tony was genuinely happy for his friend. He looked down at the footpath below. For a short time, he couldn't even muster up the enthusiasm to look at his friend, feeling almost ashamed of the situation.

There was no point in delaying it. The question had been asked and demanded a response. Tony kept leaning forward, turning his head as far around as it could comfortably go. With a deep-felt regret but unapologetic confidence, he made eye contact with his friend. The silence continued for a little longer.

The words did not come easy, but he spoke them anyway. "I'd love to, but I don't have that kind of money."

"You have to, Tony! We'd have a ball. We'd backpack, eat cheaply—it wouldn't have to be expensive," pleaded Johnny. The sole issue was money, and they both knew it.

"I'd love to go, I really would. I just don't know how I can," insisted Tony.

The boys sat on the park bench looking out into the open gardens. The spacious parklands was full of swings and roundabouts and every plaything a young child could wish for.

Families were playing with their children, kicking balls, playing on the equipment or just enjoying a family outing. It was a perfect day for a family get together.

The skies were clear and the sun shone with pleasant warmth. All around was happiness and playfulness. The only cloud around was the gloom that hung above the heads of the two inseparable friends.

Johnny stared at the ground while Tony remained content looking at the various families enjoying their day out. He tried to think of a solution, but none was forthcoming.

The frustration was written all over his face.

Both boys pondered their own shattered dreams until they could no longer stand the pleasantries going on around them.

"C'mon, let's go," grumbled Tony.

The parklands weren't far from home and the walk would do them well. The realities of the situation had been faced. Not a further word was spoken about it.

~ * ~

Back at home, Tony's Grandfather prepared his meal. He wanted and carried on with the tradition his beloved wife had kept. It had always been important to Pam that the family get together for meals and maintain an active presence in each other's lives.

Nothing could reinforce this message more than the loss of Tony's loving parents, who had died in a car accident. Despite the years which passed, the family maintained their support for one another, even under the most trying of conditions.

With this in mind, it was even more important to Arthur he honor his dead wife's traditions in the best way that he could. He did his best to keep the family unit involved in each other's lives, but the boys were all older now and each of them was pursuing their individual interests.

The year was 1986 and it had only been a handful of years since Arthur's wife, Pam, had passed away. Life went on, but the memories were still a little painful.

The three generations of men dearly missed their wife, mother and grandmother. The boys, who included Tony's uncles Jack and Chris, respected the little family tradition; it was the least they could do.

Arthur had worked hard for most of his life, earning his wages and providing all that a man should to a growing family.

The years had not been kind to his olive, sun-worn skin. The harsh sun, dry climate and tragic worries of years gone by had all taken their toll.

He had a full head of solid grey hair and the wrinkly face of a man older than his seventy-five years. Arthur was young at heart and energetic enough for his age, but the many lines that circled his face gave another impression.

Arthur was no cook, but he put on a mean Sunday barbeque. An early dinner which contained marinated meats–shashliks–and a simple garden salad.

The cooking utensils were laid out ready for use. The trays of meat were marinated in lemon juice, oregano, garlic and red wine. Copious quantities of meat lay ready to be chargrilled. There would be no empty stomachs leaving today. No one had eaten lunch today because Arthur's Sunday barbeques were lunch and dinner in one relaxing afternoon sitting.

The charcoal crackled away in the old, beaten up barbeque. This outside meat cooker had been in the family for years, looking a little like its owner, worn and ancient.

Its original red paint had faded and peeled, and every surface was either red, rusty or stained brown. Still, it kept on serving a purpose for the lives around it, holding together relatively sound and strong.

The backyard was a comfortable size for Arthur. He loved to frolic in his well-maintained garden and lawn area. The yard was almost perfectly rectangular in shape. A few medium sized citrus trees grew evenly spaced across the yard, adding a bit of contour to an otherwise neatly maintained lawn. A small vegetable patch took its place on one side and an aged, but well maintained tool and garden shed sat opposite it.

The rusty red cooker stood sound and was being used near the back fence. It smoked away without a chance of the aroma entering the house or undercover eating area.

The meat sizzled as it hit the hot metal grill, the glowing coals radiating that special aroma which penetrates so nicely into marinated steak. Everyone was in for a treat.

Arthur was well into his cooking when his sons arrived.

He stood there, cooking fork in hand, wearing his black apron and turning the meat as he dodged the intense heat that rose from the glowing coals below.

Chris and Jack had let themselves in. They lived nearby and it was convenient for Jack to pick up Chris on his way over. All in all, it wasn't at all unusual to see them both come in together.

Tony soon followed them through the door. His head was down, filled with thoughts about his discussion with Johnny earlier. His mood wasn't blatantly obvious, as everyone was too busy running around to notice. Tony kept to himself, being the quiet achiever that he was. The tournament and the flight abroad played on his mind.

"Chop, chop, sleepy head! Get a move on. We need plates,

cups," Chris demanded of Tony.

"God, he can be so insensitive at times," thought Tony. Tony looked up, but only slightly. He was only a smidgen shorter than his uncle and also considerably slimmer.

Not that Chris was fat. Like Jack, he carried a little excess weight around the stomach and disguised it well on his naturally impressive build.

His uncle did not intimidate Tony.

Tony kept his eyes still and fixed, glaring. He desperately sought to show he had no right to be addressed in this manner, but Chris was too pre-occupied with getting things in order for their lunch come dinner. All Tony could do was give in and reluctantly attend to the chores at hand.

The meat was nearly ready. It simply needed another turn and a further minute or two.

Everybody was cheery and chatting, except for Tony. He couldn't get into the swing of things, but he pretended to play along with the moment. As best as he could, anyway!

Jack was bragging about his physiotherapy practice. He had worked up his private practice into a busy little operation. "My secretary can't keep up with the workload. I'm gonna rake it in big time this year. Six figures and all mine."

Chris was retaliating with news of his promotion in the hospitality industry.

He now managed and ran one of the larger hotels in Adelaide. He was very proud of his climb up the corporate ladder. "With bonuses, I could clear one twenty grand this year. Plus the perks. There isn't a more important job in this city for hospitality," replied Chris.

Too busy with work and too focused on the dollar, the two men hadn't time to settle down with wives and families. Their respective professions certainly exposed them to the opposite sex, but they had chosen to attend to their jobs and to remain free to date.

The truth always came out with slight exaggerations. The brothers' egos were as big as their earnings.

Chris and Jack were close and wished nothing more than happiness and success for one another. The bragging was all in jest and fun, but in the background lurked the seriousness of their career ambitions.

Arthur listened as his boys let loose with the salaries and the earnings and the tax benefits and the perks. The comparisons were getting a bit much.

They had both done well in their chosen professions and that made their father happy, but the way the boys flaunted their salaries was another matter. It did not sit well with him.

A bit of a traditionalist, a man's earnings were his own private business; something you needn't share with others. All this didn't upset Arthur; it just didn't sit well with him. Arthur looked to change the topic and his grandson was the perfect alternative.

"Why the long face?"

"Oh, it's nothing, Grandpa. A little tired, I guess." Tony walked away to get some water.

For a boy who always walked proud and true, he was slightly hunched over.

Jack looked at Tony walk off and it was obvious something wasn't quite right.

"Ok, Tony, that's enough. Out with it," Jack said.

"It's nothing you can help me with. I'll be okay," replied Tony.

"That's not how it works here. That's the whole idea of these things, to work through it as a family," added Jack.

Tony stopped. He had to unload the ton of bricks that rested on his shoulders. Rightly or wrongly, something needed to be said, so Tony accepted the invitation to speak openly.

"Well, it's this competition thing. George doesn't need his airfare now, so Johnny has it." Tony paused for a second. "I really thought I had a chance to win. To fly over, all expenses paid. A bit of a wish, but I really thought I had a chance. It wasn't to be, I guess. But still, it would have been nice to travel with Johnny. Go over to see George fight and see a bit of Germany, and maybe Europe."

Tony paused for a further moment, "Look, I'll be okay. It was wishful thinking, that's all," he added.

Arthur felt for his grandson. The young man had gone through some pretty horrific events in his short life.

Tony had experienced three deaths in his family in a short space of time. The most recent loss was his grandmother. His parents had passed over a few years earlier. This had been hard enough for Arthur to comprehend, but Tony was then a child.

He did not have the life skills to deal with such serious matters and he had to learn young. And unfortunately for him, the lessons did not come easy.

"Tony, come help your Grandad," said Arthur.

Maybe that would distract the thoughts of his young grandson.

~ * ~

Quite a distance from the family Sunday meat fest, on the other side of the Earth, a father and his two young children prepared to go to church.

The children, Anita and Günter, were twins.

Eleven years old, the twins walked the town of Cologne with their heads held high.

Anita had her mother's blue eyes, while Günter's eyes were brown, like his father. Beyond the differences in eye color and sex, the twins closely resembled each other. Their blonde hair moved with the wind as if it was only just attached to their heads, almost ready to fall off. The twins' Germanic ancestry was evident and they displayed classic, sharp facial features. Their chiseled bones and pale complexion came together in a northern European way: classic child beauty.

These eleven year olds were well known in their hometown of Cologne and across Germany. Thanks to their perfectly developed soprano voices, they had been given the honor of joining the choir of one of the greatest religious monuments in Germany and even, perhaps, Europe.

The Great Gothic Cathedral of Cologne had darkened towers, with a sharp look about them. It truly lived up to its namesake of gothic. Majestic and grand would also go towards describing this man made wonder.

Many steeples reached into the air, but none higher than the two monumental main steeples that towered more than a hundred and fifty meters high.

Everything from the sculptures, statues, religious artifacts to the stained glass windows, showed no expense had been spared to build this shrine to Heaven and all things holy. The monument attracted crowds from all over the world. To be a part of its choir, and at such a young age, was a great honor.

The father of Anita and Günter took up a position in the back of the church with them. He hurriedly dressed his little boy and girl in their choir outfits. The family trio had to look their Sunday best as another service in the impressive cathedral was about to start.

Their loose white choir outfits sat over their neatly pressed church clothes like a massive bib on a baby. The outfits hung to below their knees. What remained visible were the sleeves of their tops and the lower parts of their pants and dress.

The young siblings walked out and took their place with the choir. To their side was a small band ready to accompany them. The young twins stood like little statues: perfectly still, well behaved and unquestionably prepared.

Their father tucked in his shirt. Grabbing his dark brown jacket, he proceeded to put in one arm, and then the next. He quickly pulled down at his suit, smoothing out any last minute creases.

He left the changing area and walked around and through the gathering church crowd. He took his usual seat near the front altar amongst the helpers and friends of the church. This section was reserved for those who helped out with the Sunday service.

Another Sunday.

Another show for the visitors to the town.

Another service to the people of the town.

Another Sunday in the town of Cologne.

CHAPTER FOUR
In Hell

The Devil sat on his rock of solitude, the throne to the kingdom of evil. Lucifer was grand in presence and his rocky throne was fitting to this grandeur.

The seat stood high and tall. Carved with engravings and scriptures of evil, it above all reminded the occupants of Hell that there would be vengeance on Heaven.

This was the place where the Devil pondered, plotted or devised his cunning plans. Plans to steal a soul, a plan to convert an Angel, attack Heaven or wage wrongfulness on mankind.

His hair was long and wavy and blood red in color. Protruding from his front hairline were two horns, six inches in length with a slight bend in the middle. These jutted out from his forehead and curved upward toward the sky, bony and slightly tapered on the ends.

The beast had a sharp jaw line and button nose. Many may have considered his face to be pleasantly handsome. He was once an angelic being, but any remaining good looks had been spoiled by the glaring pupil-less white eyes and his yellowy, red skin.

It was a skin that changed in tone as if there was a fire burning deep within his soul. There were signs of yellows and reds, which readily interchanged with one another. Fiery patterns danced around the skin of his face, arms, legs and torso. A body which was toned and muscle bound much like an Olympian athlete, somewhere between a heavy weight boxer and professional swimmer.

The colors could change as quickly as if a TV channel had been flipped or twirl around as slowly as a turtle's pace. One thing was certain: the texture of his skin was never still and always flowed with movement.

The back part of him was equally as impressive. His one feature stood out for all to see. It was unique amongst all the creatures that walked the land of Hades. Others had them but not like his.

A set of large, leathery, bat like wings displayed his sovereignty. A ruler of all things evil. They were far bigger and brighter than any other beast that roamed the land of fire and brimstone.

The wings had a layered color and, unlike his torso, the colors were fixed in place.

The base of the wings was the strongest of yellows and this carried all the way through to the midsection of the wing. At this point, the tone changed to a mixture of fiery red with sun-like yellow. The color transition only went for a few inches. A small band ran the width of both of the wings. And then the upper half of his wings were as bright and as red as fire. It carried on until the upper tip, where the wing was singed and burnt to a charcoal black. This impressive array of colors made for a majestic set of wings.

When they were fully stretched, one never doubted the sovereignty of the demonic Lord.

This was central Hell, the valley in which Lucifer and his band of dark angels and demons took refuge. This location was deep into the valley of sulfur and brimstone: a place far, far away from the light of God and all things heavenly.

The giant Ocean of Fire washed before the rocky throne. And like many oceans whose waves crash upon the shoreline, so too did the fires of this flaming ocean. Rolling in one after the other, the flames crashed into the ground and then retreated back to their massive origin. Time and again, the fire rolled in with a mighty crackle and retreated almost silently. The radiant yellowy red light it emitted was warm and carried itself for lengthy distances. It wasn't bright; more so, it had a way of penetrating its way through the dark.

Its gentle glow often served as a type of homing beacon for retreating demons after a heavenly encounter. It was just as useful for any heavenly intruder who contemplated the enormous journey from the Heavens. Such a journey would have them cross a line called the Transitional Border, the place where one was instantly shifted from a place of heavenly light into the darkness of Hell.

At that point, one looked for the flickering glow in the distance. This was the giant Ocean of Fire. Visitors crossing the Transitional Border into Hell quickly came to realize two things. Firstly, Hell's headquarters made for quite a journey and secondly, the Ocean of Fire and its gentle glow would point the way.

But there would be no heavenly visitors today.

Lucifer was simply at home with his sadistic court of demons and dark angels, and his home was a place whose barrenness was surpassed only by its threatening evil.

The grounds were relatively open and there was usually lots of devilish traffic around. Foot soldiers snarled and chatted on the ground while dark angels flew above, practicing their aerial attacks and acrobatics. They flapped hard and flew in a diabolical fashion.

Demonic foot soldiers gathered on the ground, snarling and snickering to one another. They had skin charred and singed, unlike the Devil. Their eyes were large and took up much of their upper skull. Their pupils remained dilated and darkened, taking up most of the eyeball. This feature served the dark angels well in the darkness of Hades, but unfortunately played havoc on their eyes in the brightness of Heaven.

And this was now the problem. There was a glowing heavenly light in central Hell. A special gift from the Angels. This heavenly light had unfortunately become a permanent part of Hell and had been shining for a little while now.

And as each Hellish day passed, Lucifer had to contend with the reminder of a little angelic present delivered in the most unusual of ways.

It was only in recent times that Tony and Johnny, the two young mortal warriors, were entrusted with an angelic mission to create a heavenly disturbance in Hell.

And once they crossed the Transitional Border, they were guided to their destination by a glimmering point of light, the giant Ocean of Fire. They didn't know it at the time, but they were heading right towards central Hell.

Once there, they broke two orbs. They contained the light of Heaven in a package no bigger than a golf ball. It shone with the intensity of bright search lights.

As hard as he looked, Lucifer could not detect its source. It shone with a loving intensity that did not fit in a place of evil and hate. Its origin was never detected nor could it be destroyed.

Hell was no longer Lucifer's place of retreat. The light of God did indeed play havoc on the occupants of the Valley of Evil.

Every time a demon shaded his eyes, or an acrobatic maneuver went astray, or a mid-air flight turned into mid-air collisions, it usually had something to do with God's light.

Lucifer ran this thought through his evil mind. Again!

How could two mere mortals catch Hell off guard and cause such an ever-lasting disturbance? This did not sit well with Lucifer. His ego was larger than the rocky throne he sat upon. It was even larger than the empire he had built up from nothing.

The thought he had been outsmarted by two everyday humans stirred vengeful emotions deep within his fiery soul.

Suddenly, the Devil's face turned bright red and then, just as quickly, his torso burst with a brilliant flash of fire and flame. The color of his skin mirrored the fiery oceans that regularly crashed upon the hellish landscape before him.

The anger inside him had built up like a run-away forest fire, and the display on his skin was just as awesome. An array of fiery skin colors twirled erratically for all to see.

The Devil's body colors expressed the emotions that stirred deep within the mighty beast.

All of those in his immediate demonic presence sought shelter for fear they might be caught by his anger.

Until Lucifer's fiery rage subsided, all beings in Hell were on alert. Anyone could be Lucifer's next victim.

Everyone before the mighty beast froze and watched in anguish. Lucifer muttered to himself, mumbling with rage. The demonic angels dared not move suddenly, no poor soul wanted to draw unnecessary attention to itself.

Lucifer's muttering dragged on and on.

From yonder, a dark angel flew in, back home from a day out on patrols. The dark angel flew in carelessly, unaware of recent events.

Lucifer jumped out of his throne and leapt high and fast.

The Devil's wings guided and propelled him towards the demonic flyer. Like a homing missile, the Devil reached his unsuspecting target in next to no time. He laid his hands on the weary dark angel and threw him towards the ground. The dark angel hit the charred surface of Hades hard and fast. The patrolling beast could not resist the might and force of Lucifer.

He bounced once and then twice and then lay on the floor rolling in pain and agony.

"Get him out of my sight," ordered Lucifer in a language of squeaks and clacks—a language only understood by those of Hell.

Immediately, nearby foot soldiers came to escort their wounded, winged colleague off to a place out of sight and out of mind. Two foot soldiers supported their winged comrade, keen to follow the orders of their demonic king.

Watching his victim being dragged away, calmed the ruler of Hades. Normality was returning to the Devil's composure, the signs of serenity were returning to his skin. The changing of skin colors slowed to a gradual twirl.

Soon all was calm and back to normal. Lucifer sat back on his throne and acted as if nothing had happened.

All in his demonic presence returned to their normal duties—at least until another event caused the vicious cycle to begin again.

On the other side of the Hellish valley was Sebastian. He was one of Lucifer's most prized warriors; the general in the army of darkness. He had fought many a battle in Heaven and had been by Lucifer's side for centuries.

Using the language of shrieks, screams, clicks, grunts, moans and everything unworldly, Sebastian gave newcomers helpful advice on dealing with the heavenly light that glowed intensely in the middle of the Valley of Darkness. He was a natural leader who generally did his best with what he had.

Lucifer sat in his throne and looked at Sebastian in the distance. Lucifer appreciated the natural leadership skills of his trusted general.

Surrounded by foot soldiers, Sebastian was teaching hand to hand combat. Lucifer smiled slightly. His old friend was as loyal as anyone could want. His devotion to the preservation of Hades was second only to Lucifer himself.

Heavenly light was now part of everyday life in Hell. It was difficult to get used to, but life in Hell would have to go on.

Lucifer turned to the flaming ocean, sat back in his rocky throne and shut his white eyes. He needed to separate his thoughts from his vision.

~ * ~

Back on an Earthly plane, in Arthur Gretsis' backyard, four men gathered to devour red meat, drink a little beer and enjoy a family gathering. Tony had lightened the mood as he spoke about Johnny and the competition fight disqualification.

"You should have seen him, all crouched down and covered up. Johnny had lined him up and BANG! Down for the count. He was holding his jaw and then off to the Docs to have a little wiring done, I would say. He won't be chewing meat for a while, I can tell you that for sure." Everybody laughed and Tony couldn't help but giggle along too.

Part of him felt bad. Perhaps he shouldn't have laughed at someone's misfortune, but his friend was disqualified via unorthodox tactics. For the moment anyway, the thought did not bother Tony too much.

As soon as the laughter died down, the reality he was not going abroad with Johnny entered Tony's mind again and he withdrew from the gathering. He was there in body, but not in mind and spirit.

Showing it outwardly, he wanted the rest of the family to feel his disappointment to which he would not be joining Johnny on a trip he was wanting more than anything in the world.

Arthur couldn't bear to see his grandson in this state, so he immediately got up and made his way through the back door and into the house.

Tony wanted to separate himself from the family gathering, and he could think of no better way to do so than by surreptitiously walking over to the old barbeque. The red coals were as good for company as anything else. Jack and Chris continued to chat away about nothing in particular.

Arthur was only gone for a short while, but when he came back, he held a small bank book. "Your grandmother was saving this so we could go back to Greece," said Arthur. He handed over the book and Tony opened it to look inside. "Here, it's yours, we can go to the bank tomorrow and get your tickets," Arthur continued.

Tony looked at the sum. There was more than enough money to cover flights, accommodation and meals.

"I can't, Grandpa. I can't take this," said Tony.

"And why not? You want to go to Germany don't you?"

"Well, of course I do," replied Tony.

"Then let me hear no more of this. We'll sort out the finances tomorrow when the bank opens."

Tony's smile reached from ear to ear. "I got to tell Johnny," he said as he hugged his grandfather. He ran off with excitement to tell his dear friend the news.

Jack approached the outdoor table and picked at some of the cooked meat. Chris walked over to his father.

"How could you, Dad? The money was for you and Mum," said Chris.

"Well, Mum's not here anymore and I want Tony to have it," replied Arthur.

"Well, if you were going to give it away, then why didn't you share it? I might like to go for a holiday someday," said Chris.

"Are you in your right mind, son? How much more do you want?" Arthur replied abruptly.

"A moment ago, you and Jack couldn't make more than enough money and now you want even more. The kid just wants to go to Germany. He's never asked for much. Don't you think he deserves a bit of a break?" Arthur took a moment to look at Chris. "You really need to do some growing up, son." Arthur didn't even wait for a reply and walked straight back into the house.

Jack looked up at all the commotion. He saw his brother standing alone and his father disappearing through the back door.

He was not even contemplating on entering the debate. His older brother was determined and set in his ways.

His father was usually diplomatic but now he was angry.

Jack concentrated on being a little hungry and keeping out of other people's business.

CHAPTER FIVE
The Parents of Anita and Günter

Simone prepared the dishwashing water while Josef gathered the last of the plates from the dining table.

"I'll take care of the dishes, dear," said Josef. "You go put your feet up."

"I'm okay," replied Simone. "You've been at it all day, I'll finish."

Josef walked up to his wife, who was awkwardly trying to place herself in a comfortable position to do the dishes. She had to maneuver her pregnant mid-section so it rested on the kitchen bench. She had managed to do this throughout her pregnancy and although it got harder by the week, she succeeded.

He walked up from behind and gently put his arms around her. He was quite a tall man with great reach, but even he found this task difficult. He offered the little support he could, with his hands tucked around his wife's underbelly, a part of her body that currently bore a significant weight and strain. Eight months in and carrying two babies was not an easy task, but Simone was not one to complain.

He tilted his head near hers as they both faced the kitchen window. He closed his eyes, lifted his head and gently kissed his wife on the cheek. They both stared out the window for a moment more and then he let her go. As he did, he affectionately stroked her pregnant bump and in jesting return, she patted his little beer-loving belly.

Simone continued with the dishes as Josef moved into the bedroom. It was time he got out of his gardening clothes. They weren't dirty, but he had been wearing them for most of the day as he did odd jobs around the backyard.

Simone picked up the hand towel and began the duty of drying her dishes. She adored her dinner set. The plates had been given to her as a house warming gift by her now deceased parents.

It wasn't just the sentimental value of the set; she also loved and admired its beauty.

The outer rim was a thick band of light, antique blue. It looked like multiple layers of scales. It was followed by a thick band of white and then another thick band of blue. The center artistic piece was what made this dinner set so strangely beautiful even as it maintained a classic, English antique look.

An old Japanese temple in a traditional Japanese garden overlooked a nearby shoreline, stylishly depicted in blue and white. The detail and quality of this dinner setting was adored by both Josef and Simone.

Simone moved around the kitchen, hindered by the massive weight of her pregnancy. Tidying up the kitchen was not as easy or as quick as it used to be.

"JOSEF!" she screamed. Her scream was immediately followed by a crashing sound. Josef stopped what he was doing and rushed towards the kitchen.

Simone was standing in a small pool of liquid mixed with shards of blue and white plate. Her pants and legs were soaked with amniotic fluid.

As Simone had been instructed in her neo-natal classes, a hospital suitcase was already packed and ready to go. She was calm and her thoughts were collected.

This day had come a little sooner than she had anticipated.

Josef grabbed the suitcase and put it into the car and then dashed to escort his wife. Simone leaned on the kitchen bench, supporting her tummy.

The first of the contractions had set in and she did not want to move just yet.

Huffing and puffing and breathing heavily were what she had been taught to try and relieve some of the pain.

"What should I do? What should I do?" asked a nervous Josef.

Simone noticed his shaky hands. She thought it was cute.

"It'll be okay, we have plenty of time," Simone tried to calm her panicky husband, but Josef took little notice of her rational explanation and continued to support his wife as best he could as he tried to get her into the car as quickly as possible.

Before he knew it, he was dodging what little traffic was on the road. The trip to the hospital was quick and he knew exactly how to get the immediate attention of the nursing staff.

It wasn't long before Simone was admitted and lying comfortably in a maternity ward bed. "I told you, Honey, nothing to worry about. But thank you anyway." Josef half smiled back at his wife, his hands still nervously shaking.

Simone took her husband's hand and gently stroked it, anxiously awaiting her next contraction.

Like clockwork, there it was. The muscles in her lower abdomen cramped up as she resumed the breathing exercises she had been taught.

She let go of Josef's hand and tried to take control of the situation. The task before her was demanding. She was losing the battle of self-control, and her face cringed with every gut wrenching cramp that pulsated through her lower abdomen.

She inhaled and exhaled as heavily and as quickly as she could. The cramps tied her belly in knots; her legs quivered from the intense, short, multiple bursts of contraction pain. The breathing exercises took the edge off the pain, but even so, suffering and strain were written all over her face.

She took Josef's hand again and squeezed it as the

contractions continued. It offered some relief as the tension within her abdominal cavity grew in both strength and duration.

It was finally over–or at least until the next set of contractions.

Each new set of contractions was only a little longer than the last set, but they still felt like an eternity. This did not help Josef's shaky hands. He was living on an overdose of adrenaline and it didn't look like he was going to get any relief in the near future.

The midwife had gone to fetch the obstetrician for his opinion. The doctor walked in. His composure was cold and analytical.

He had an Albert Einstein look about him and was determined to get on with the task.

"Let me have a look," he said. He washed his hands thoroughly in the washbasin as the nurse put Simone's legs in the correct position.

"Hmmmm," said the doctor.

He went to one side and consulted with the nurse and midwife. Simone was busy in anticipation of her next contraction. She could feel her abdominal and cervical muscles prepare for the next round.

Although Simone reached out for her husband, Josef was more intent on listening to the doctor's conversation.

She was seeking comfort, but at the same time, trying to listen to the medical opinions. She would have really liked to have joined in on the medical discussion, but all she could manage was bits of the doctor's conversation. There was not enough information coming forward to make any sense of it.

"Contractions?" "How far apart?" "Dilation!" "Examination!" "Diagnosis?" The key words meant nothing. They were words that left pieces missing such that she could not complete this close and personal puzzle.

"OK. I think it's best we prepare you for a caesarean section," said the white haired and elderly obstetrician.

They both heard this quite clearly.

"The midwife will fill you in on the details and answer any questions you may have." And with that, the specialist left the hospital room. The nurse and midwife were left behind to fulfill their duties.

This wasn't an emergency, but nor was it a case of "taking your time" either.

Josef insisted on being present at the birth of his children and the nursing staff was not opposed to accommodating this.

Josef went off to don surgical dress, and Simone laid patiently in her bed waiting to be rolled into theatre.

Even with the agony of labor pain, Simone enjoyed the journey and she let the event take its natural course. Josef, on the other hand, was experiencing things quite a bit differently. His heart pounded as if it was about to blow his chest open. His nervous system had automatically responded as it had evolved to do so.

The body was ready for fight or flight. His pupils were dilated, his heart was pumping hard and fast and his mouth was as dry as a desert sand dune. Josef's life was not in danger and there was no threat nearby. Simply put, he was about to witness the miracle and marvel of childbirth.

Josef emerged wearing surgical garb. His plain white top, loose fitting blue pants and protective hair net made him look the part.

Her head resting on the hospital pillow, Simone turned slightly to look at her husband as he approached. He walked so proud and true. They exchanged smiles.

There was no need to speak. Simone was very excited and while Josef hid behind his nervousness, he was excited too. The thought of a non-natural birth and all the hospital procedures scared them both a little—but the greater thought of parenthood made it all worthwhile.

Josef was directed into the corner of the operating theatre, which was normally reserved for teaching medical students. There were no medical students on hand today and the hospital was willing to accommodate participating fathers here.

Two hospital assistants wheeled the mum-to-be into the operating room and transferred her onto a stainless steel table.

It was cold and Simone wiggled around trying to make herself a little more comfortable. In the background, the necessary preparations took place. Josef approached his wife, gave her a loving kiss on the forehead and resumed his position in the corner. He didn't want to interfere with the medical staff and their ability to perform their surgical duties.

Three nurses wandered around the room, checking their equipment and supplies. The anesthetist, a tall burly man, hovered over the instruments that soon delivered anesthesia.

The pediatrician, a small framed, timid man discussed the unborn baby's needs with one of the nurses. Although relatively small and softly spoken, when this professional discussed his medical duties, he received the attention he deserved.

The obstetrician hovered over Simone. His analytical mind was running through the routine caesarean birth procedure. He had performed this duty many times in his long, professional career.

He made the necessary preparations, sterilizing the area of skin he would soon cut. Once the operation began, time was of the essence.

The anesthetic was now working and all medical parties were at the ready.

The obstetrician began. He sliced away cleanly and precisely at the layers of skin that led him into Simone's womb. Small patches of blood appeared, running out and over the fresh incision. It was not a sight many tolerated, but Josef didn't mind. He suspended his nervousness to take in the miracle of the human body.

As soon as the cut was complete, the nurse pressed down on Simone's upper abdomen and soon enough, little Günter appeared. Crying as most babies do, the nurse held him high to show him off to his father on the other side of the room.

The anesthetist's main duties were completed, yet the need to remain in the surgical room was standard hospital practice. He was utilizing his time well, sitting back in his chair and catching up on some routine paper work when he looked up for the first time in a while.

"Could go for a schnitzel, this one. Going to be a big boy. Ya!" said the burly anesthetist. His strong German accent was very pronounced and his voice was full of life and joy.

Günter was soon in the hands of the pediatrician, wriggling and squirming, trying to make sense of the new world he had entered. His young vocal chords produced murmurs mixed with short bursts of cries. The pediatrician and the nurse were keen to start with the baby's first routine medical checks.

The strategically placed spinal block made for a pain-free delivery. The long labor had taken its toll on Simone. She was worn out, but she was not going to miss out on the experience.

Josef, on the other hand was wide awake and overwhelmed with emotion. His eyeballs swelled with teardrops and he could not hide from wiping his eyeballs dry. Everyone else in the theatre was too busy to notice, except for Simone, who smiled as she caught the teary eyes of her emotional husband.

Being so enthralled in the moment, Josef lost track of time. But before he knew it, there was another little surprise. As she had done before, the nurse raised little Anita for her proud father to see.

Josef looked upon his beautiful little girl and smiled.

Suddenly, Simone flat-lined. One moment, the medical machinery showed heart beat peaks and troughs, but suddenly it showed one straight, endless, worrying line.

Bells and whistles sounded as Simone's pulse went from a normal rhythm to nothing. A second later, Anita slumped in the nurse's arms. The nurse's face looked shocked, knowing the baby girl had stopped breathing.

The people in the room turned back into busy medical professionals.

Under protest, Josef was escorted out of the room as medical staff worked to revive both mum and daughter.

Josef sat outside the surgical theatre. His heart was pounding so hard, his windpipe vibrated and breathing became difficult.

Josef wanted to get the bear off his back. The imaginary beast was crushing his rib cage, making each breath a little more difficult than the one before.

He sought distraction by seeking answers.

He was trying to get anyone's attention, but all the hospital staff were running in and out of his wife's operating theatre.

In the theatre, the medical staff had broken into two teams.

The pediatrician was asking the world from the two nurses. They were incubating young Anita, monitoring her for any life signs, trying to bring life back into her body.

A few meters away, the obstetrician and anesthetist were in constant communications. The obstetrician's primary task was to stitch up the wound to stabilize Simone. The anesthetist was trying anxiously to get oxygen to Simone's brain.

"Where are those damn paddles?" he demanded.

The trolley was being wheeled in at that very moment. The defibrillator was being charged and ready to go.

"Clear," the anesthetist shouted, placing the two paddles diagonally apart on Simone's chest. The charge sent her body heaving into the air.

"Again!" The sound of the 'zap' was haunting. The room waited for Simone to respond.

Just then, Anita began to cry. Her shriek was a welcome relief. The pediatrician and nurse went about warming the young girl and setting up her crib.

"Where you taking my baby?" asked Josef. He watched the crib as it was wheeled out of the room. The nurses were keen to get the baby into intensive care.

The pediatrician followed the nurses He stopped to speak

to Josef.

"She appears fine, but we will monitor her closely for the next few days," he said.

"What happened? Where's Simone?" asked Josef.

"I don't know. I was busy with your little girl. You will have to wait until one of the other staff members comes out."

The pediatrician saw the worry on Josef's face. "I am sure they will let you know as soon as they have any news." The soothing softness in the pediatrician's voice did little for Josef's anxiety.

Before the pediatrician left for intensive care, he grabbed Josef's shoulder and squeezed it as a sign of support.

No sooner had the pediatrician left the theatre area, nurses emerged from the main birthing theatre, weeping and clearly distressed.

The obstetrician walked towards Josef.

This man who was usually so cold and analytical became compassionate and warm. He walked towards Josef with a look of remorse, his body lightly slumping.

"No! It can't be!" said Josef. His hands were trembling more than ever.

"Not my Simone!!!"

CHAPTER SIX
Simone's Journey

Josef stayed slumped, his head buried in his hands. He sat in a black lounge located outside the surgical operating theatre.

His heart no longer pounded heavily. Instead it was suppressed, as if someone had reached down deep into his throat and had grabbed the beating muscle. Anxiety of the body had quickly changed to anguish for the mind.

Right now, Josef wanted the world around him to disappear, but all he could do was hide his eyes. His palms were tightly fixed against his face, his eyes covered by his palms. There was plenty of light around him, but still, he sat in his own creation of complete darkness.

The noise of conversation and hospital foot traffic continued, but Josef stayed in his dark little world.

Simone walked out of the surgical theatre. Her surgical gown was draped loosely over her weary body.

It was all a bit hard for her to comprehend.

Nursing staff and doctors were passing right by her, busy with their medical duties. She wanted answers, but there were too many people around her asking questions.

Out of the operating theatre, she stopped to look around. She looked right and then left and saw her husband sitting down, head buried in his palms.

Simone approached Josef. Josef had chosen to sit in the

middle of the sofa, but there was room for two or even three people. Simone didn't need much space and so she gently squeezed in next to her husband.

"Are you okay, honey?" she whispered.

She raised her arm and lovingly laid it on her husband's shoulders, but her hand moved right through his body.

She tried it again and again, but each time her hand moved straight through him.

Turning herself towards him, she threw out her hands and tried to grip her husband's hair, tried to pull his body to hers, tried to do anything that brought them into physical contact.

Nothing worked.

All this time Josef remained in his dark, private world. He was none the wiser to Simone's presence, his eyes were clenched shut, and his palms were fixed to his face.

He was not going anywhere for a little while.

Simone could not stay. She was always the rational type and, although she was frightened by the experience, she was also curious. This mystery had to be solved and it could not be solved here.

As much as she did not want to leave her husband behind, she did so.

She stood up and took a good look around, trying to work out why no one was noticing her, even though she could see them. She hesitantly returned to the surgical theatre.

The hospital foot traffic had settled a little. There weren't as many doctors and nurses walking in the passageways, but the frantic pace of medical staff rushing in and out of her surgical room remained.

Two nurses left the theatre, stopping to look in Simone's direction. Their eyes were red and swollen from crying and they were consoling each other.

For a moment, Simone thought she had their attention, but the nurses were looking beyond Simone and towards the heartbroken Josef. One of the nurses could not contain her emotion and howled in immense sadness. With the support of her colleague, she turned and walked the other way.

It had been an unhappy day for all who were in the theatre.

Simone stood there and watched the nurse's march away from her. She turned to look at Josef again. He had not changed position since she had first laid her eyes on him.

She had to make a move. But where?

She was only a few steps from the entrance to the operating theatre so she turned the corner and walked in.

As soon as she had turned, she stopped. It was as if someone had suddenly thrown up a solid brick wall in front of her. Her head jolted back as a shockwave ran through her. Her physical body lay motionless on the operating table in front of her. She looked at her lifeless body, utterly unable to comprehend what was happening. Denying it, defying it.

"No, no, no! This can't be."

"No! Impossible! How can this be?" So many unanswered questions, thinking of the unthinkable.

Simone cautiously approached her body. She tried to touch it, but she could not. Her hand swept through her body. Try as she might, Simone could not grip her own arm or touch her hair.

She had no choice but to give up trying.

The only thing left to do was to stand there and give into the reality of her death. She was in spiritual mourning as she came to terms with it all. Things were starting to make frightening sense.

Simone took one long last look at her dead self, running her eyes from the tip of her toes past her slightly swollen ankles. Her gaze continued along her legs.

She was in conflict, part of her gripped with terror and part of her refusing to believe the obvious. And now, she just stared at her knees. No thoughts, no emotions. She daydreamed of nothingness.

This only killed a little bit of time. Simone continued, brushing her eyes past her knees and then over the length of her surgical gown. It wasn't until she reached her lifeless face that she stopped.

It all finally took its toll and the emotion of grief turned to anger.

Simone turned and stormed out of the theatre, demanding answers.

But from whom? Where to now?

She looked left and right, but had no idea what to do next. Josef had not budged. She felt for her husband, she understood his grief, but she had to move on. And so she walked down the surgical passageway, away from her distressed husband.

She did not look back.

Simone continued through the maze of passageways looking for whatever it was she was supposed to look for. Whatever it was, the answer did not lie in the surgical theatre. Of that, at least, she was certain.

Finally! Up ahead lay a set of theatre exit doors. On the other side of them lay a series of passageways and rooms to a large metropolitan hospital. A hospital whose layout was somewhat foreign to her.

She approached them eagerly, but stopped suddenly, a few meters from the doors.

She waited and waited and waited and then turned to look behind her.

It was now late and most of the operating ward was being cleaned and prepped for the next day. The few people visible were all involved with their hospital duties, including those arising from Simone's death.

Simone turned to face the doors again, but they stood motionless and shut. Growing impatient, she stepped ever so cautiously towards the surgical theatre doors. Although they were very close, like a lioness to her weary prey, Simone moved ever so slowly and gracefully towards them. She took one little step. And then another, and then another, until she faced the doors.

Just then, the tall burly anesthetist came barging through the theatre doors. They swung open with force and speed, swinging right through Simone. The operating theatre doors swung back and forth after the doctor's overblown entrance into the theatre ward. The anesthetist also passed through Simone in a hurry as he was keen to get back to the delivery room.

This left Simone feeling very disturbed.

By the time she had gathered her thoughts, the doors were completely shut. She once again put her foot hesitantly forward as if she was testing the cold water of a pool before a swim. Simone left her foot dangling out. And then she did it; her foot passed through the solid door. And then her ankle, her knee, and her loosely fitted surgical gown. And then her face and head.

She advanced with no resistance, passing through the hospital doorway and making it to the other side. The young mum stopped for a moment to look back and to try and comprehend the reality of it all. She had just broken a thousand biological, mathematical and physical laws. These laws belonged to the human species, a physical world she was no longer an active and participating member of.

She was now an observer, an unbiased spectator, in a new world with its own rules and agendas.

If Simone tried to apply logic and reason, the experience only became more confusing. She had to let it go for the moment as she continued with her journey.

She walked down every passageway, walking through doorways, making her way to a place she had never been before.

She didn't know why she had this feeling of urgency, but she had to follow a certain path. There was a right hand turn up ahead. It felt like it was a hundred miles away, but it wouldn't be long. This was the place for her to go.

She knew.

Simone picked up the pace, speeding up from a walk to a low paced jog. The jog got a little faster and then even a little faster still. She didn't stop until she reached the end of the corridor.

She turned and there it was. Slightly ahead, a big glass pane faced her. The glass window ran for a fair length down a new and different passageway. The wall which supported the glass was only waist high and the glass windows ran right up to the ceiling.

Simone could see a door further down, but she didn't need to use it. Still, Simone was content at stopping at the glass pane, as any physical being would. The habits of a lifetime on Earth were hard to break.

She looked in, and all the babies of the nursery were on display like fruit in a vegetable shop. It had been a busy time for the hospital. The nursery was full and, except for the odd, restless cry, the babies were all settled for the night.

The nursing staffs were having a relaxing night sitting in the far corner trying not to disturb the tranquility.

Simone looked over at the nursing crew. They were engaged with their own little work matters.

The excitement of being in the hospital's nursery made her forget about her spiritual worries. Like a capricious teenage girl browsing and buying at her favorite shopping mall, she giddily cast her eyes over the rows of babies before her.

Three rows deep and she saw them, sound asleep: her brave little princess and her knight in shining armor.

She clasped her hands in front of her face. Even death could not take away the joy of seeing the miracles of her life.

She was in awe. It was bittersweet. Simone knew the reality of her situation, but it did not diminish the beauty that lay in the two hospital cribs on the other side of the glass.

Not far behind the row of cribs was a wall running parallel to the glass pane. Diagonally opposite Simone, near the door and away from the nursing staff, stood two adults, a man and a woman.

They were standing up against the far wall, leaning back in a relaxed manner. Their arms and legs were crossed and they both had the cheekiest grins on their faces.

The two of them looked out of place and Simone did not want to stare.

Out of the corner of her eye, Simone glimpsed at the two individuals. It had now got the better of her. She raised and turned her head to get a better look. The adults looked Simone's way. By this stage Simone had quickly grown accustomed to the living looking right past her so she turned to look behind her, but there was nobody there.

Simone quickly turned her head back and returned their gaze.

"What are they looking at?"

She turned her head again, looking directly behind her, but there was still nothing there. Turning and facing forward, she looked back, puzzled and confused.

The manner of these two individuals changed. The cheeky smiles had been replaced by a stare so intense and serious that it pierced Simone's spiritual existence. It was now obvious the two adults were looking right at her.

Simone experienced confusion, fright, anguish and worry all at the same time. She was frozen with emotions and did not know what to think or do.

The two individuals stood up, tall and proud. As they did, gentle smiles returned to their faces. They wanted to make sure Simone had taken notice of them. And notice them she did!

The spirits of Charlie and Mary Gretsis walked over to the crib. Once there, Mary raised her arm and she waved Simone over.

At first Simone hesitated and then Charlie waved too. They were now both encouraging Simone to pass through the glass pane to take a closer look at her babies.

Simone instinctively knew it was okay.

She took her step through the glass pane and made straight for her babies. She walked through the rows of cribs until she was standing between the male and female entities.

For the first time, she looked down on her little miracles,

the most beautiful things she had ever seen in her life —and even in her death.

The male and female entities had not said a word, but now they both raised and put their gentle, loving arms around Simone. Simone felt the touch, the warmth, the comfort and the love of another being.

As quick as a flash, Simone raised her open palms to her eyes.

In the same way as her husband had, she used her palms to shield her eyes from her immediate environment. Quivering in her own world of complete darkness, Simone was overwhelmed by emotion.

Even in the spiritual world, there was a place for tears.

CHAPTER SEVEN
The Spiritual Medium

The twins grew fast. It had been nearly a year and a half since the family lost their wife and mother. Life was hard at times, but the family had found a new routine.

Josef had become quite the dad. And the mum! He took the good with the bad and fortunately, the children were very well behaved.

One spring weekend, Josef was lying in bed. The children were mumbling to each other as they so often did. The conversation was baby babble and made Josef smile from his neighboring bedroom.

The chirps, the garble and the gurgles amused the dedicated father as his little girl and baby boy conversed in a language cutely incomprehensible to him.

A little time passed and Josef snuck in to have a look through the doorway.

He saw both children facing the corner of the room with their backs to their father. Their heads were slightly tilted up and they seemed to be conversing with the top back corner of the room.

Josef had witnessed this kind of scene before, but lately it appeared to be happening more frequently.

This time, however, there was something noticeably different about the baby talk. The babies were reaching out, reaching out as if they wanted to grab hold of something —or someone. Josef stood in silence and watched as the babies gestured towards the back of the room.

All of a sudden, their hands and arms rose simultaneously. They excitedly hung there for a while, shaking then trembling and then after a short moment, their arms dropped as quickly as they had risen. The rising and falling was almost synchronized to perfection.

After a little more conversing, a little time to rest the arms, a giggle here and a giggle there, the hands and arms were raised again. This pattern repeated itself several times as Josef watched.

This performance was only slightly stranger than scenes he had previously witnessed. Josef had learnt to observe and then to ignore the behaviors.

One thought had been with him ever since the birth of his children. He knew the twins were inseparable and had a very special connection to each other. He believed their dead mother was looking over them and that she had some sort of spiritual connection to them.

Life is one big journey and right now, life was one big system of routines and schedules.

Today was no exception. Josef had completed his morning chores and had prepared all that was needed in order to have his children cared for until he returned from work.

The neighbors took it in turns to help out with the babysitting. Josef had the perfect kids, the perfect house, and the perfect neighbors in the perfectly located street. All that was missing was the loving mum, who happened to also be the perfect wife.

The morning ritual was now complete and Josef was on his way to work on the tram. Josef worked as an administration manager in a busy office complex in the heart of Cologne. He was good at his job and well respected.

His lunchtimes were mostly spent walking the busy streets

of central Cologne. He mainly spent it window shopping, admiring the views, enjoying street theatre acts or simply taking some time for himself.

Between his needy kids and even needier employees, these lunchtimes helped him retain a degree of sanity. It was the only part of the day he dedicated to himself; to his own needs and wants.

Today the streets were full of theatre acts, foreign visitors and locals. They all came out like any other day.

The afternoon was grey and overcast, but the weather didn't stop the people from walking the streets, nor did it stop Josef from taking his much needed work break.

Josef paid attention to all the street theatre acts. There were fewer today than usual, but that didn't matter. The performers helped distract him from the worries of a working single parent.

There were acts of all sorts: young and old, male and female acting, singing, all performing for the donation of spare change.

Something new was parked in the main street today: a caravan done up with the frills and lace of travelling gypsies. Material, chains, and candles, this little caravan was decked out with all the trimmings. It really looked the part of a gypsy woman on her travels.

"COME AND HAVE YOUR FORTUNE READ," read the sign out the front in big, black, bold letters. The sign was an old piece of wood, hand-lettered with some rough looking black paint.

"ENTER SAYS MADAME LIZ," read another similar sign hanging below. They weren't professional signs, but today they caught the eye of a man named Josef.

Leading into the trailer was a small, two-step ladder.

Josef climbed it slowly, trying to peek in through the curtains, lace and chain that dangled in the doorway. Josef could not resist the temptation to walk through the curtains, even though he was a bit skeptical.

"Come in, come in," said a middle-aged lady. She was sitting in the far corner of the trailer behind a medium-sized card table.

Her crystals, fortune cards and decorative stones were neatly packed on one side of the table. On the other side stood a long, thin candle, its flame flickering ever so gently.

"Take a seat and I will read your fortune," said the gypsy lady.

Her long blonde hair fell elegantly over her shoulders. Her deep blue eyes captured Josef's attention. Her features were pleasant and well-proportioned on her oval shaped face.

With very few wrinkles or signs of aging, the mysterious gypsy looked like a much younger woman. Her face shone with a peacefulness that was contagious. Her voice put Josef at ease immediately.

He listened closely to her.

"My name is Liz. And you are?" Liz shuffled her cards, eagerly awaiting the response.

Josef, slightly mesmerized by his surroundings, snapped out of his trance once his brain had the second or two to process the question. "Josef," came his eventual reply.

"This is how it works," said Liz. "You may ask me questions at any time. My guides are the Angels. With their help, we will meet your spiritual guides. Guides are those you may know or even not know but who have an interest in your wellbeing. They are spiritual entities that had once crossed over. Which once lived a life on Earth." Liz then stopped to make herself a little more comfortable on her seat.

"I will relay the message as I get it. Some of it may make perfect sense. You may come to recognize the importance of other messages at a later time." Liz was still fiddling around, re-organizing her decorative stones, playing for time. She looked up.

"Angels also help out. Sometimes they have a message to convey. Angels have never walked the Earth, only served in Heaven. Safe keepers of all that is right and heavenly. They will also offer any future visions and information—if they think it is of purpose and intent."

Liz then stared into Josef's eyes. "Are there any questions?" she asked. Josef shook his head from side to side. "Then I will take my payment and begin."

Josef's curiosity got the better of him. He first parted with his skepticism and then he politely parted with his money, ready to enjoy a venture into the unknown.

"Ok then…" Liz re-organized her crystals and fortune cards one more time. She was ready. Her eyes glanced to the left and right of Josef's face, looking over and past his shoulders. Liz listened closely as her spiritual guides conveyed their message.

Josef looked at the candle. Its flame flickered awkwardly. *"Strange,"* Josef thought. There was no wind in the caravan, yet the flame was being blown about, dancing precariously on its thin, blackened wick.

"I see a male and a female entity," said Liz. "They both died tragically in a car crash. A long time has passed. A long, long time. I'm being shown ten. Ten years ago? Hold on!"

Madame Liz looked above and beyond where Josef was seated, acknowledging a spiritual conversation in her own special way. Signs of frustration appeared on her face. She jolted in a "what are you all trying to tell me?" fashion as her shoulders shrugged and her palms pointed outward and upward.

Liz looked at Josef. She was puzzled by the message she was about to deliver. "But they don't know you and you don't know them."

Liz looked beyond Josef's shoulders. None of this made any sense to her. She was looking to the left and then to the right of Josef's face, shrugging her shoulders at the ghostly entities who were trying to communicate through her with the physical being they all knew as Josef.

She kept on trying to make sense of their spiritual message. It was mixed and difficult to understand. She had never experienced such confusion in her years as a spiritual medium. "They are telling me they come from a place far away." Liz continued to listen to her spiritual guides. "I feel you don't know them, but they are here to protect your children. To guide them and keep them from harm's way."

"What's going to happen to my children?" asked Josef anxiously.

"Nothing! As far as I can see, your children are healthy and safe," replied the gypsy lady.

Josef did not know what to think. His opinion of the experience had changed. He wasn't thrilled about the fact that his hard earned dollars were being thrown away to some gypsy woman for a whole lot of useless information. Josef was a patient man, but this was beginning to aggravate him.

"Wait, there's more!" said Liz.

Liz could sense all of Josef's frustrations. This had never happened to her before. Liz was genuinely talented in her spiritual readings.

She could not understand why she was being misguided by those who had crossed over, by those who had helped her help others for so many years. Even Liz was frustrated at what appeared to be unethical behavior by the guides. This was not Liz's style.

"Two spiritual entities are standing behind you now. A male and a female. Their arms are around a loved one of yours. She comes across as a young adult, a young female, someone close to you who has passed on recently. I see a sudden death, an unexpected death."

"Did your sister die young?" asked Liz. Nothing was entirely clear and Madame Liz was still trying to seek clarity. "I see a pregnant woman and broken plates. No, no. Not plates, more so a blue and white plate. I see it, a whole plate, patterned. A lovely little blue and white design. A very intricate and special design. I perceive an important attachment to this patterned plate. Wait! They are now showing me pieces. Pieces of the plate, as if it has shattered into lots of bits."

This made a bit more sense. Josef was now very attentive.

Just in time, Liz had regained some of his respect. Josef had been only seconds away from storming out of the gypsy caravan and Liz knew it.

"I lost my wife a short time back. Suddenly. Unexpectedly."

"Does the plate hold any significance for you?" asked Liz.

"My wife. When she was pregnant. When she broke her water, it must have caught her suddenly because she screamed my name and then dropped the dinner plate. We both adored the dinner set we own. It has some…" Josef paused for a moment and took a little sigh of sadness.

"…Had some sentimental value for both of us."

Josef looked into the top corner of the caravan and sighed some more. This meeting was stirring up some sadness from deep within him. He then looked back to Madame Liz and continued. There was a definite change of tone in his voice as he unhappily drew upon memories of the past.

"By the time I ran into the kitchen, she was standing in a pool of her fluid mixed with broken plate bits," Josef said, adding, "Yes, it makes perfect sense."

"She is using this message as a means of clarity, so you can relate and be sure the message is from her to you," said Liz.

"But I find this strange," said Liz. She sat back and observed the spiritual world for a while. There was what appeared to be a little dispute between the spiritual guides. As Josef sat in awkward silence, Madame Liz concentrated and lost track of time. Close to five minutes passed. Her concentration was broken by Josef's much exaggerated movements to look at the time on his watch. He could not see what Liz was seeing.

"The other ones that are here will no longer let her speak directly to me. I don't know why. She is being protected by these entities and they are being very selective about what is being said. She sends her love to you. She is sending her love to two others. Little children. One girl, one boy. Does this make any sense?" asked Liz.

Josef nodded.

"Like I said, when the time is right, you will make sense of this message," said Liz. "There is always a purpose to their message. You needn't look for it, just remember!"

Josef walked out of the caravan, it was time to get back to work. The experience had made him think about many things. But soon enough he was back to his needy staff and his mind was quickly occupied by work chores and the functions of a busy admin team.

Another day passed and he was quickly back into the family routine. Josef slept restlessly that night. The day's experiences and the confusion of the mixed messages kept him awake.

The next day, he hoped Liz was still around. He had to find out more. Once he arrived at the office, he excused himself from his morning duties for a little while. This errand could not wait until lunchtime.

Josef found the gypsy caravan and entered it via the same two-step ladder. "Hello again," said Liz. She was sitting in the same spot re-organizing the same crystals.

Liz looked up. "My message is what it is, please do not enter my trailer in search of a refund."

"No, no, not at all. I would like to ask something of you, please, if you will. Could you come to my home? I think I need to introduce you to my children."

Liz looked up and leaned back in her chair. For once she was not fidgeting with her crystals. She simply looked back at Josef. Her face was peaceful and pleasant, but an awkward silence filled the room.

Josef cut through the silence with a no nonsense statement. It was his last attempt to get what he wanted. "I wish to pay you for your inconvenience."

Another momentary pause. Liz leaned forward and played with the crystals again. She looked up like she had done many time s before.

"The one thing I have learned, the one thing my special gift has taught me is there is a purpose to everything. Our paths cross with others to serve this purpose. Be it negative or positive, there is still always a purpose. It's a shame many do not reflect or learn from these interactions, but nevertheless, there is always a point to be made, a lesson to be learned, a life experience to be gained and held onto." Liz saw the sincerity in Josef's eyes. His eyes showed the pain of recent years. Liz leaned back again. "I can make time this weekend, on Saturday morning."

"Perfect," said Josef. He grabbed his notebook and jotted down the relevant details.

"Thank you, Madame Liz." Josef's gratitude was heartfelt.

What felt like the longest working week followed for Josef. Time passed ever so slowly.

The days dragged on and the nights had Josef's mind racing with thoughts and questions.

Saturday finally arrived and so did Madame Liz.

"Please come in. Is there anything I can get you?" asked Josef.

Madame Liz declined the offer and walked through his home freely, trying to get a general feel of things. Josef didn't mind. After all, this was in part, the aim of her visit.

As Liz ventured around, she found nothing unusual. The house was serene.

She made her way towards the back of the home, looking into every room. Neither the toilet nor the bathroom was exempt from her visit. She circled around, winding around the furniture, looking up towards the ceiling and down towards the floorboards, tiles and carpet.

As she did so, Anita decided to crawl away from her brother and make her way into the main passage.

"Hello, sweetheart, you must be the little princess I have heard so much about," said Liz. A smile lit up Liz's face and just as quickly disappeared.

"Oh, my!" Liz remarked. Liz was startled by what she saw in the spiritual world surrounding little Anita.

Then she immediately searched and made her way over to little Günter who was sitting on the floor amused with his stuffed toys in the children's bedroom.

Liz stopped suddenly.

"Josef, we need to have a long talk."

CHAPTER EIGHT
In Flight

Tony and Johnny walked through the airport. It was functional enough, but compared to other airports in nearby capital cities, it was old and looked worn and tired.

Tony waved his brand new passport in the air. It was his first ever and he was very excited.

Tony was only catching a domestic flight from Adelaide to Melbourne and then flying to Germany from there, but that didn't bother him. He wanted everyone around him to know he was going somewhere far away.

Johnny was just as excited, but it was for a different reason. He was looking forward to seeing his older brother compete in the Cologne International Karate Finals. George was picked to represent his home country along with five other Australians and the boys couldn't be prouder for their mentor and sensei.

Johnny and Tony lined up to book in their luggage. A small queue of people stood before them. Behind them were Johnny's parents, Marlene and Nick. They were chatting with Tony's grandfather and his Uncle Jack.

"And where's Chris?" asked Nick.

"He got caught up at work," answered Jack, knowing all too well Chris still held a bit of a grudge against his father for giving Tony the money to travel abroad.

His stubbornness would dissipate in time. Jack knew what

his brother was like, and Arthur definitely knew what his son was like. Tony, he was just too excited to worry about these little differences of opinions.

"Next please," called the lady behind the ticket counter. Tony and Johnny approached the counter. "Could you stand back, sir, we can only book one at a time. If you wouldn't mind, a few steps back from your friend. I will be with you in just a minute," she said.

Johnny stepped back as instructed. He left the main queue and stood on a worn carpeted area a few meters back from where Tony was checking in.

"Just the one bag, sir?" The lady's smile extended from ear to ear.

"Yes, Ma'am," replied Tony. "We're off to Germany," he added cheerfully, bending to add his luggage on the loader.

"I know. May God bless you," came the reply from the lady behind the ticket counter.

Tony put his luggage down and looked up. He stared intensely but politely at the lady behind the counter. "I beg your pardon?" he replied.

"Would you prefer aisle or window?" she asked.

Tony stood still, his mind churning over the reply. The moment seemed to linger.

He turned to Johnny who was busy daydreaming, staring out into nothingness. Tony looked at Johnny for a moment longer and then hesitantly asked him, "What do you want—aisle or window?"

"Window." Johnny's reply was instant.

"Aisle it is for you sir, window for your friend." The lady strapped the appropriate stickers on the luggage and printed off the ticket.

"Now you take care because the Angels are looking out for you." The lady stared into Tony's eyes in a caring and tender fashion. Tony's face crinkled and he carefully walked back towards

Johnny.

He didn't take his eyes off the ticket lady nor did she off him. Johnny was looking into his flight itinerary and the relatives were too involved in their own conversations to notice. Tony continued to step back.

Tony turned to Johnny and was about to say something when he was interrupted by the ticket lady. "Sir, you can now step up to the counter."

Johnny walked forward past his friend. He went straight to the luggage conveyor and lifted his suitcase on the loading deck. Whilst Johnny was busy getting his tickets and luggage into order, the ticket lady leaned slightly back and smiled with tenderness at Tony.

In the time it took Johnny to organize himself, the lady gazed upon Tony with genuine non-romantic affection.

Johnny lifted his head and she went on with her airport duties as if nothing had happened. Tony turned and walked towards his family.

There was an awkwardness in his manner. His mind was preoccupied. The ticket lady had stirred something within him.

"Are you okay?" asked Arthur.

Tony looked at his grandfather and then back at Johnny who had finished booking in his luggage. Johnny excitedly waved his window ticket in the air and at his friend. Tony smiled half-heartedly at his grandfather. "I'm fine, Grandpa. I guess I didn't sleep well last night. You know, excited and all."

"You'll be alright, sport. Plenty of time to sleep when you check out of Melbourne. Your flight to Germany's got to be about twenty hours," said Jack. It got the small gathering of family friends smiling.

But Tony could not get his mind off the ticket lady. He thought about it for a little while longer and then resolved to dismiss her as the overfriendly, religious type.

Tony joined in with smiles and the family chat.

The boys checked their hand luggage through the airport security x-ray and set off for the waiting area.

A long passage separated the airport security from the waiting lounge.

Along the way, there were all sorts of cafés and merchandise shops. They too had aged. While all the merchandise in the shops was modern, stylish and new and the cafés offered everything you would wish to drink or eat, the shop fronts were not as bright or glamorous as one would expect to find in a modern shopping mall.

The family walked and talked between themselves as they made their way to gate eleven. The gate was a fair walk away, but that didn't matter; there was still plenty of time before the flight.

"George!" shouted Johnny. Johnny was both startled and surprised to see his brother at the gate lounge. It wasn't a surprise to the family members, but George had insisted the boys not know so he could have the opportunity to talk with them.

Johnny and Tony ran down the passageway through all of the small crowds gathered at the various gate lounges.

"What happened?" asked Johnny.

George shrugged his shoulders and pointed to his forearm, which was in plaster and supported in a sling. "Copped it nice and sweet on the forearm," replied George.

"Is it broke?" asked Tony.

"Yep. A nice one, too. I'm still taking some pretty strong stuff to help with the pain. Just one of those stupid training things," replied George.

"How's it going, mate?" asked Jack. He couldn't help but do his physiotherapist thing. He walked over to George and lightly held the cast. He was quick to notice George flinched at the slightest movement.

"Come and see me after a few days. I'll do some work on the shoulders and relieve some of the tension and get the blood flowing to the damaged area."

"Gee, thanks, Jack. I'll do that," replied George.

George then turned his attention to his little brother.

"I've spoken with Mum and Dad and we want you and Tony to have a good time abroad. Go enjoy yourselves."

George reached into his pants pockets, awkwardly scrounging around with his good arm and hand. "By the way, look after these for me." George handed over some tickets.

Johnny looked at the print and excitedly turned to Tony. "I can't believe it, front row seats at the Internationals! But how?" asked Johnny.

"Well, it's the least the national coach could do for me. I can't travel to Germany. Flying back from Melbourne was bad enough, so you boys enjoy."

The boys were very excited. Arthur in particular hadn't seen his grandson smile so widely in such a long time. Arthur instinctively knew the trip was worth every dollar and he was not wrong.

Tony's happiness was Arthur's happiness.

Arthur turned to Jack and quietly whispered, "If only Chris could see this."

"Dad, you know what he's like. Don't worry about it. I mean, look at Tony. He's beaming from ear to ear. What you do with Mum's money is your business, not Chris's." Jack looked up. "Boys, I think it's time."

The passengers were looking at the monitors for the flight announcement. Some had started to line up at the gate. The plane was in view and the last of the suitcases had been loaded into the cargo bay.

"Would all passengers flying Qantas Flight Q, F, Six, Six, Three please make your way to Gate Eleven. Your plane is now ready for boarding." The announcement had the occasional electrical crackle in it, but the message was loud and clear.

The families said goodbye to their two young adventurers and off the boys went onto their flight.

In next to no time, the plane was in the air. The excitement and his restless night caught up with Tony. Johnny sat patiently in his chair watching in-flight movies as Tony caught up on some sleep.

Before they knew it, the plane touched down in Melbourne and they were off to the international airport. Their luggage had automatically transferred over and all they had to do was check in.

They lined up to validate their tickets. "Wow, look at the size of this place," said Johnny.

"Makes our airport look a bit shitty, doesn't it?" replied Tony.

"Next!" came the call from one of the ticketing windows.

The boys approached the young lady. "Where are you lovely boys off to?" the young lady asked flirtatiously.

"Europe. Germany," said Johnny. His warm smile earned him an even warmer smile back from the pretty little airport employee.

"I'll tell you what, boys. Today's your lucky day. We've got a couple of business class tickets that are only going to go to waste." The young lady leaned forward as if she was going to whisper a secret. "Why don't you have an extra special trip on me," she finished with a sexy little wink.

"You're the greatest," said Johnny.

"Yeah, that goes for me, as well," added Tony.

"My pleasure," said the young lady.

Johnny took his ticket straight away and made for the customs area. Tony would only be a few moments.

The young lady handed Tony his ticket, but she did not let it go.

Tony played a little game of tug of war with her over the ticket counter. Her playfulness disappeared.

Whispering loudly, her words were fast and furious.

"We will make sure you burn in Hell." She was direct and to the point. She let go of the tickets as she spoke her final words to Tony.

Tony was in a disbelieving daze. His eyes flickered as he shook his head from left to right in small movements. In a way which signified denial. His arms crossed over one another. The body language was defensive and self-protective; the surprise attack had caught him off guard.

"Did I hear what I just heard," wondered Tony.

He wanted to get as far away from the ticketing area as possible. He would have confronted the lady, but the look in her face told him to leave it alone.

Tony followed his friend and got ready to board his first international flight.

~ * ~

On another plane, a spiritual plane deep in the depths of Hell, Lucifer sat on his mighty throne.

Behind him, the heavenly lights shone through Hell like searchlights cutting through the night sky. Lucifer faced his mighty ocean rather than the heavenly disturbance behind him.

"You called for me, my Lord," said the dark angel, Sebastian, communicating in the language of the winged demons; a blend of sharp clicks, eerie screams, loud moans and deep sounding grunts.

Lucifer turned and acknowledged the presence of his long-time friend and trusted companion.

"It is time we gathered more souls, two in particular.

As it cannot be done in Heaven, it will be done on Earth," said Lucifer. He looked out onto the horizon, casting his eyes out into the vastness of the great fiery ocean. The roar of the flames crackled as the fire crashed onto the shoreline.

"Your soul will not survive long on Earth. You will need to replenish it often. You know what you have to do," said Lucifer.

Sebastian bowed before his leader and moved on. He was now entrusted with the unholiest of tasks, one that he'd undertake with honor and pride.

Lucifer was left with the difficult task of getting Sebastian past Heaven and onto the grounds of Earth.

He sat back on his throne as his eyes gazed across the mighty fiery ocean. Soon, and within his own evil ridden mind, his plan would be complete.

Execution of all that had been thought through was the next step.

CHAPTER NINE
Sebastian's Mission

Josef and the children were getting in their car, soon to return from another Sunday service at the cathedral. The children had sung beautifully and had once again performed with the well-respected church choir.

It was a short and uninterrupted drive back through the minimal Sunday morning traffic. For most of the citizens of Cologne, Sunday was either a day for church or a day of rest and relaxation.

After a brief and leisurely drive home, the children and Josef re-entered their home still dressed in their Sunday best. "Get changed, children. Auntie Liz is coming to say hello this afternoon. She tells me she has something special for you. A little treat for you both."

The children cheered and jumped with excitement as they made their way to their rooms. The children knew the routine and took their church clothes off with care. They neatly laid them down on their beds for their father to attend to.

In next to no time, the children had changed into their everyday play clothes. Loosely fitting black pants and T-shirt to match for Günter. Anita wore old jeans with a white T-shirt that hung a little below her belt line.

Günter went out to play outside while Anita stayed in her room sitting on the edge of her bed.

The hymns she had sung this morning were still bouncing around inside her head. It didn't take long before she was singing the hymns from the side of her bed.

The church songs harmoniously reverberated around the room, never losing amplitude or pitch. Her sweet voice echoed through the house and out into the backyard.

Her young brother continued to play outside, enjoying the rhythm of his sister's sweet, angelic voice and the hymns they both adored.

Josef tidied up the house in anticipation of Auntie Liz's visit. He could not think of any better accompaniment to his home duties than his daughter's immaculate singing voice.

The children loved music and the only thing Josef loved more than their music was the children themselves. Music made this house a home, bringing the family even closer together.

"Where is my beautiful songbird?" asked Madame Liz as she entered the house. The operatic voice had caught the ear of their favorite auntie.

"Auntie Liz!" Anita abruptly finished her singing and ran into the hallway. Her brother heard the excitement and hurriedly ran in through the back door.

The children rushed to Auntie Liz together. She was not an aunt by blood, but her title had been given to her out of respect.

The cuddles lasted several seconds and Liz kissed her favorite little children on the tops of their heads.

Liz had stuck to the image she had presented the day Josef first crossed her path. She was dressed in her gypsy attire; neat and colorful with all sorts of draping and patterned material. Her hair was tied back and secured in a red and green patterned scarf. Her gold earrings stood out a mile; big circular hoops that dangled and glistened elegantly.

The sunlight bounced off her earrings with a sparkle that caught all eyes. The earrings were only outdone by the jewelry around her neck. The necklaces did not shine, but the beads of various sizes and colors demanded attention.

Liz had picked up some hard-to-come-by Swiss chocolates for her favorite little people. "Here you go, children. Enjoy!" The kids thanked their Auntie by giving her another cuddle and kiss and then left their father and Liz to catch up.

The gypsy was a regular visitor to the household, but Josef hadn't seen Madame Liz for a couple of months. Normally they caught up fortnightly, but every now and then Liz's travels prevented her routine visits.

"Are they still there?" asked Josef.

"It never ceases to amaze me," said Madame Liz. "All spiritual guides, or at least I thought up until I met you, will walk by their chosen human companions. But your children's guides are walking within the children. It's like their souls are an extension of your children's'," said Madame Liz.

"But that shouldn't be. The image I see before me is foreign. Different, because I don't speak with the souls of the living, just the souls of the dead. And the souls of the dead do not walk within the souls of the living."

Josef and Madame Liz made their way to the back door to look out onto the yard. Günter and Anita were sitting in the corner with their heads lowered, focused on their sweet treats. The children were trying to make every little bit of chocolate last an eternity.

"I see them as plain as day," said Madame Liz. "They're looking our way. They are here with the best intent for your children. This I know for certain."

The spirits of Charlie and Mary Gretsis stood out of the children's bodies as if they were standing inside a potato sack ready for a sack race. "What are they saying now?" asked Josef.

"Nothing. Nothing before and nothing now. I find this so strange. Every spirit I have encountered offers some sort of guidance. They may pick and choose what or how they may guide you, but nevertheless you always get some sort of guidance. The spirits see me. I see them. We acknowledge the presence of each other, but other than that. Nothing! Nothing before and nothing now." Madame Liz looked at Josef. "I don't know what to say, Josef, other than I need to be around. I need to find out why we crossed paths. This was no blind luck. As I have said to you so many times, people enter our lives for a purpose."

Madame Liz turned to look at the children in the back yard, gazing directly at the images of Charlie and Mary, which were only visible to Liz herself.

Her gifts enabled her to see on the other side. She had thought she understood the other side until she met the spirits of Charlie and Mary. Again she said, "This has now become my chosen destiny. I am not sure why, but I need to be around."

CHAPTER TEN
The Demonic March

In the dark depths of Hell, a massive army of hellish foot soldiers and winged demons were making their way to the Transitional Border. The march was long and laborious.

The main kingdom of Hell sat far away from the Transitional Border and the journey did not end there. The march from the Transitional Border into the main kingdom of Heaven was as long and just as arduous.

The demonic foot soldiers marched in blocks a hundred wide and a hundred deep. Formation after formation, they marched in unison like soldiers on parade.

They weren't marching in perfect military precision, but if the aim of the game was to progress copious numbers of able and willing soldiers, then they were on target.

In total, they numbered in the many hundreds of thousands. Above them, and almost equal in number, were the winged demonic beasts.

They flew in triangular formations, with one at the point and then two, three, four behind them and so on until the triangle was thirteen deep. Each aerial formation triangle contained ninety-one winged demons, ready to die for the cause.

One triangular block followed, and then another and another. As far and wide as the eye could see, they moved forward like a dark cloud rolling rapidly across a clear blue sky.

The spacing between one aerial formation and another hardly ever varied, but the spaces within the formation did. Like the foot soldiers below, each aerial grouping flew in an erratic unison. Some had their wings up, others had them down. Some flew straight and steady and others sped up then slowed down, twisted and then turned.

Once again, the aerial numbers were not on parade but were there to maim and kill.

It was not pretty and perhaps even looked quite awkward; however, the massive march progressed towards their long-time enemy. It was not the largest attack Lucifer had ever thrown upon the Heavens, but it was certainly close.

Their first check point destination was the Transitional Border where they crossed over from the darkness of Hell to the brightness and warmth of Heaven.

This light was warming to any loving or godly soul but disruptive and disturbing to those who chose to live a life of brimstone and sulfur. In one step, the Transitional Border had you make the transition from Hell to Heaven or vice versa, as the case would be, dependant on your travels and final destination.

Hell's occupants found the smell of angelic beings putrid. Equally, the Angels and all those who occupied Heaven found the smell of burnt hellish flesh as disgusting.

At this point in the march, everyone of a Hellish origin was keeping to their side of the border. They did not want to cross over and alert Heaven of their presence.

Not just yet, anyway.

In the deepest parts of Heaven and as far as one could be from the Transitional Border, the Archangels Michael and Gabriel were welcoming new souls into their holy land.

Pam had been chosen by the Angels as the spirit who helped counsel the once young and adventurous Earthly souls. Pam had proven her worth when it came to young souls who had died in tragic circumstances. Her ability to provide loving, but stern direction helped the newly deceased make a smoother transition from life on Earth to their existence as spirits of the light.

The Angels were coming to the end of their preaching. The well-rehearsed script gave new visitors an understanding of the laws of the spiritual and eternal kingdom.

Soon, Pam put it all into a more meaningful perspective. As lovingly as the Angels delivered their message to newly arrived souls, the need to finally accept one had crossed over from the living to the dead was a responsibility Pam was honored with.

The former mother and grandmother did this exceptionally well, particularly for those who were young and had died tragic and sudden deaths. This was her strength and contribution to life in Heaven.

The Archangels stepped back and allowed Pam the honor of performing her heavenly duty for those who had arrived. She was about to start when the Angel Raphael ran.

"Do you smell it?" asked Angel Raphael.

Simultaneously, the Archangels Michael and Gabriel stood up. All angelic heads were raised in unison and they sniffed the air like dogs trying to catch the scent of a not-so-distant fox on a traditional English foxhunt. The Angels scanned the air for that all too familiar pungent scent.

"They're here," shouted Michael. The Angels screamed like air-raid sirens as they took to the air. The Angels flew fiercely throughout the heavenly sky, searching as a hawk would for field mice.

Instantly, thousands upon thousands of winged Angels and spirits joined them. They were diving and soaring, flying erratically in the sky. Tension was high as they remained on the lookout.

Pam gathered her new recruits. Lucifer was on the hunt for new hellish souls and Pam's recent arrivals were easy targets. "Come this way. Quickly! We must get out of harm's way." Pam knew her group of souls were highly vulnerable and with that, she had to act fast. She knew all about the potential dangers that were about to hit the Heavens.

"What are we running from?" asked a newly arrived soul.

Pam cleverly avoided answering the question. "In war we are all soldiers. If this is not the case then we help the cause." The newly arrived souls had bigger things to worry about and discussing the current circumstances was not appropriate.

All around, the souls and Angels of Heaven were on the move. They took to the air or to the ground; they scurried for safety, ready to support the battle. The scene was frenzied; one of complete chaos and mayhem and not what one would consider typical of Heaven.

The souls, Angels and spirits took up their position ready for battle. Not all, however, prepared to fight. Some sought to find and protect those who didn't have the resources and skills to take on a demonic assault.

All in all, a significant part of the heavenly population had lined up ready to do his or her bit for the fight ahead.

The population of Heaven included all Earthly souls and the angelic hierarchy; it was an extremely large force, one to be reckoned with.

The enemy accounted for the rest: the occupants of Hell and sundry doers of evil and destruction.

During a time where Heaven did not know what to expect from Lucifer and his followers, there was one thing that provided comfort. The heavenly light helped heal any wounds. It was a kind of home ground advantage.

Still, any war has its losses and casualties. The name of the game was to fight; to protect or to be protected.

The stench in the air grew stronger and stronger. The Angels and spirits recognized the smell of burning and charred flesh all too well.

As the smell became more intense, so did the Angels and spirits become more aggravated. As they lined up, the spirits became restless, spread across the heavenly grounds. The rolling white mist seemed to go on forever. The heavenly population stood ankle-deep in the fluffy mist, eagerly looking out into the near horizon.

Some Angels and spirits had taken to the skies. In flight, the Angels soared throughout the blueness, showing off sharp turns, brilliant acrobatics and ferocious speed as the lesser flying spirits hovered, floating up high and trying to gain the best aerial view possible.

The Angels' siren-like screams rang out loudly. The screams jumped from one Angel to the next, but this was no pleasant conversation. The screams, like amplified trumpets, were more like a series of warnings that continued to echo throughout the Heavens.

In the distance they appeared.

A mix of foot soldiers of the underworld together with flying dark angels.

Their formations had already started to unfold. Ready for the inevitable attack, aerial demons and foot soldiers positioned themselves for battle. The time for military formations was over and individual beasts did what they thought best for the coming onslaught.

Their presence in Heaven signified a breach.

God, with the help of his Angels, had cast Lucifer and his followers out of Heaven. To return to Heaven usually signified that Lucifer longed to sit in the Holy throne to rule Heaven and Earth.

This normally would have been the case, but this time Lucifer had another objective.

Back on the angelic front, Raphael, Michael and Gabriel grouped up.

They looked to each other and knew what had to be done. The cost of the battle was understood by all. "Victory to the Heavens," shouted the three angelic friends.

Leading the way, Michael flew towards the swarm of dark angels. Raphael and Gabriel were not far behind as they followed the lead of the great angelic warrior. They picked up tremendous speed as they drew their great wings down harder and faster than before.

Gathering incredible acceleration, they approached the oncoming army. At the final moment, the Angels tucked in their wings and executed a half forward rolling somersault with perfect timing. Their legs and feet now faced the oncoming Dark Angels.

Maintaining great momentum, the Angels plowed through the dark angels, using their feet as powerful weapons; angelic foot against demonic head. Mindful of protecting themselves from damage, the large, white feathery wings remained tightly tucked in.

Like a bowling ball crashing through a set of bowling pins, the Angels moved through the cloud of dark angels, causing damage and injury.

The Angels had greater maneuverability in the air and far greater dexterity in hand to hand combat.

They rammed, swooped, hit and did whatever it took to defeat their winged enemy.

In the air, the Angels attacked promptly.

They grappled and rammed, making sure the hellish invaders hit the misty ground hard and fast.

The heavenly light annoyed the dark angels and demons. These were beings of dark, fire and brimstone, after all.

The spirits were quick to pounce on any injured dark angels that hit the heavenly floor, taking advantage of injury and the desired effect of God's heavenly light. There was no holding back as heavenly spirits punished the fallen dark angels. Their attacks were swift and without mercy.

This was to be a long and drawn out battle.

~ * ~

After several grueling days, the Angels had almost cleared the sky of winged demons. Gabriel, Michael and Raphael had done the most damage by far, but many hundreds of thousands of others had also performed their heavenly duties.

A few demonic winged beasts remained scattered around in the blue, heavenly sky. They circled like vultures, not particularly interested in joining the battle on the ground.

The long duration of the battle had taken its toll on both sides.

In the skies, the heavenly victory was relatively brief and the celebration was short.

Taking only a moment to rejoice, the Angels quickly realized the struggle below. Their spiritual comrades on the ground were overwhelmed with massive enemy numbers. The Angels were stunned by the vision below them.

There were demons aplenty on the ground. Hell's ground forces were greater than any of the Angels had anticipated. It should have been an easy victory for the spirits and Angels, but they were caught off guard by the unusually high numbers.

Michael, Gabriel and Raphael turned to each other. They and the other Angels and winged heavenly souls took only the shortest time to regroup, immediately joining the troops below. Angelic screams echoed across the Heavens, sending a clear message it was now time to support the ground troops.

Heaven had suffered no angelic losses, but was starting to lose many souls and spirits.

One of the dark angels that remained in flight was the loyal Sebastian.

With almost all aerial heavenly beings on the ground, it was time to make his move. Sebastian flew ferociously into the depths of Heaven. He flew with speed and determination, flying as hard and as fast as he possibly could.

He passed the crowds below unnoticed.

A lone winged Angel saw Sebastian and made pursuit, but Sebastian was fresh and uninjured, unlike the holy warrior who had done battle and was weary from some intense fighting.

The chase did not last long as Sebastian pulled away from the pursuing Angel.

The lone Angel called for help, but all below were too busy in battle.

Sebastian flew deeper into the sky, passing through the many layers of Heaven, rising up from one heavenly layer to the next.

He dare not stop as the likes of the Holy trinity would destroy him in an instant. Sebastian's only chance for success lay with the element of surprise.

He continued to fly higher and higher into the heavenly pyramid. Flapping with ferocity, rising with power and speed, the dark angel was beginning to tire, but he was almost there.

Suddenly Sebastian was thrown into turbulence.

He could not maintain any sort of stable flight pattern. Tumbling and turning in the strong eddy currents, Sebastian had no choice but to go with the turbulence. An opportunity to re-orientate would come soon enough.

The sky was dark. Wherever he was, it was definitely night, and Sebastian was now approaching the ground fast. The currents subsided and Sebastian was able to pull up a little, but he still hit the Earth hard.

It was agonizing, even for a beast of Hell.

He rolled on the Earth, writhing with pain. He was surrounded by the shadows of large trees. The immediate area was thick with greenery and plant life. The demonic beast snarled and cursed the ground on which he rolled. But he had been successful and had achieved his mission of going through the Heavens to reach Earth.

He got up. *"Where am I?"* he asked himself. He was so excited.

What an achievement! Like a dog wanting to dry his wet, furry body, Sebastian dusted himself off, shaking his body vigorously from side to side.

Back on heavenly grounds, another lone winged demonic being hovered in the sky. Sebastian had made it to Earth and this lone winged warrior was honored with the privilege of delivering the good news to Lucifer.

He yelled out to the skies with the news. It was time to retreat. The hellish mission, or at least the important part of it, had been accomplished.

Demons that were still able were quick to retreat. Injured demons were quickly disposed of by the ground gangs of Heaven without hesitation and without mercy.

Their attacks were precise and swift. The remaining angels and spirits hit their opponents hard and fast. With the battle now over, the remaining angels and spirits watched the enemy flee in the distance.

Raphael was hurt.

An injury from an earlier battle had been aggravated in this one. His right wing had been snapped in half and his right side, particularly his chest, had taken quite a beating.

Raphael was not happy with this all too familiar outcome.

Try as he might, he needed to rest before he could choose flight or fight. Gabriel had also taken a number of hits to the head. He was swollen, but otherwise fully functional. Archangel Michael had, except for some minor grazes, sustained no injury.

Heavenly light healed all in due course.

The news that Sebastian had reached Earth quickly spread across Heaven. They knew he would create havoc on Earth. As much as Heaven would have liked to do so, they needed to wait before they followed Sebastian.

Heaven simply could not spare the resources after such a great battle.

The need to attend to those who had passed was a priority. This involved nurturing the injured, rehabilitating those who had died from a life of heavenly existence. And then there was the opportunity to convert many evil souls over to a life under God's rule.

The latter was the most demanding task.

Even though he didn't know it, Sebastian was free to do as he wished.

Lucifer had given him only two conditions: complete the mission and avoid drawing attention to yourself.

CHAPTER ELEVEN
Earthbound

One could not apply any logic to the apparently illogical.

Their respective worlds couldn't be farther apart.

The same laws did not bind them, whether they were physical, biological or other. Time also had its own agenda with each world, but Earth and Heaven still maintained a bond.

It was a unique interaction. Nothing like it could be found between any other astral, physical or spiritual body.

Of all the items man had invented, it was the good old record player which best described this connection. A vinyl record waiting for the tone arm to swing across and lay the needle into the spinning record's groove. Yet where the needle fell was totally random.

It could land anywhere and everywhere. Having Heaven touch onto Earth in the middle of the Atlantic Ocean, on the top of Mount Everest or in the middle of downtown Los Angeles were all distinct possibilities. Essentially, the Earth spun away like a record and Heaven dropped in on it at any randomized point and location.

Not even God himself could control the point of interaction. It was simply the law of the physical world meeting the spiritual world, a law completely and utterly unto itself.

Down on Earth, which now housed a beast from the depths of Hell, all was dark. The night was eerily still and not a creature stirred, not even a single breeze.

Even the plant life remained dead still. With no wind to rattle the leaves, all was completely silent.

Sebastian had been standing on solid Earth for a while. In all his short time on Earth, he had done nothing other than recover from his hard landing and then marvel in the fact he had arrived on Earth.

He stood there mesmerized at his new world. Not that he could see much; he was surrounded by the dark of the night.

Accompanying him were minor wounds, scratches and a few superficial grazes that would heal in next to no time.

As if he were falling back into bed, Sebastian relaxed and let out a sigh of approval as he allowed his body to fall backwards. He landed in the dirty Earth below. Small rocks and dry leaves scattered around his fallen body. Fine brown dirt was stirred up from its resting place.

All these physical laws were in action, yet it was too dark to notice, even for a creature whose sight was used to dark and dreary conditions.

With another, much deeper whine, Sebastian reflected on his journey from Hell and was grateful; at the very least, he had landed on solid ground. He was also humbled by the efforts of the many who helped get him here.

The journey from Heaven and Earth was a major step towards achieving his objectives.

It had been quite a while since Sebastian was last on Earth. To have gotten this far was a testament to a clever, devilish plan.

The mission in the eyes of Sebastian was already a success.

Accordingly, he grinned with the cheekiest smile.

It had also been a grueling trip and he needed to rest a little more.

Sebastian gazed into the darkness above. It was a phenomenon his eyes were used to, but he did not know where he was. The trees and dense foliage that surrounded him did not help matters.

Sebastian rose to his feet and dusted himself off once more. As if he were royalty, Sebastian took the time to clean himself with dignity and pride, carefully brushing off the fine dirt and organic debris from his legs and arms.

The action was strange for a beast that spent his time living amid sulfur and brimstone. Strange for a creature that would, without remorse or hesitation, strike or degrade another one of its kind. For here stood a creature who had no morale or self-value. And still Sebastian continued to dust himself off with the dignity of a king before a public parade.

He then looked around, gaining a three hundred and sixty degree perspective of his surroundings. Sebastian tried to get his bearings but it was all dark and too dense. He looked for a higher vantage point to help him get out of this immediate area.

He needed to rise above the thick foliage that surrounded him.

A nearby tree gave him the out he was looking for. Climbing with the ease of a monkey, Sebastian jumped up from one tree limb to the next. His claws gave him excellent grip to climb thick trunks and he gained height with every move.

The tree limbs and branches went from thick to thin as Sebastian climbed higher. Maneuverability was becoming increasingly difficult, even for a dexterous beast like Sebastian. This did not concern him because he had found what he was looking for.

Out of the darkness of the thick foliage, high in the parkland tree came a new perspective. The full moon shone bright above the tree line, its glow danced off the treetops. The soft, lunar light provided great visibility above, but had trouble penetrating the dense foliage below. Still, things were a lot clearer from this new vantage point.

The forest before him was well manicured and it was evident it was not a wild forest, but a well maintained, manmade garden. As he panned around him, he realized he was in a massive parkland.

The trees and parks went for what seemed like miles in every direction. In the distance, on the outskirts of the park, there were tall buildings and skyscrapers.

Clearly, there was a big human population nearby. It was time for Sebastian to move with urgency.

He climbed down from the treetop, jumping effortlessly from branch to thicker branch to tree limb until he was back onto the ground with a thumping crunch.

The noise he made was loud enough to echo in the silence.

Sebastian looked around with the furtiveness of a would-be robber. It was not in his best interest to be noticed and this was one of the clear directives given to him by Lucifer.

Contemplating his next move, Sebastian looked around again, scanning the immediate area. It didn't really matter what direction he took. It was all unfamiliar to the beast of fire and brimstone. So he picked a direction and walked through branches, over plants, bushes and small trees of all varieties.

Sebastian had lost track of time, a concept which didn't carry a lot of value in the spiritual world, but was closely linked to the sunrise on Earth. Sebastian's primary goal was to go unnoticed; his secondary goal was his mission. There was nothing more that mattered to him.

Sebastian walked along the edge of a walking path, one of many that ran through the English Garden parklands of Munich.

He kept as close to the foliage as possible, scurrying for shelter wherever he thought it necessary.

Up ahead was a being known to Sebastian as a "Son of Adam." This term was widely used in the spiritual world to refer to humans.

This man, as he had done on many nights before, had taken rest on one of the park benches located in the massive parkland. His pants were old and tattered, held onto his waist by a makeshift belt. His jacket was loosely fitted and might have been considered stylish if it were being worn new, properly sized and ten years earlier.

Newspapers made for a substitute blanket and a scrunched up jumper gave his head something soft to lean on. A lonely brown paper bag with a greenish bottle protruding from it lay underneath the park bench. The man slept in a semi drunken bliss.

Sebastian had to walk on the path, for the parklands' organic matter would crunch and break beneath his feet. Silence was needed to keep his presence a secret.

Sebastian snuck up to the park bench and gazed upon the human's face. It was a sight he had not seen for some time. The drunk was certainly no great representative of the human race, but he gave Sebastian the chance to reunite himself with mankind.

Sebastian stared for the longest time, admiring the grunts and snorts that emanated from the man's mouth—along with breath, putrid from a mixture of last night's alcohol and bad dental hygiene. The smell did not worry Sebastian, who had come across much more vile and vulgar odors.

Suddenly the drunk repositioned himself and opened his eyes for the briefest of moments, closing them just as quickly.

His eyes immediately re-opened.

Horrified by what was staring back at him, the drunk froze in silence.

Sebastian became tense, so tense, his head trembled. The expression on his face turned to anger. His eyes focused on the human before him. He snarled at a barely audible volume. His tone was low and deep and it resonated like a sound of a downpour on a bituminous road.

The man's heart pounded hard and fast.

The bass sound continued to resonate. It travelled directly from the mouth of Sebastian and on right through to the core of the homeless man.

The beast's face became more and more intense, his face trembled with incredible speed and tension. Anger had turned to hatred. Sebastian's head vibrated so fast it blurred out of focus.

The drunk stared back, hypnotized with fear. The very essence of his being was being shaken. Even if he had wanted to, he could not move. He was paralyzed like a victim of a venomous snakebite.

The body was simply a shell of flesh and blood that housed the only thing of value to the beast, the soul. Then a crack came, a sound all too familiar to spiritual beings in battle.

The sound signified the spiritual shell cracking, releasing the soul for its onward journey. By default and by the laws of the spiritual world, the onward journey meant a trip to heavenly rehabilitation.

"About time," thought Sebastian. The task was enduring and tiring, even to one as skilled and determined as he. The human's soul had now moved out of the shell of this homeless drunk. The empty shell of human flesh and blood now belonged to Sebastian and was to become his shelter.

The drunk was no longer a Christian servant of God, for his body was now soul-less.

The shell that walked the Earth only moments before would soon house the devilish beast.

Sebastian stepped into the man as one steps into a doorway. He was quickly absorbed into the man's body. Sebastian was now able to wander incognito, unrecognizable to the outside world.

~ * ~

Onward, the homeless soul went. It was quickly thrust into the Heavens and re-emerged in a corner where all was quiet, without a single soul or Angel in sight.

The soul stood in the rolling white mist, a totally unfamiliar landscape.

Beyond being puzzled by the location in which he stood, the homeless man's mind was blank. Not a single thought ran through this being. He kept on following the trail of rolling mist.

91

He saw no end to the fluffy white clouds that went on as far as the eye could see.

He then raised his head, looking up at the strange and foreign sky. The blue of this sky was as pretty as any color could ever be. He had no reaction to the beauty of Heaven.

Where most were taken aback by, or at the very least warm to, the love, irresistible peace and comfort of Heaven, the drunk did not. His soul was in the deepest of shocks.

This man's soul did not travel to Heaven in a typical manner. It had been raped and pillaged by an occupant of Hell, traumatized into leaving the homebody that it once occupied.

Normally, cinematic images would begin to play when a soul entered Heaven. One would begin to view images of one's life against the blue backdrop of Heaven's serene skies, as if one was in a panoramic picture theatre and the blue surrounding sky was a movie screen.

But there was too much shock involved in this passing. Even in death, the souls of human mortals were not programmed to cope with such horror as invasion by a devilish soul.

Heaven was instantly alert to the newly arrived soul. He required the special attention of an experienced Angel. Although Raphael was still healing from the wounds from his battle, he was given the mission of nurturing this poor soul to the point where natural entry to Heaven could take place.

Raphael's healing would not interfere with the challenging task ahead.

The Angel Raphael was soon standing by this soul. "Welcome, my fellow Christian. Do not be concerned, for I am a friend."

Raphael then extended his wings. His wing injury still had not healed completely and a little discomfort was displayed on Raphael's face as he spread them out.

Truly beautiful, he demonstrated the warmth of Heaven and the love and protection of Angels through standing with wings at full stretch. Raphael bravely hid the pain of his injuries, remaining in as full a stretch as possible.

For the very first time, the newly arrived soul showed a flicker of interest as he gazed upon the beauty of Raphael. It was a good start to an out-of-the-ordinary entry into Heaven.

Raphael had to go back to basics and withdrew his wings into a much more comfortable position. His initial greeting to Heaven was over.

The challenge ahead for the great Angel was to reprogram the soul into understanding the connection between God and man. "We're all connected to Heaven," said Raphael. "It's just that common man forgets to check the connection from time to time. But let's go back to the dawn of time, the dawn of man.

"We all gathered; Angels and Holy spirits. A gathering of angelic beings surrounded the divine God, listening to his words of praise and the master plan. The inception of man, woman and child was about to be born. Man would rule over an animal kingdom that would come to fill the skies, the oceans and the different types of landscapes. This place would be called his home. His home would exist on this planet that would be eventually recognized and named Earth," said Raphael.

What started as a blank gaze onto a heavenly misty floor and open blue sky, quickly transformed to learned interest.

The homeless man with the traumatized soul had lost his memory of all that was important to make the transition into Heaven. There were some fundamental teachings that needed to be relearned.

Raphael continued with his lesson, going into every detail about man and God's intentions for him. The conversation went on for some time. It covered many topics, all with a common theme: the unbreakable connection between God and man and between Heaven and man.

Raphael stopped and walked away, far enough to allow the disturbed soul to process the information and make the connections for himself. As with any posttraumatic therapy, the healing process was slow.

Then Raphael walked back and blurted out suddenly in a loud but friendly way. "Give man free will, let him have free choice!" This put the discussion point into total perspective.

The drunken soul reacted to the delivery of the loud, firm message. His head jolted back as if he were being threatened, even though this was not the case. The point had to be made loud and clear, and consequently, it had sunk into his soul.

Lesson one was over and now for lesson number two.

"Where there is good, there will be evil. One cannot appreciate light unless they are to stand in complete darkness." Raphael spoke these words as if he was announcing the title of his masterpiece. A momentary pause followed before Raphael continued.

"Lucifer, one of God's most trusted Seraphs, the highest order of any Angel," said Raphael. "How power easily corrupts one whose ego is out of control.

"It was my friend, Archangel Michael, who was asked to put an end to the disharmony Lucifer had put upon the Heavens. Lucifer could no longer be trusted. Blasphemous was he!" Raphael shook his head in disappointment. "What Lucifer had done and accomplished is worrying to all in the Kingdom of Heaven," he added.

"The friction caused by the Angel Lucifer, an Angel I once called my friend, was affecting Heaven and its ability to effectively perform its earthly duties. For a short time in man's evolutionary history, his journey went astray as heavenly guidance was little to non-existent. For the very first time, man experienced the opposite of God's intended everlasting love and harmony. Primitive man had suddenly come to know extreme violence, famine and disease. And above all, primitive man had defied God's will of living in brotherly love and respecting the life and landscape that surround him. Because of one Angel's misdoings, an entire generation suffered.

"Enough was enough. Archangel Michael had the unpleasant task of addressing this. And so be it. Michael respected the hierarchy and angelic order and took to his heavenly duty immediately."

Raphael then turned and pointed to the blue sky above. The homeless man raised his head and eagerly waited. The event played out like one big movie.

And like in any story, the opening act was about to start. Michael had invited Lucifer to the Transitional Border. All that existed in this time was the end of heavenly light. No one had ever ventured into the darkness, as there was never an incentive to do so.

The Transitional Border simply marked the end of a vast and extensive Heaven.

The Archangel's words were harsh and direct. Michael, who had a reputation for being loud and direct, laid it on the line. There was no mistaking the message being conveyed to Lucifer.

"We are of the source, you must stop this at once," shouted Michael.

"You are but an Archangel, do not defy me! I sit near the throne of God, and given my way, I will one day rule the Heavens. I will one day rule you."

Lucifer's ego had truly exceeded the expectations of Archangel Michael. It was worse than he had first thought.

"Never!" shouted Michael. The Archangel angered instantly at such a preposterous idea.

The homeless man glanced up at the movie screen. The forgotten memories that lay deep within were starting to make sense. Subconscious memories were starting to heal and connect.

Even though this was emotionally draining and physically challenging, there was no choice. The disturbed soul looked on, observed, listened, witnessed and absorbed event after heavenly event.

The movie rolled on. Like rowdy drunks at a broken down

old pub, Lucifer pushed Michael around. His hands thrust down on Michael's chest, pushing the Archangel backwards. He thrust and prodded, forcing his authority over the mighty Archangel.

Michael was a patient and loyal follower to the throne, but he was also not to be pushed around. Everyone knew where they stood with Michael and he certainly did not appreciate what was turning into physical abuse.

And before you knew it, the pushing turned into a fight. No angelic beings had ever really gone to battle with each other before. Archangel Michael and Gabriel were both members of the warrior class of the angelic beings. Lucifer was outclassed as Michael retaliated.

The warrior Angel could easily have destroyed the once loyal Seraph. Had he persisted and killed Lucifer, rehabilitation would have meant his spirit would re-enter the Heavens.

But sadly, it would only be a matter of time before Lucifer would be led back to the same ideas and intentions. Before he would, once again, rebel against his God and all that he stood for.

Archangel Michael was sure of this and so was left with only one plausible alternative. Without any remorse, he cast Lucifer into the darkness beyond the Transitional Border.

A millennium slowly passed for the outcast Seraph. Lucifer had no choice but to make the darkness his kingdom.

Suddenly, weird images flashed onto the blue sky. They were pictures of Lucifer's transformation, snapshots of the hellish landscape, fire and brimstone, dark angels and winged demonic beings. All these horrors appeared before the wide eyes of the homeless man.

After all, an appreciation of good can come from the knowledge and birth of evil.

"To truly understand the glory of God, one must understand and never underestimate the evil and ultimate purpose of Lucifer's reign. We Angels live with this knowledge and in turn, man must never forget," said the Angel Raphael.

The man's soul was beginning to show signs of healing, but there was more to come. He observed the battles Lucifer unveiled upon the Heavens and learned from them. He also came to quickly realize why the Devil himself rarely took part in any battle.

As mighty as he was, if Lucifer were to lose his kingdom, the fiery skinned demon would have no home and no kingdom in which to reign.

The ruler of Hades had, through the ages, attacked all which was good and godly. The attacks occurred at irregular intervals, so Heaven remained on guard at all times. Angels, souls and spirits all took part and battled fiercely to protect the Heaven they loved so dearly.

The demonic attacks inflicted relatively little physical damage, but they imposed great emotional anguish on the Heavens and those who lived in the glory of the holy light. The former drunk needed to acknowledge the important interrelation of Heaven and Hell.

In order to do so, the movie event had come to a sudden stop to give him a break in which to think.

There was silence.

A lot of information had passed through the disturbed soul. Gathering all this data, processing all the emotion, trying to make sense of the unthinkable—it was all tiring.

As if they were taking a half time break at a football game, Raphael and the homeless soul both took time to rest and recover. Although the break was lengthy, it passed quickly.

Then Raphael approached the homeless man once more. He put his face next to his. The next set of words to leave Raphael's mouth were yelled but not shouted, loud but not deafening. They needed to be driven home with a firm impact.

Raphael took a little time to position his face in such a way that he was eye to eye and nose to nose with the homeless man. The Angel drew in a large, slow breath and prepared for the loudest delivery this man had ever heard.

The homeless man was not afraid; rather, he was open to the copious amounts of information that were being reinscribed onto his very soul.

Raphael's voice was so penetrating that any mere mortal would deafen in its presence. Not so was the effect on spirits and souls and creatures of the afterlife.

"Celebrate in God's presence! Communicate God's will! Demonstrate God's love! Educate yourself about all that is heavenly! We welcome thy humble servant into God's family." The words were spoken so loudly, they echoed for all the Heavens to hear, but the message was only directed to the one soul.

Raphael's speech had made an impact. He stepped back and let the soul respond. And as expected, he started to process thought after heavenly thought.

The trauma this soul had experienced had nearly all but subsided.

There was a little bit more to go.

With no warning, lesson three began. The movie images played again. The sudden explosion of sound and picture had the homeless soul snap out of his trance.

The images and information he had witnessed had to be processed at a later stage.

This time, the scenery in the film was different. A much more pleasant and serene setting in ancient Jerusalem, where a beautiful young lady was given the opportunity of a lifetime.

Under the instruction of God and through the efforts of the angelic hierarchy, the Immaculate Conception of Jesus Christ took its place in the history books of humankind.

And in a wooden shed full of farm animals, the Angels bore witness to the birth of the man who was destined to become the savior to all mankind.

In his life, they guided the young man until the day he faced those who persecuted him for his religious practices and beliefs.

The images of Lucifer appeared on the sky above.

His efforts to try and sway the Son of God were wasted.

Jesus would have been a great asset to the demonic King of Hades. Try as he might, the efforts of the Devil were in vain and Jesus remained true to the holy cause and to his heavenly father.

The homeless soul looked on. He grew more aware, more attentive, more connected as the lessons progressed.

The film images showed the Angels hovering around the place where Jesus stood, nails protruding from bloody hands and feet tightly fixed to the sturdy, wooden crucifix.

Dry blood mixed with dirt mapped the lines across his torso, back and limbs; a sign of the cruel lashings he had only recently endured.

The thorny crown lay embedded in his forehead, blood dripping from his near lifeless face.

But still this unique individual showed compassion to his fellow man and even to those who inflicted his pain and suffering. And in turn, Jesus tried to alleviate the worry of his loved ones who came to bear witness to this awful event.

And then the moment of moments came.

Jesus raised his weary head and spoke to the Holy Father above. "Forgive thee, Father, they know not what they do."

Out of the cruelty of many men arose one man's forgiveness. Jesus had done the Heavens and the Angels proud.

To the left and the right of this brave and divine individual were two common thieves, who also stood crucified. They did not have the misfortune of being nailed to their wooden stakes; instead they were bound tightly by rope and twine.

The homeless soul flinched as he began to comprehend the pain and torture endured by Jesus and the two thieves. The awareness passed through his rehabilitated soul like an electric shock.

The moments and experiences flicked by rapidly. The soul stood exhausted, unwillingly watching and feeling what became one of man's most celebrated events.

Jesus endured the most pain and suffered the longest, knowing he would be the last of the three to pass on. The movie slowed down and the images appeared at a rate which was close to real time. It was now the time to experience the passing of the Son of God.

The skies darkened as grey clouds emerged from the corners of the upper atmosphere. The Earth seemed to tremble and shake as an intense, but short quake celebrated the final moments of Christ's existence on Earth and his entrance into the Heavens above.

The awfulness and beauty of the moment came together rapidly and the emerging emotion was unexplainable. It drew many a tear to the rehabilitated soul's face and even drew upon the emotions of the Angel Raphael.

The homeless man watched on, Raphael close by his side. The Son of God was now the new ruler of the Heavens, answerable only to the Holy Father himself. The Virgin Mary was honored in the unanimous decision of the Choir of Angels to award her the title, Queen of the Angels.

These beautiful and loving memories impressed themselves upon the once lost soul. The healing process was approaching its finale.

The soul anxiously stood there waiting for more. The movie had paused for only a moment, giving time to briefly reflect on the importance of the angelic order and on heavenly friendships.

As often as Raphael had come to see these images, he was still moved to a tear or two.

"Lucifer was always in competition with the Heavens. Good and bad always fought for the right to win an earthly soul forever. History came to acknowledge the preachers and the prophets. Of equal glory were the tyrants and mass executors. All souls entered the Heavens by default. Some stayed to live a life in the glory of the light. Others were reincarnated in the hope a second chance would eventually lead to a better and more fulfilling heavenly existence.

Some were simply so enraged with hate that their only option was a life of brimstone and fire." Raphael spoke these words staring intently into the face of the homeless soul.

Raphael continued. "Masses of souls and beings came to fill the Heavens and Hells. When Lucifer saw fit, another battle exploded on the grounds of Heaven. On the odd occasion, Heaven chose to retaliate. It was not the way of this godly place and at times the costs were too high in terms of lost and rehabilitated heavenly life. Heaven's advantage was fighting its battles on its own ground."

Numb with emotion, the former drunk had spent what seemed like an eternity in Heaven whilst on Earth only a small fraction of time had passed.

The homeless man finally sat down with his legs crossed. The man's head remained bowed down in deep thought.

Raphael walked away.

His job was done.

Soon after, the homeless one's concentration was broken by the big blue sky above. The panoramic theatre was about to start again.

But now, as every soul that enters Heaven does, the man would spend many days reflecting on his own lifetime, watching his life in surround sound on the heavenly sky above.

This allowed the homeless soul the time to reflect on his own life experiences and ensure a smooth transition into Heaven.

He was entitled to this transition, but, unfortunately, it had been demonically stolen from him. Now this right had been returned to him.

Ultimately, Heaven was there to offer him a love and warmth he had not experienced back on Earth for some time.

CHAPTER TWELVE
Over to the Skies of Germany

Today was a picture perfect day.

In the heart of Munich stood one of Germany's largest landscaped gardens.

This giant park had creeks, rivers, fauna, wildlife, beer gardens, pathways, jogging tracks and everything else to entertain the locals and visitors to the region. The English Gardens were a credit to both Munich and to the people of Germany.

However, today walked a wolf in sheep's clothing. In the gardens there was a beast of darkness hiding inside the skin of a poor homeless man.

The sun rose, shining through the atmosphere unhindered. Not a cloud in sight to dissipate the sun's rays, its brightness or its gentle warmth.

It lit up the picturesque beauty of the gardens.

Creeks and streams glistened as the sun speckled off the rippled, watery surface. Trees danced in the light breeze, creating moving shadows on the grounds below. Animal life was out and about, too, seizing the opportunity to warm up from a cold and frosty night.

Man was also getting ready for another day in a busy German city. Some chose to have breakfast in the English Gardens, taking their morning meal in a natural setting. Many, however, chose to walk one of the many paths, taking in some exercise and fresh air before the hustle and bustle of a busy working day began.

In amongst all this stood a homeless man who was not of this world. He walked around trying to not be noticed, but noticed he was. The beast could not comprehend he now occupied a shell of a body that made him inconspicuous.

All he had to do was play the part of a misplaced drunk.

Instead, Sebastian desperately sought shelter, trying to run away anytime he was within sight of any man, woman or child.

The evil beast awkwardly walked around in tattered clothes. His guilt was as evident as the stale body odor which emanated from every fiber in his tattered clothing.

Many noticed the beast, but they were unaware of the evil soul that lurked within. Instead, they took pity on this apparent misfit, choosing to view but not look at him, to notice but not to stare, to care but not get involved.

The attitude was typical of busy people in this modern, crowded city.

Desperately seeking shelter, Sebastian made his way through the thick foliage to a corner of the park where he could sit in peace and quiet. The foliage was dense enough to keep him out of sight and attention. It was the place where he had started his journey on Earth and for now, he had made his temporary home there.

All human activity was now audible to him. He listened to couples talking as they walked by on a nearby track. From much farther away came the sound of a child throwing a tantrum and a mother telling him off for some wrongdoing.

For the moment, Sebastian could rest. He didn't have access to the healing and replenishment that emanated from the depths and warmth of Hades. His only choice was to gain some rest through sleep and meditation. The surrounding sound of humans was of no concern. For the first time since landing on Earth, Sebastian closed his eyes.

~ * ~

Tony and Johnny were on their way to Germany; their destination was still several hours away.

Up in the skies somewhere over southern India, the boys sat in their business class seats. They had finished their meals and were looking through their monitors to pick one of the many in-flight movies. This would help a few hours of their long journey go by.

Johnny put on his headphones and turned to Tony. "This hasn't even hit the big screen back home!" He continued, "I'll see you on the other side." Johnny sat back and prepared to enjoy the entertainment.

The credits of the movie started and Tony perceived every indication that Johnny was not to be disturbed until the movie's end.

Tony got up to stretch his legs.

He had been in one place for a little too long. To the left of him was the passage to economy class and to the right to first class. He chose economy, walking down one of the two passageways that ran through the length of the plane. He steadied himself with every other step.

Even in the smoothest of flights it can be awkward to walk down the aisle.

Johnny looked up to catch his friend leaving the immediate area. He glanced only for a moment and then was quick to get back into his movie.

Tony had only just passed the curtain separating economy from business class. The plane passageways ran by the rows of economy class seats. There were three seats, a passageway, then five seats then a passageway and then three seats again. The flight was pretty full.

Tony took his first steps into economy class, making his way in a very casual sort of fashion. The walk helped get the blood flowing in his legs. He hoped that it loosened up some of the stiffness which had set in.

He walked through one dividing curtain and then another until the inside of the tail end of the plane was in sight. He continued on his stroll until he reached the end of the plane. In the back galley, Tony bent forward and lifted his legs in an effort to do a series of leg stretches.

Tony then crouched to retie his shoelaces and then took his first steps back.

The quiet sound then arose. Tony looked up and all eyes were upon him.

They all looked upon the young man with pride and joy as if there were a bride walking down the church aisle on her wedding march.

"There he is," Tony heard. The softly spoken words came from a seat near the second passageway. A young man smiled at Tony and looked upon him like a parent looks upon a newborn child.

Tony didn't want to be rude and threw back a half-hearted smile.

"God bless this young man," came another whisper. This time it was from a passenger sitting between the two aisles. The passengers were talking quietly between themselves. The noise of the combined voices created a type of murmur that carried itself throughout the economy class.

A flurry of complimentary tones, one after the other.

Tony caught the odd comment in amongst the many whispers. It didn't make any sense. The attention gave Tony goose bumps and he picked up the pace of his walk, refusing to look left or right, down or up. He steadied his eyes on a curtain that returned him to his seat.

A stewardess had broken through the curtain from the business class section. Her trolley in front of her, she was cleaning up plates from the meal. "I will only be a minute, young man, and then you can come through."

Tony had no choice but to wait patiently.

An elderly lady covered in a blanket was making herself comfortable in the first aisle seat of economy class. Tony glanced over her finished dinner tray and raised his eyes to meet hers. He politely smiled at her and she at him. "God bless you, son," said the old lady.

Tony was taken aback with surprise. He tried to maintain his politeness through his smile but failed to do so. Tony felt unworthy of the many compliments that came his way.

The old lady's comment was the final straw.

Whatever Tony chose not to acknowledge had now caught him off guard. His smile quickly turned to a look of polite disapproval and his head simultaneously pulled back in sheer astonishment.

As Tony looked up and away, he met the eyes of the airhostess. She was still cleaning dinner trays down the economy aisle but took a moment to look up and back at Tony. She had her dinner cart with her and it appeared as though she was about to head back to the central kitchen. "Excuse me, sir, we must clear the dinner trays. You are welcome to wander the cabin, but please keep clear of first class."

She then maneuvered her trolley to allow the young man to pass. As Tony walked by, the stewardess leaned forward and whispered sternly, "Please heed my warning!" She took a few more steps and turned her head. "By the way, young man, you better tie those shoe laces. You don't want to be tripping in the aisles now, do you?" She smiled back pleasantly one more time and was then back into her duties.

Tony politely returned the smile and looked down to notice his laces were untied. He felt that the laces could wait just a little longer.

Tony walked back into business class.

It was dark outside and the lights had been dimmed inside the business class section. The trays had been cleaned and it was time for some sleep or some movie entertainment.

106

Tony looked over to his friend who was now fast asleep in his comfortable chair. Everyone else was noticeably involved in his or her own activities.

Tony was pleased to be back. It was a welcome relief from his experiences down at the other end of the plane.

He stood at the curtain trying to make sense of what had happened. It had started at the airport and then continued on the plane.

What next?

He waited for it, wondering whether something would happen in business class.

He bent to tie his shoelaces and then stood and waited.

He waited some more, but all he noticed was that one by one, the passengers were getting ready to sleep or had already fallen asleep.

Tony had lost track of time. He had been standing there long enough for the stewardess to come breaking back through the curtain. She had finished her duties in economy class and was making her way to the front galley. "Excuse me, young man."

Tony politely moved to one side and let the stewardess through. He deliberately stood his ground waiting for something to happen, but she completely ignored him as she passed him. It was as though they were complete strangers. As if they had never exchanged looks or words.

It might have been that she was busy and concentrating on her work.

Maybe it was self-inflicted? Or maybe Tony had become too sensitive to his surroundings and how people reacted to him.

Tony wondered about it all, while he stood by and watched her continue into first class. She wheeled her dinner trolley through the curtains and then disappeared out of sight.

He watched the curtains sway to a close, wondering whether she would pop her head back out with some sort of weird message. As patiently as Tony waited, there was nothing. He looked around business class. Everyone was asleep. Some, like Johnny, had fallen asleep in front of their monitors; others were lying comfortably in their chairs enjoying some well-deserved shut eye.

Tony looked up towards the first class curtain. Things were getting a little bumpy and Tony had to steady himself against the turbulence with the help of the surrounding seats.

He made his way towards the curtains. The bumps and thumps were a little more pronounced than before. He was careful not to wake any of the other passengers as he steadied himself on their seats. Tony eventually got to the end of his journey. All were still and sound asleep.

He scanned his surroundings and paused for a moment longer by the curtains which separated business class from first class.

He then slowly pushed one of the curtains off to the side, gently brushing it so as not to disturb the passengers. The first class section was not as busy, with only a dozen or so passengers to cater for. There were many spare seats, which allowed the lucky passengers to spread themselves out in the first class cabin.

Things appeared a little livelier in first class. Everyone was awake and sipping on a post meal alcoholic beverage.

With no stewardesses in sight, Tony could not resist the temptation to see what the best seats in the house were like. He made it all the way through first class to the front curtain separating first class with the front galley.

Peeking his head through, he saw the meal preparation areas and the passageway leading up to the cockpit. He pondered going further but decided he would not push his luck.

There was nothing more to see here. Tony turned his head.

It was suddenly dead silent.

All first class cabin eyes were set upon him. All the passengers were simultaneously sipping their respective drinks methodically and at an extremely slow pace.

They glared angrily right into Tony's core. It was as if he

was on trial for murdering a loved one. The first class passengers continued with their meticulous drinking, and their eyes did not move off him.

Tony, with fear and reluctance, looked back. Everywhere he turned his head, a set of glaring eyes was upon him.

Tony made for a quick exit. Back into business class he went, and this time he did not look back.

Nothing had changed in business class. All were restful and asleep. Tony sat next to Johnny.

"Johnny," he called, bumping his friend to awaken him. Johnny brushed him aside and turned his body so he could be left alone to his blissful sleep.

Tony's eyes were wide open and his heart was pounding with adrenaline and nerves.

Under the current circumstances, all that was left to do was to sit back in his chair and allow the remaining hours of the flight to pass.

CHAPTER THIRTEEN
Hell in Munich

The moon glowed with limited intensity. Its small crescent shape did not give the sun enough area to provide a reflective light to illuminate the Earth's surface.

Instead, a tender lunar glow, which barely penetrated the night time sky, made its way across Munich. It hardly made an impact given that it was faced with the need to combat the bright city night lights and street lamps.

Sebastian sat up and stretched his arms back and high. Even with his well-developed night vision, he found it awkward to see to the ends of his now human hands.

Sebastian crawled out of his shelter of dense shrubs and surrounding trees. A faint glow shone through some of the greenery. He knew he was headed for the right direction as he made his way back to one of the main pathways in the English Gardens.

The light became brighter as the flora became sparser. Sebastian was out in the open and could finally see.

His eyes, however, needed a little time to adjust from complete darkness to the light shed by the brightly illuminated park lamp on the side of the parkland path.

Like a baby child awakening from sleep, Sebastian rubbed both his eyes with the palms of his hands. He twisted them left and right, left and right again, giving his eyes a good old rub.

Sebastian's hands felt a bit gritty. A strange sensation came over the beast of Hell. He looked down to see his cupped hands full of flaky dead skin. The beast dropped the dead skin onto the ground and quickly reached for his face.

It felt the same: dry. It was unusual.

He turned his hands over in a concerned fashion, checking his adopted body.

It didn't look right, A dermatologist's nightmare, as bad as any dermatitis could be. The skin was flaky. Sebastian checked the rest of his body only to find the same occurring all over him. This had come sooner than expected.

Heaven's golden rule: all souls default to Heaven and God's light. To pursue an eternity in fire and brimstone is an entirely different matter.

No matter what path you take, be it Heaven or Hell. But when on Earth, no human shell can survive without its soul.

Sebastian was a slave to the physical and spiritual rules that dictated his necrosis. He quickly came to the conclusion that he'd soon have no shell of a human body in which to hide his beastly manner. His mission would be jeopardized if his identity was discovered.

And so the hellish beast returned to dodging pathways and moving in the dark. The beast searched the parklands, looking for his next victim, but all was quiet. It was a working day and an ungodly hour. Try as he would, he could not find a human shell to occupy.

Sebastian was left with no option but to leave the security of the giant parkland. He scanned the skies where the skyscrapers met the tree line. The distance to the edge of the park was not great and soon he found himself on a dainty little street on the northern side of the park.

The antique street lamps were painted a deep green. The street was more open and spacious and located in a more luxurious part of the city.

In this new environment, there was a greater chance of

being discovered and, therefore, it was a little more difficult to navigate without being noticed, but Sebastian managed.

Cautiously, he looked around and ducked from one hiding place to the next.

Trees in streets, front yard greenery, sides of houses or anything that was out of the light and away from potential, prying human eyes was a short term hiding place.

There was little traffic, with only the occasional car making its way through the tastefully decorated, tree-lined street.

Sebastian became desperate. The skin which once covered his arm had almost completely peeled off. The muscle underneath was revealed and had lost its pink fleshy appearance. It oozed with pus and smelled rotten. Movement was difficult, too, as the mechanical system of the human body had stiffened, hindering the beast's ability to move freely.

The appearance and smell of his body did not bother Sebastian, but he knew it could give his presence away.

The limitations to his movement were also becoming annoying. Sebastian moved around as if he were wearing several tight pieces of clothing. It would not be too much longer before he was ready to contemplate leaving this shell and walking the streets in his natural form. He would no longer have to contend with the current necrotic smells and he would, at the very least, regain the ability to move with speed and agility.

But at this point in time, he remained in his homeless man's shell.

He heard a ruckus from a nearby house.

A taxicab had pulled into a laneway to let a couple out. They were drunk, but cooperative and paid the cab driver the fare. The only thing left for the cabbie to do was to look for the next paying job on this quiet night.

The cabbie sat in his car a little while longer. The inside cabin light was on and he finished some paper work while considering what part of Munich gave him the best chance of finding another passenger.

Sebastian looked into the near distance. The couple staggered up their driveway as the cab driver reversed his car ready to get to his chosen destination.

The taxi headed in the direction of the hellish human shell.

Sebastian jumped out into the street and the headlights glared upon him as the cab came to a screeching halt. Sebastian raised his arm to shield his eyes from the brightness. He hoped the cab would stop without inflicting further damage on his human host.

The cabbie jumped out of his car. It took him a little while. He was tall, well-built and carried a fair degree of excess weight.

"You stupid son of a bitch! Who jumps out into the middle of the road in the middle of the night like that?" Sebastian seized the moment, jumping out of his human shell and revealing his true form.

The cab driver was set upon by one of Hell's finest and he was frozen with fear. His soul went into a state of shock and was shaken at its very core.

The beast shook his head, vibrating it from left to right, staring with the greatest of intensities. The vibrations strummed faster and faster. A deep sound emanated from the beast's mouth. The cabbie's soul was now being asked in the most intrusive of fashions to exit his body.

Excess weight combined with a sedentary job had taken its toll on the cabbie's health. This soul would not have walked the Earth for much longer.

The task of removing this soul to give Sebastian a fresh shell was not as the last one. It happened with relative ease.

With a heavenly crack, the former human soul exited for the Heavens and Sebastian jumped in.

This human host was a difficult one to move around in.

Standing next to an open door of the idling taxi was a big burly body that now housed a beast of Hell. In this new form,

Sebastian looked down the road and focused on the middle of the taxi's beam lights. The homeless man's body was now a corpse lying motionless in the middle of the road. Two headlight beams shone upon the still and rotting body.

This was once the human host Sebastian had come to inhabit. And just like that, it was deserted and left to rot in the middle of the road with no remorse and no respect. It was simply a last minute opportunistic choice that came by the way of a dark angel and its continual need to occupy the bodies of human beings.

The demon struggled with the choice before him. Thoughts ran through the beast's mind and he entertained ungodly considerations, balancing ease of movements in a body whose flesh is rotting versus a body who was so overweight, to move expended much energy and effort.

Ultimately, the beast wanted speed and agility, neither of which was really available in the bodies before him. The beast tested out the shell of a body it currently resided in. He tested its large frame and freedom of movement as if he were taking a car for a test run.

The taxi was still running and the headlights were still shining down the tree lined street.

He walked up to the human body that lay on the road, kneeling beside his former host and looking at his skin. The corpse looked artificially aged.

The skin and muscle had lost much of its integrity and elasticity. Sebastian played with the skin like a child playing with a rag doll. It tore with ease, revealing more muscle and flesh. It was stale, with faded color and pungent with rotting stench.

His choice was simple.

Regardless of the inconvenience, movement on Earth without arising too much suspicion was his ultimate goal. Sebastian got up and headed back to the cab. He then walked past the idling vehicle.

He was not of this world and although he knew what the

vehicle was used for, he made no attempt to either understand the technology nor to use the resource.

He left the scene of the crime as it was: motor running and rotting corpse in the spotlight.

He continued to struggle with the movement and mechanics of his new host. Every movement was jerked and out of sync. He could not easily accommodate himself to the excess weight.

As awkward as the task was, he was soon in the shadows of the parkland again.

The night time was soon to come to an end and it was evident he had to see another full day out before he could once again hunt in the dark.

This was some twenty long hours away so he sought the refuge of his favourite resting place in the English Garden, far away from prying human eyes.

Sluggishly and awkwardly, the beast made his way to the edge of the gardens. Sebastian had tired and sat down on a park bench at the northern end of the gardens.

He dropped his chin to his chest and relaxed his body, trying to release some of the tension and stiffness that had built up. He closed his eyes and focused on loosening up the burly frame of a former taxi driver. Relaxation quickly and unintentionally turned to sleep.

Time passed.

A parkland lamppost shone nearby.

Its light flickered a little. On and off. On and off. On and off and then off for good.

On the park bench, the big, burly man lay stretched out, fast asleep. The creature lurking within the shell of the sleeping man was none the wiser to what was going on. After all, it was the beast that was asleep, not the man.

The parkland lamps had automatically switched themselves off as the massive gardens witnessed the sunrise. The fiery skin of the sun appeared on the horizon, and the first rays of sunlight filtered across the city landscape. The black dark night turned a shade lighter.

Soon the skies were a navy blue and becoming lighter by the moment. The first signs of warmth only made Sebastian sleep more soundly. Indeed, his sleep became deeper in proportion to the warmth that beamed down onto his tired body.

Time passed and Munich woke up.

An hour or so later, rudely awoken by humans hurrying on a working morning, Sebastian opened his eyes and was startled by the foot traffic before him. As quickly as he could manage, he scurried for shelter.

The track Sebastian was looking for ran off one of the main pathways. He could see it up ahead.

The beast was looking for a place where the greenery and foliage were thick. He needed an isolated location to keep him out of sight and feeling comfortable and secure.

The beast turned onto the track, scurrying through the plant life and making his way to familiar shelter. Once there, Sebastian laid his weary head on the dirt and closed his eyes. He could still hear the sounds of nearby humans using the parkland pathways.

As before, the noise did not bother the beast.

Sebastian closed his eyes and returned to a deep meditative state.

In this sub-conscious realm, he re-energized in preparation for another night's work.

CHAPTER FOURTEEN
A Fighting Competition in Munich

Jack sat across from his father, as he had done on many occasions. He was chatting with his dad, talking about events in general.

But he was also checking in on his father to see if everything was okay.

He could see in his father that he was still troubled by the lack of communication that existed between him and Chris.

Jack was worried about his father. He was a strong man, but the events of the past few years had taken their toll. The grey haired man tried to put on a brave face, but Jack knew his father well enough to perceive life was catching up with him real fast.

Arthur's olive complexion didn't have the luster it used to. His face looked tired and worn, riven by a series of very deep and well seated wrinkle lines. This all came together to give the impression of stress, worry and a hard life.

Arthur had finished up the plates. Jack had dropped by for an evening cup of coffee. Father and son had chatted about nothing in particular until they got to the subject of Chris; a topic both knew had to eventually be raised.

They then discussed Chris in detail, particularly his attitude. The discussion was pretty one-sided with Jack doing most of the talking.

"He's being pig-headed, Dad, and you know it!" Jack spoke

firmly to his father, but it was like throwing a tennis ball to a brick wall. The comment simply bounced back to where it had started.

The dispute over the giving of the money to Tony had gone on longer than he had anticipated, and while the disagreement itself was not cause for worry, the fact it had not resolved itself by now was. Jack did not enjoy seeing his family divided and he knew his father felt the same.

~ * ~

The house was lonely.

Arthur didn't have his Pam anymore to talk with, his grandson had gone overseas and his sons had moved out many years ago. Arthur would have liked to have shared his concerns about the issue between Chris and him with someone.

He had his chat with Jack, but there was more that needed to be said, more that needed to be discussed and shared with someone of his own vintage.

Jack kept talking as Arthur's mind aimlessly wandered.

For a short time, Arthur was reminded of the things he used to take for granted. As he thought about these moments, he let Jack speak, but did not pay attention to the detail.

Jack continued and Arthur withdrew into his own world. Still, the loving father kept his manners and at the very least, pretended to be attentive to Jack's discussions and opinions.

Arthur was reminded of the special family interactions that made his house a home. He was reminded of the day when the family pulled together in the hope his daughter survived her horrible injuries. They were the injuries that came from the car crash which instantly killed their son-in-law and eventually claimed Mary's life.

Mary was the only daughter of Arthur and Pam Gretsis. She was the only sister to Jack and Chris Gretsis and most importantly, the only mother to a young and influential Tony.

Her injuries were so severe, she succumbed to them in a very short time.

As difficult as it was initially, it was different now.

Many years had passed and the pain of the loss of his daughter had settled. Arthur now reflected on how the love and support surfaced so strongly at a time when the family was in their deepest mourning. How the family pulled together during the short period when Mary fought for her life and eventually gave in to her injuries.

As hard as it was, life went on for the Gretsis family.

But soon after, relatively speaking, Pam had succumbed to a heart attack. The family was once again thrown together to support one another and carry on with only loving memories of the dearly deceased.

Almost like clockwork, the family went into automatic mode when tragedies hit. Having Pam around had made Mary's death bearable.

Losing Pam had artificially and very quickly aged the loving father and adored grandfather. He had generally worn his years well, but two close deaths was a strain.

Arthur knew he shouldn't ponder such things. He very quickly got into a vicious cycle of depressing thoughts. Not that he was depressed. His mental state was more a pool in the sunshine.

The pool represented the repressed memories. No matter how pleasant the day was, one could not resist jumping in the pool and swimming around for a while. But no matter how long you swim for, you eventually get out to dry yourself off.

It wasn't time yet.

Arthur had to swim around for a little longer and take one more lap around his pool of intermittent depression.

He needed to wallow in his memory for a bit more as his thoughts turned to his immediate family members.

His mind's eye recalled the vision of that dreadful day. Deep in his memory, Arthur watched each and every one suffer and torment themselves in their own special way. This hit every Gretsis family member hard, but none harder than Tony. His one and only grandson, a young man who had learned to grow up fast.

Arthur's eyes almost welled. This was a big deal for a man who had witnessed the hardships of war. Men of his era did not cry.

An army of tears was waiting at the command, but Arthur raised his hand and wiped away a single lonely tear, the only tear he allowed to stroll down the side of his cheek.

He cleverly hid this from Jack.

Jack was too busy talking. In a non-egotistical sort of way, he was too busy with the sound of his own voice. Even so, his concerted efforts to get this issue out for discussion had left him none the wiser about the wandering thoughts of his father.

Jack did notice one thing.

It was getting late and his father's eyes were tiring. This was a tell-tale sign it was time to wind up and leave his father to deal with his night time rituals before retiring to bed.

Memories were there to be dealt with. These reflections came every now and then and there was no point in dwelling on them.

This was Arthur's life motto: Acknowledge it, deal with it and move on. (Or at least do the best you can!) And with that thought it was time for him to jump right out of the depression pool.

It was time to dry himself off. Shake off those repressed memories and move onward.

Arthur had seen his son off, locked the house up and was now in his bedroom.

He took a look at the marital bed Pam and he shared for many years. As big as it was, Arthur still kept to his side, the habit of a long and successful marriage.

He looked at the neighboring pillow and placed his hand at its center. This was Pam's pillow, the place where she laid her head every night.

He lovingly stroked it a few times, slowly arcing his hand, back and forth. Pushing into the pillow enough for the firmness of the pillow to push back. Back and forth he went again until it was time to turn off the bedside lamp light, roll over and close his weary eyes.

He quickly fell into a deep sleep.

~ * ~

On the other side of the world, the boys had settled into their new destination and were enjoying the trip away.

Today was the day of days! With their special tickets, they were soon seated in some of the hottest chairs in the house, watching a tournament as big as they come in the world of Karate competitions.

Karate had a stronger following in Europe and the Munich tournament was attracting spectators from many of Germany's neighboring countries. The crowds were walking into the giant stadium. Many were avid supporters, dressed in their home country colors and waving the home flag. Others were dressed in casual attire to see the fight of fights.

The boys were thrilled. It wouldn't be too soon until they found themselves merging into the crowd of nations and swept into a stadium of tournaments.

This was not European football. Such events may attract many tens of thousands of fans and supporters. This competition was different. The following was more loyal and personal in most cases. The tournament was expected to attract fifteen or so thousand. And this was considered to be a successful event.

As was the case with many elimination tournaments, three fighting arenas were set up with seating all around and up into the length and breadth of the stadium. The seating was pre-allocated at first, but not many people stuck to their assigned places, moving around to other locations to get better views of fights of interest.

The young adventurers held onto their special tickets. They were right up front, giving them both an unobstructed and slightly elevated outlook over the middle and main fighting mat. The view onto the neighboring arenas was also more than satisfactory. The boys were thrilled with their assigned places. There were fighters in every corner, differentiated only by the small flag on the upper corner of their fighting Gi.

The traditional Karate uniform was marked with the flag of the fighter's country of origin. Nothing more and nothing less. Many fighters representing many countries were out in the open areas, stretching and flexing their kicks and punches.

The warm ups added to the electric atmosphere.

The Australian flags were in sight and the Australian team could be seen in the distance. The boys remarked on the familiar faces. They talked about the different fighting styles they had come to recognize while competing in the qualifiers back home several weeks earlier.

None of it meant much; it just killed some time while the crowds and competitors settled in.

Tony took his eyes off the fighting floor and let them wander. The conversation then strayed a little.

"Got to say this about the Germans," said Tony, "very well organized indeed!" Tony observed the giant board which marked the fights by surname and country. Times allocated were to the minute and it was clear they were going to push through each fight like a production line.

~ * ~

Back in the land of Australia, all was dark. The night sky was clear and there was an array of stars to pick and choose from.

These, however, were far from Arthur's mind as he lay fast asleep. He wiggled to get comfortable, continuing with his deep and much needed sleep.

Eddie Georgonicas

Arthur's subconscious mind was communicating with his conscious mind, dealing with the day's events, the thoughts and the worries. His mind was working at two different, but unified levels. Ultimately going about and doing its diligent duty of maintaining oneself.

The moment was quick and brief. Somewhere deep in the thought process came the message to open his eyes and awaken.

With the strangest feeling of being looked upon intently, Arthur snapped his eyelids wide open. He didn't have to look for long. With his head firmly set on his pillow, he looked straight ahead and was startled by the image before him.

An image of Pam's face was outlined resting on the pillow next to him.

At first, Arthur thought he was still in the dream state, but he soon realized he was not. The image was crystal clear and doubts about the vision soon disappeared from Arthur's mind.

He could see every feature, every wrinkle drawn out in white and shades of grey. The image was better than any sketch artist could ever think of doing.

Arthur realized the image was not still.

Pam let out a gentle smile, looking back at her husband with caring eyes. The picture before Arthur changed. Pam's face now reflected care and gentleness.

The seconds passed slowly.

Arthur's startled response quickly turned to joy and comfort.

The introductions were over.

Pam was expending much energy and even spirit entities tire. Sounding like an athlete who had been interviewed immediately after running a marathon, her words were blurted out as if she was out of breath.

"Don't worry, all will be okay," spoke the spirit entity of Pam. "All will be okay. Tony, Chris and Jack. You needn't worry. Especially my Tony. We are all looking out for him." As soon as the

123

last of these words had been spoken, the image of Pam's face disappeared.

Arthur's heart was pounding. He searched for the bedside lamp switch, bringing light into an otherwise pitch black room.

The image remained long enough for Arthur to have no doubt about the message or the person bringing in the message. This didn't help him calm his pounding heart.

Arthur reflected on Pam's words, but could not fathom the meaning of her cryptic message.

All was okay!

"Could it not be?" He wondered.

He did not know what to think, but the one thing he did realize was that he was not going back to sleep in a hurry.

He was wide awake like the people in Munich on the other side of the world.

The only difference was it was day there and the middle of the night in Adelaide, Southern Australia.

His thoughts turned to Tony. Was he okay? What was he doing?

His grandson was a responsible child, and Arthur had to rely on his motto in life.

Acknowledge it, there's nothing here to deal with and so move on.

Tony, on the other hand was none the wiser.

Thoughts of his grandfather or any other family member had not crossed his mind. Both he and Johnny had enjoyed a jam - packed evening watching the Karate competition.

Australia had been eliminated in the first round, which left the boys with nothing to do but to enjoy some fine fighting.

And fine fighting it was. The boys were as pumped up as the fighters in the arena before them.

At this stage, with the event coming to a close, the crowds were moving around and the numbers in the stadium were dwindling. It had been a long afternoon. Some had seen enough and had called it a day. Others had sat for many hours and were now moving around to get some blood circulating into their stiff bodies.

Tony and Johnny, except for the occasional refreshment or rest break, had remained in their original front row seats the whole time.

The fighters were still being put through their paces as fight after fight was run in line with the schedule on the board. As Tony had suspected it would be, the competition had been efficiently run and all was on time.

It was mid-afternoon and the boys spotted a large man walking in awkwardly with wobbles and jerks.

The movements did not look natural and they attracted attention from the boys and spectators. The boys took their eyes off the fight for a brief moment to watch the obese man make his way to his seat. It was likely this man needed the space of two or more seats. His massive weight interfered with his maneuverability to the point he could not even walk without looking out of place. The stares of the crowd soon reverted back to the fighting arena.

Tony and Johnny, however, kept their eyes on this individual for a little bit longer. More so because of the flag he carried and waved. The large man did not look or acknowledge the boys, but he had chosen to walk in their general direction.

The Australian flag was being waved a bit late in the competition, they thought. Soon the boys forgot about it and returned their attention to the main fight.

The tournament was into the first of the semi-final fights with the host nation up against one of its European neighbors. The host nation looked to eliminate Russia as the fight settled into its last minutes. The boy's eyes remained fixed on this engrossing battle for the finals.

Suddenly the large man appeared within a few feet of the two youngsters, vigorously waving the Australian flag. He then made his way up the stairs and continued to wave the flag, not once removing his eyes from the boys. And the boys kept watching him, too.

Johnny stood to confront the man, but Tony grabbed his friend and sat him right down.

"Ignore him, he'll go away," Tony sternly whispered his words of caution to Johnny. Tony resumed watching the fight, but Johnny had to look back.

The large man for the briefest moment stared intently into Johnny's eyes and vibrated his head with the smallest of movements. Low sounds vibrated from his mouth as he gave Johnny a taste of his power.

Sebastian took long enough to disturb Johnny's soul, but not long enough to draw attention to his actions.

Johnny went into the briefest of trances and sat down. He felt ill to his stomach and had lost track of where he was or what he was doing for the moment.

"Johnny, Johnny! Are you all right?" Tony asked, but there was no response. "Johnny, Johnny!"

At that point Johnny snapped out of his miniature trance and held his stomach. "No!" He held onto his stomach for a little longer. "No, I'm not feeling well. Not well at all."

"Do you want to go?" asked Tony.

"Yeah! I don't think I'll last. I really have to lie down." Johnny stood up, feverish and weak. Tony helped his friend as they made their way down to the platform.

Once on the lower platform, Tony could not help but look back up into the stadium at the large man who sat several rows behind the seats Tony and Johnny had enjoyed for most of the day.

The man sat back with his arms folded and resting on his large belly. He laughed silently and directly at Tony. It was a long and sinister laugh.

Tony's eyes did not leave the obese man until Johnny moaned and Tony's concentration was broken. Tony then reverted his attention back to his friend and did not look back at the man whose soul was now possessed by one of Hell's most powerful.

Sebastian let out a half smile as he kept his eyes on the youngsters, tracking their movements until they were out of the main stadium.

Sebastian looked, but did not follow them.

CHAPTER FIFTEEN
A Trip to Cologne

The Devil had many spies.

His eyes and ears were in the street, on the police force, the quiet neighbor and even the odd clergy man.

These people didn't know it, but when communication or information was required, their souls betrayed the bodies they occupied.

Strategically, they were placed in all sorts of places to serve whatever hellish purpose was required. Of particular interest were the transport depots and airports, which helped Lucifer and more importantly, Sebastian, keep track of the movements of Tony and Johnny.

Word had got to Sebastian. Tomorrow and late in the afternoon was when the boys were to catch a flight to Cologne. The reason for their flight was not important, but Sebastian following them was.

The clock had ticked a little past midnight. Sebastian sat on the outer edge of his dense patch of greenery. He was only a meter from one of the walking paths that cut through the English Gardens in Munich.

Behind him was the place where Sebastian went to get rest and to keep out of sight. But at this ungodly hour, he stayed on the outer edge of the path and shrubberies. For now, he did not venture deep into the scrubland where he could be secluded from the prying eyes of human beings.

He was not alone.

Sebastian was conversing with a stranger in the hellish language of clicks and clatters.

Like a spy on a mission, Sebastian stayed partly hidden by the cloak of the night. He chatted away with a human who had been summoned to deliver a message of great importance.

This earthly soul was none the wiser to the deed he was performing.

He was a middle aged man who worked in the airport. He came to the park at just after midnight and enlightened Sebastian about air travel. He did as he was asked subconsciously, by the power of hellish suggestion.

Unknown to this man, the subliminal message had travelled long and far to get to him.

They were collective thoughts, originating from a hellish landscape, traveling through the Heavens and onto Earth. An evil wavelength of thoughts, ideas and instructions. The suggestion came from another existence altogether, but it served its Earthly bound purpose.

The airport man completed the task, but would never remember doing so. He had carried out a number of hellish tasks in his forty-five years on Earth, but all paled in comparison to the importance of the task before him now.

Sebastian listened intently as he was taken through the process of air travel.

Everything was covered in immense detail. From checking in to getting on the plane. Sebastian needn't worry too much as there were people to help him get through the ticketing area, through the security checks and even when boarding the plane.

These people did their best to make Sebastian's first time experience of flight a memorable one. They ensured the objective of getting Sebastian to Cologne was completed inconspicuously.

In the language of the beast came the final message from

one of Hell's human servants. "You cannot board in that body," he said. "You will attract too much attention."

The clicks and clatter were very clear and precise about this.

With that, the informant left a flight schedule behind and then walked hurriedly away from the meeting place. No other person was about and all was secure and safe for Sebastian.

Sebastian looked at the piece of paper. A nearby street lamp provided the light to make out the writing. The words meant nothing to him, but he knew it was a piece of paper he needed to guard with his life as this was his key to a flight between German cities.

He folded the paper with care and inserted it into the front pocket of his baggy pants.

Time was now of the essence. He had his orders and so, as instructed, he walked and wobbled awkwardly to the park's edge. This time he chose to walk in the opposite direction of the beautifully tree lined street that he had stumbled across previously.

This was a long walk.

Sebastian had inadvertently chosen the longest path to the outer edge of the park. He tired and stopped on many park benches to rest.

There were times he resented his directional choice, but he persisted, stopping, resting and walking.

He didn't know Munich and he did not know where his chosen direction would take him. Not a single soul crossed his path as he walked for the longest of times to eventually reach a previously unexplored part of Munich suburbia.

He was now well into the streets of his newly found suburb of Munich. Sebastian soon found himself in an abandoned industrial lot. Sebastian rolled his eyes and snarled, "More walking!"

There was housing in the immediate distance, but he had to get past and out of the rundown industrial section.

As he walked across the abandoned factory sites, Sebastian noticed the first signs of morning. At this point, the sun had only let out a hint of its fiery glow.

The factory site was behind him and the houses had begun.

There were some well-maintained homes with nicely manicured gardens and others which were rundown and in need of some attention. It was a mixture of working income and lower class homes on a worn and aged street.

The street lamps were basic and had been vandalized. It didn't compare well to the beautifully tree lined street that he had wandered into only recently.

Not that Sebastian noticed.

Beauty and art. Presentation and working class status. They were all meaningless concepts to him.

Sebastian made his way along the streets, struggling with each step. The large frame was drawing on his strength. He was a fighting class warrior and as fit as any hellish soldier, but this was taking its demand.

On he went.

Up ahead walked a middle aged lady. She was neatly dressed in a fashion that suited a professional office worker. Her dress was dark grey and extended a little past her knees. It sat tight and firm against a body that was shapely for a lady of her age.

It was complemented by a dark and matching jacket. One that covered most of her upper half.

She carried a little bit of excess fat, but then again, who doesn't at that age? All considering, she kept a neat and fit looking body.

Her looks, however, were odd. Her hair was short and dark, in a style more fitting to a man. The face and head was large and round, and unattractive.

Her eyes were large and piercing, but well-proportioned to the features of a larger head. Even her mouth looked like it was overcrowded; holding a few more teeth than it was designed for.

But it wasn't all bad. Her graceful features included a delicately placed nose on a skin that was as smooth as that of a teenager and lips which, had it not been for her overcrowded teeth, would have been inviting to any gentleman.

This was a mixture of beauty and disaster. A face which, wherever she went, often elicited a second glance.

The morning sky was clear and the wind that shuffled from street to street carried a cold chill. The lady was talking to herself as she hugged her arms around her.

Trying to keep warm in the cold morning air, she muttered to herself.

As Sebastian drew closer, he could hear a conversation. "It's going to be a busy day. Busy! Busy! Busy!" She wobbled her head from side to side. Her eyes moved in all sorts of directions as she continued with her talk. "I got to get to the office. My boss is an arsehole. He works me hard. Busy! Busy! Busy!"

Sebastian had to stop.

He had never witnessed such behavior before. The lady was still several meters away and closing the distance. Her head down as she talked to the pavement. Her head lowered to cover her face from the wind.

"Work! Bloody work! Busy! Busy! Busy! Got to get to work!"

As the lady reached Sebastian, she stopped. She looked Sebastian straight in the eye.

Her eyes moved erratically, from side to side and up and down. She rolled her eyes, almost revealing the whites of the eyeball. For that moment, all was strangely relaxed. She rid herself of any chilly feeling and stood true and proud. She spoke directly to Sebastian in a confrontational fashion.

"Busy! Busy! Busy! Got to get to work." She said the words with a tone of disturbance and anger.

Sebastian grabbed her shoulders, restraining her from any further movement.

At the same time, he looked around to check if they were hidden from prying eyes. It was only the two of them. There wasn't another soul in sight.

His head shook from side to side as a low tone resonated from his hellish voice. Sebastian was now in communication with her soul and he demanded it vacate the shell in which it resided.

Sebastian found this difficult because this soul was disturbed. It was in mental anguish that carried right through to the spirit of this entity.

As a result, the spiritual communication was difficult for Sebastian. The lady's soul was almost defying the demands of the hellish commander, jumping to irrational places.

On a spiritual level, Sebastian cornered the inner soul and threatened it. But this spirit was more interested in ghostly fun and games. It cleverly played with the hellish soul, treating its demands with laughter and a type of disturbed defiance.

Sebastian was chasing down a spiritual entity that did not sit still long enough to be violated.

His head now vibrated with a speed which blurred his face to any outside spectator, not that anyone was watching.

The tone had changed from low in volume and in pitch to mid volume, high pitched shrieks.

Under normal circumstances, Sebastian would vacate a human soul easily. This time, Sebastian had to resort to shouts and screams. These sounds were still directed at a level only another soul could communicate with. It was draining for the hellish beast. This lady was schizophrenic and highly disillusioned.

She had not been a normal child, and her perception of the world was largely formed by the media.

Whatever the reason, she saw it fitting to walk the streets in her office attire religiously every morning until she had vented all her frustrations and illusions. She was well known in her immediate neighborhood and as a result, generally ignored and mostly avoided.

Sebastian screamed at the soul. He shrieked at it, chasing it spiritually around the body. This disillusioned soul kept fighting back in a way that was disturbing and challenging to Sebastian.

Sebastian's patience was drawing to an end. The thought of killing the individual was now an option.

But for his last attempt, Sebastian took a completely different tack.

He chose to not attack the soul but rather the subconscious mind. He unlocked a brain whose wiring was so messed up that no amount of psychotherapy could ever cure it. He then returned to the soul who now had to contend with the deepest of disturbances of her own subconscious mind as well as the presence of an invading hellish being.

In essence, her own inner demons were tormenting her, as well as a real life demon in the form of Sebastian.

Together, they made a formidable enemy.

It didn't take too much longer.

Suddenly!

Crack!!

The soul had been vacated. Her disturbed spirit could now be attended to by the Heavens above.

And as far as Sebastian was concerned, they could have the package. Sebastian knew she would keep the Heavens busy. And they were welcome to her and everything she came with.

Disturbed mind, disillusioned soul and the rest!

The overweight body in which he resided slumped to the street floor. It lay motionless in a position that almost represented crucifixion.

The fat taxi driver lay with arms extended to either side and with legs straight down. The feet were almost aligned on top of one another.

The position in which this man lay reminded Sebastian of a man who once walked the Earth as a preacher and who had died on the cross to bear all of man's sins.

He snickered briefly and then spat at the soulless corpse.

His objective had been achieved and it was now a matter of getting to the airport. Sebastian didn't have to worry about luggage.

A change of clothes came with a change of souls.

But there was one thing he dare not forget: his airline ticket.

Most of all, he now had the maneuverability he sought. There was no remnant mental anguish as Sebastian was now the driver of this human shell.

The objective was to get to a nicer part of Munich, somewhere near the location where he first met the overweight taxi driver. From there he (or should we say, she) would be taken to the airport and walked onto the plane.

There were many waiting to help the devilish cause.

The Devil even had spies and servants who drove cabs. Cab drivers who, for the short time, will serve a hellish purpose and assist an evil objective.

Sebastian begun on his next task: to meet up with a servant of Lucifer whose occupation was driving cabs. But this would not occur soon.

He needed some rest.

For now, Sebastian's remaining journey would be, as the saying goes, a walk in the Park.

CHAPTER SIXTEEN
The Disturbed Soul

Archangels Michael and Gabriel were discussing battle strategies.

As warrior class Angels, it was their task to protect against the raiding terrors that lived in the depths and darkness of Hell.

The Angel Raphael ran up, approaching the two Archangels at great speed, frantic with concern and worry. He interrupted their conversation, believing his worry to be much more important than their discussion.

He was at a loss as to what to do and his voice expressed the ambiguity.

"There's another one here. She's different. The anguish in this one is far worse than the other two. Far worse than I have ever experienced." Raphael turned and drew his wings to full span. The Angel flew quickly deep into the far reaches of a counselling corner of Heaven.

With looks of concern, Michael and Gabriel followed close behind.

In moments, they were all there. Raphael landed and with the momentum of speed still behind him, he ran for another eighty meters or so.

He was impressively fast by any standard and Michael and Gabriel were only seconds behind.

Pam and four other heavenly helpers tried to assist the

disturbed lady, but she resisted their help.

She crouched and cowered in the open grounds of Heaven with her arms over her face and head as if she was being beaten into a corner by a maniac. But there was no malice here, just good hearts wanting to offer helping hands. The disturbed soul could not see this. Even though she was in Heaven, through her demented eyes she could only visualize demons.

She saw souls that looked like disfigured monsters. Angels appeared as dark demons with deformed, blackened wings and ugly, demonic faces. Her perception was hideously distorted.

Ultimately, she was resisting Heaven and its beauty with everything within her. Resisting the Heavens, resisting spiritual aid and most of all, resisting angelic assistance.

By now, Pam had worked closely with many souls which had died suddenly and tragically. She had witnessed all sorts of grief, but this one was incredibly different.

The well respected grandmother turned to Raphael. The mighty Angel stood there feeling as useless as Pam, who shrugged her shoulders, shaking her head from side to side. Pam was lost for words and could not offer further aid.

Archangel Michael intervened instantly. "We have no time for this. Send her back to Earth. Re-incarnate her," he demanded.

"She may turn out worse. We may not be able to help her next time." There was anguish in Raphael's voice. He pleaded with his friend, Michael.

Raphael, Pam and the others worked tirelessly on the disturbed soul for what seemed like an eternity. Sebastian now occupied her shell down on Earth and Heaven had to deal with her infinite insanity.

Raphael didn't like giving up as easy as the rest seemed to do on this occasion.

"There is more at stake here, my friend," said Gabriel. "Release her," he asked as he put his hand gently on the right shoulder of his long-time friend.

Raphael knew what was going on. He knew of the greater threat that could rise from the depths of Hell at any time.

Heaven was in rebuilding mode and dealing with the casualties of war, with rehabilitated souls who had died in spiritual battle.

Those that had been killed in battle were now, by default, sent to Heaven. These souls put pressure on the counselling resources of Heaven. The results were never guaranteed. Heaven could turn around a hellish soul, could convert a soul of evil into a doer of good, but all this involved time and resources.

Sometimes the outcome was great and at other times, made much worse.

But it was worth the extra effort. The opportunity to try and convert another evil soul over to Heaven could never be missed.

Nevertheless, this woman's soul was different. It was a disturbed soul to begin with, and it had then been invaded by an evil terror. A soul which had to vacate its Earthly shell before its rightful time.

Raphael knew what had to be done and walked up to the disturbed woman.

With his feathers at full span, he wrapped his massive wings around her, squeezing her like a boa constrictor. With every second that passed, Raphael squeezed harder and tighter until the disturbed lady collapsed on the misty white floor of Heaven.

For the first time, the disturbed soul was at some sort of peace.

"Be reborn, my Christian soul, and live a good life. We will do what we can to guide you on a path of righteousness." Raphael knew his words meant nothing to her, but he spoke them anyway.

This soul needed more time in Heaven, but she would have demanded more resources; resources that could not be spared for the moment.

Raphael leant over and kissed the disturbed lady on the forehead. And just like that she disappeared, only to be born to unsuspecting parents down on Earth.

The heavenly collective knew the parents of this child would suffer as the soul was destined to become mentally anguished and highly disturbed.

Only the parents of this poor soul would unsuspectingly come to know of the additional effects that come when you mix a disturbed soul with one that has been violated by one as evil as Sebastian.

This would be an unfortunate set of circumstances to inherit.

The Heavens would need to keep an eye on this one.

CHAPTER SEVENTEEN
The Healing Has Begun

Tony sat in his hotel room.

The TV was turned down and his friend lay in the neighboring room fast asleep. Tony flicked over the channels, catching one German show after another. No subtitles and no interpreters; everything was in German.

Tony stopped at an in-house kids' channel.

A pretty young woman was counting to a small group of young children as she flipped through the number cards. The cards served as much of a purpose for her TV children as they did for the audiences watching.

The sweetness in her voice complemented her gorgeous looks and for a short moment, Tony was mesmerized by her presence as she counted from one to ten.

"Eins, zwei, drei, vier, funf, sechs, sieben, acht, neun, zehn."

As soon as she reached the count of ten, Tony snapped out of his loving trance and moved on. He took a moment more to admire her beauty and then flicked to an entirely different TV station.

Tony stopped and stared at the television screen.

He was pleasantly taken by surprise, but for an entirely different reason. He saw familiar faces on a familiar show. In fact, one of his favourite shows.

He always liked the stars and the mystery of space. And

there was probably only one TV series that tried to address them all.

Star Trek!

He looked upon the familiar faces of a new crew on a relatively new TV series. Star Trek: The Next Generation. The story was set approximately seventy years after the original series. The new star ship, the Enterprise–D and her new crew were led by Captain Jean-Luc Picard.

Tony watched the scene intently.

The crew were in silence and hid behind an asteroid belt. An enemy known as the Borg was passing in the vicinity. Their ships were Gothic looking and shaped like giant metal cubes.

It wasn't hard for Tony to pick up what was going on. It was intense and exciting. The threat soon passed and the silence gave way to conversation.

Tony was then in hysterics. Literally doubled up, his eyes watered as he had never laughed so hard for such a long time.

Johnny walked out in his bed clothes and rubbing his face. "What's all the commotion about?"

"These Germans. I tell you, they really know how to stuff up a good show. It just doesn't quite sound the same." Tony stood tall and at attention, military style.

"Warp Factor Eins!" Tony said, still laughing to himself. "Cracks me up!" He exclaimed.

Wiping the tears of laughter from his eyes, he looked at his friend. His tone was a little more serious as he asked, "How you feeling? I must say I got a bit worried for a while."

"It's weird. I can't explain it," said Johnny. "It just hit me hard. I don't know what super bug got into me. I've never been so sick in my life."

"You okay now?" asked Tony.

"Yeah, I'll be fine. A bit of lunch and a hot drink and I'll be right." Johnny never knew this was no super bug, but simply a little trick Sebastian chose to play on his soul.

"Well, you go get ready. I got to know what Captain Warp

Factor Eins does next," said Tony.

The young sci-fi fan struggled with the Star Trek story line from then on. He knew the characters and the enemies, but the script was foreign and lip reading was not his specialty. The action scenes kept Tony interested as the Enterprise played "cat and mouse" with the Borg Cube.

It killed a bit of time.

The TV series was nearing its end, moments from the storyline's climax. There may have been many Germans watching and sitting on the edge of their seats, but Tony struggled to put it all together.

From the hotel bathroom emerged a young and refreshed Johnny. "Hey, Captain!" Johnny said jokingly. "I'm starved."

"I can't get the hang of this anyway," Tony said as he sat up and switched off the television.

"We better get them bus tickets after lunch. You feeling up to it?" asked Tony.

"I'm much better. Really!" said Johnny "Hey, I'm sorry, too."

"What for?" replied Tony

"You know, the lost money. You paid for the flights to Cologne and I would have gone if I…"

Tony interrupted Johnny. "You were in no state to fly. You really had me worried. You were sweating and hot and feverish and all sorts of things. I'm glad I didn't catch what you caught. It didn't look pleasant." Tony picked up what he needed for the trip into town.

"The tickets. Don't worry about the tickets. It only means sometime soon there are going to be some empty seats on the plane. We can miss this one. We'll see more on the bus anyway."

Tony locked the door behind him as the two friends made their way for some overdue lunch and some bus ticket shopping.

CHAPTER EIGHTEEN
The Hellish Flight

Several kilometers away, Sebastian was riding in the back of a taxi cab approaching the airport terminal.

It had all been planned carefully.

He conversed with the cabbie in clatters and squeaks and chirps. The flight instructions on the piece of paper Sebastian held were being reinforced. The devilish soldier tried to make more sense of the instructions he was handed back in the parkland.

The hellish soldier who had last travelled to Earth several centuries ago was about to have a lesson in the protocol of travelling from airport to airport. The human cab driver was being used as a messenger for Hell's master plan. The human messenger would be none the wiser after the event and would simply go on living once he had served his purpose.

A protocol most took for granted was becoming a problem for a slightly anxious Sebastian. He'd rather walk to his destination in the dark shadows.

He found the days of horses and carts so much simpler, but the world had changed since then. The massive distance between Munich and Cologne made walking an impractical option.

He stepped out of the cab as instructed and lined up at the ticketing area.

Looking like a lady secretary, Sebastian slowly made his way towards the check in area. A Walkman radio with ear pieces was given to the hellish soldier to help him (or her, as it was) avoid any unnecessary conversations.

Sebastian made his way uninterrupted to the airport waiting lounge. Another aid escorted Sebastian onto the plane as a special passenger. And with the aid's support, Sebastian was sitting in a sole seat that was not to have him disturbed or interrupted.

The human aid put a night eye mask on the hellish beast and then gently inserted the ear pieces of the headset into Sebastian's ears.

As others boarded and got settled, the flight attendants went through their usual spiel about flight safety and what to do in the case of an emergency.

Sebastian was oblivious to all that was around him. His eye mask and headset isolated the beast from the rest of human society for a while.

Before too long, the plane was accelerating down the runway and into the air.

Whatever the experience or sensation, Sebastian was not to budge. This instruction had been reinforced by all those who helped get him onto the plane and this was very much in line with his own objective of not wanting to be noticed.

Sebastian took the time to meditate. In the spiritual plane one did not sleep. They meditated to put them in touch with their source and their spiritual surrounds. No matter where they were, be it on Earth, in Heaven or in Hell, meditation was one way of getting back to your source.

Time passed conveniently while on an airplane seat in the meditative state.

And it remained this way for most of the flight.

The hellish beast tried to keep as isolated from the rest of the passengers as possible and he managed quite well.

The flight was nearly over. In less than a quarter of an hour, the flight would be parked and Sebastian would have completed his flight to Cologne—a first of firsts for this demon of Hell.

On the flight descent the stewardess walked up to Sebastian.

One of Hell's human aids, she gently lifted the headphone earpiece and whispered in clicks and clacks. "The ones you are after. The young men born of a country far away from here. They did not board. We do not know their whereabouts. We are looking and we will let you know as soon as possible."

The flight attendant repositioned the earpiece into Sebastian's feminine ear.

The demon within the shell struggled to control his emotion. Sebastian boiled with rage and anger. The external shell of a person was being controlled by the hellish being within.

Like a puppet master to a puppet, Sebastian was in control of the body.

The former troubled soul closed her eyes as if a terrible migraine had taken hold. The beast was not in pain, but livid with anger.

The troubles he had gone to, the coordinated efforts, the human aids, his mission and even just the bigger scope of it all—it had all fallen apart within the space of a small conversation.

Suddenly, Sebastian exploded out of the shell of his female carrier. The fireball burnt his human host to a charcoal crisp within a few seconds.

A spontaneous combustion of sorts.

At the same time, Sebastian's hellish form punched through the upper layer of the aircraft.

The fire and gaping hole lasted only seconds. There was not even enough time for passengers and crew to put into place the instructions given in the case of an emergency.

The whole plane disintegrated with a deafening bang.

The explosive fireball hovered in mid-air for a couple of minutes. There was only one survivor: a beast who served in the army of Hell.

His only thought was to use the fireball as a distraction to avoid detection.

No other thought, regret or concern passed through his evil mind.

CHAPTER NINETEEN
The Queen of Angels

Pam was performing her heavenly duty. She was preparing for the arrival of two hundred and thirty-one souls who had died tragically, mid-flight, only a handful of miles from the outskirts of Cologne.

It was a massive task and she sought the help of fellow souls and Angels.

Many of the arriving souls were caught unexpected and did not know what had hit them.

The explosion on the plane was quick, followed by instant death.

Some, however, had witnessed the devilish soldier. Some saw the creature of the dark, if only for a second or two, before he carelessly broke through the top of the plane's carriage.

The end result was still the same for them: sudden and unexpected death!

All Angels, souls and spirits were running around with some urgency, setting up areas to counsel those who had died a tragic death.

This volume of souls was not normally a problem, but resources were already stretched as Heaven recovered from a devastating hell-sent attack.

Archangel Michael stopped what he was doing. He stopped to observe, listen, look and notice. This was not productive.

Heaven usually didn't take this long to get back on its feet. There was foul play at hand and it was the work of Sebastian.

The reason for getting Sebastian to Earth was unknown in the Heavens, other than it was linked to some sort of wrong doing. Some sort of evil and sinister plan.

And there was a small stream of evidence to support this. It was like a trail of breadcrumbs; only in this case, the breadcrumbs were violated souls.

Michael continued to gaze over the spiritual souls like a shepherd scanning his flock in the fields. Michael took notice of each and every one: Pam coordinating a group of spiritual souls; several spirits meeting and greeting them to make them feel welcome; Angels at the ready to deliver the message of transition into Heaven. They delivered the same message that had been delivered in one way, shape or form with every single passing since the beginning of mankind.

Michael stopped to have a really good look; his regard was deeper and philosophical in a way as he sought to see what was beyond the obvious.

It didn't take long to realize enough was enough.

And with that, Michael spread to show his impressive wingspan. The wings stretched out within a split second. Normally, Michael would spread his wings to show off the beauty and grace of an angelic being, but this time, it wasn't for show.

The mighty Archangel was on the defensive, annoyed at his home having turned into chaos.

A second after, Michael was headed into the sky, flying vigorously to gain height and momentum.

Heading for the upper layers of Heaven, Michael flapped with strength and intensity, gaining the speed and push he needed to fly higher. This was always tiring, even for a warrior class Angel.

Michael flew onto heavenly grounds way up and high above the crowds of spirits and Angels below. He landed with such speed and momentum that it took a good length to come to a running stop.

He had positioned himself perfectly.

The contact he sought was nearby and so, upon stopping, Michael knelt and simply waited.

A white mist floated above the ground, ankle deep. The ground appeared soft and fluffy, as if it was made of white cotton wool. The light that illuminated the sky, unlike the sun, had no single source. Its warmth, brightness and goodness were omnipresent. This was an upper level of Heaven and it housed the upper hierarchy of Angels.

The grounds and light were very much like they were on Heaven's floor, way below. Only it was brighter, warmer and, in a way, more loving up here.

On the higher plane, you were closer to God's light and all that it represented.

Michael had knelt down immediately upon coming to a stop. One shin lay flat on the white billowy floor while the other remained upright with knee bent.

Michael rested his right forearm on his upright leg and bowed his head. He was almost in a position like an olden day field soldier in line to fire a rifle. He remained in the kneeling position and kept his head bowed. He did not look up until commanded to do so.

Michael waited and waited and waited.

It was unlike his Queen to make the Archangel wait. Curiosity finally got the better of Michael and he slowly raised his head and eyes enough to glance upon the lady he so admired.

And there she was in a deep and meaningful conversation nearby, surrounded by a higher order of Angels. There was only ever one way Michael could describe her: beauty in presence and beauty in spirit.

Set against the blue backdrop, she presented an incredible image. She wore a white veil that fell loosely around her face and came to rest upon her shoulders. The face of a true Angel, she had hazel eyes, a petite nose and small, ruby red lips.

Her hair was long and brown, curled at the shoulders.

Around her head was a bright light, as if the morning sun had set behind her pretty face. It glowed behind her. All in her presence felt a reflective light that was warm and soothing.

She wore a white, full-length gown, only exposing her bare feet. The gown was tied up with a blue ribbon, which was darker than the blue sky of Heaven. Resting on her shoulders and on her white gown was a dark blue cape. The cape fell behind and to the side of her, dropping almost to the ground.

The Holy Mother stood with hands out and palms exposed; a gesture of warmth and acceptance.

In her stance, beams of light shot out to the ground from under her loosely fitted sleeves. The white misty floor of Heaven appeared to stir where beams of light hit. This caused small clouds of pure white to lift and hover so the heavenly floor showed where she travelled. A trail of sorts.

The Holy Mother was talking to Angels of all levels.

To an outsider, they may have looked like a freak show, but to Michael they were old trusted friends. Their friendships literally spanned the existence of man and Earth.

Standing next to the Holy Mother was the right hand Angel of God, the Seraphim called Zophiel.

A light emanated from Zophiel that was bright. Most souls found it close to unbearable to look upon the great Angel. But to surrounding Angels, the Holy light emanating from Zophiel made no difference.

He was a creature of one head but four faces. The faces resembled human faces, but the bright light shined so intensely from the Seraphim Angel, it distorted his looks.

Zophiel's body was serpent or dragon-like and attached to his leathery body were six leathery, bat-like wings. His legs and arms were lengthy and muscular with claw-like paws.

All the Angels stood of a similar height to a tall human man.

All were around six foot and three inches in height—plus or minus an inch or two. However, Zophiel stood out from all the Angels.

Special was he, standing taller than most, closing in on almost eight feet in height. Indeed, he was as impressive in height as he was in build and presence.

Next to Zophiel was Ezekiel, the Cherubim Angel, second in order only to the Seraphim.

The Cherubim stood in stature like a man. Six white feathery wings gave this Angel an impressive appearance. The head, however, was out of proportion, being three times larger than you would expect. The head was full of eyes: colored eyes, blue, hazel, green, black, brown, aqua and yellow. Each eye blinked simultaneously with the others.

The more the Holy Mother talked, the faster the eyes blinked. The movement of the eyes was an indication information was being processed.

Michael judged a lot of knowledge was being processed right now.

Next to the Cherubim stood Oriphiel, the Throne Angel. Oriphiel had a reputation that was well known and respected and for him to be involved in this discussion concerned Michael, for he had witnessed many of Oriphiel's doings.

Being the dispenser of God's judgment, this Angel acted with what looked like little mercy. He was there to act with impartiality and humility to bring about the desires of the Lord.

Historically, he was best known for his reign of disaster during man's early existence, famous for the bringing of stormy, heavy rains in the form of fire and brimstone.

Sometimes the combination of God's will and Oriphiel's doings had devastating results for the Earth and mankind.

Oriphiel was shaped like a giant truck tire wheel, only without the treads. He was black and circular and looked sort of leathery and rubbery. Every square centimeter of this being held an eye of a different shape and color, similar to Ezekiel.

The big difference being each eye had its own little blinking sequence. Some eyes blinked rapidly, some not at all, while others again had their own little unique pattern. Every eye on this being was loyal to the blinking pattern it held and they each held their pattern indefinitely and precisely.

The Queen of Angels was done with her little crowd of Angels.

Michael knew better than to ask.

If he needed to be involved, then he would find out when the time was right.

Michael was not here to join a meeting. He was looking to find the Holy Mother.

"You seek me, Michael?" asked the Virgin Mary.

"Yes, my Queen," replied the Archangel as he simultaneously rose from his position of kneeling and respect.

"Walk with me, Michael," requested the Holy Mother.

The two walked side by side as they casually strolled the upper grounds of Heaven.

"Mother, there are terrible troubles below."

"Yes, I am aware," replied the Holy Mother. "There are evil doings on Earth.

Even Lucifer will be disappointed at the recent events. Even he does not go about killing human masses on leisurely flight. It is not his way, not his doing."

"Send me, Mother, for I must stop this reign of terror," begged Michael.

"Respectfully, Michael, you must trust in the greater plan. Your work and skill is needed here. Deep down, you know these words to be true." The Holy Mother turned to Michael. "There is much to do. May the lights of the Heavens warm your heart and keep you true and holy."

"As always, my Queen," replied Michael, as he knelt as he had while waiting for the Holy Mother. The Virgin Holy Mother kissed her long-time friend on the upper forehead and turned to resume her duties.

Michael rose and returned to the lower grounds.

Going down was far less strenuous than going up and his journey home was to take a fraction of the time.

His arrival on lower ground was timely, as the plane victims were making appearances, wandering aimlessly along the lengths and breadths of the heavenly grounds.

Gabriel, Raphael, Pam and her dedicated team all went about their counselling duties with dedication.

These souls had been touched by Sebastian and they had died a tragic and sudden death.

The amount of rehabilitation required varied. The sooner it was attended to the sooner the souls could start their normal entry and transition into the Heavens.

These were duties everyone performed without quarrel or argument. This was no job. Instead, rehabilitating souls was a labor of love and dedication to the heavenly cause.

All involved worked for this cause diligently.

Michael looked up into the skies. He spoke softly and slowly. Only he heard the question that came out of his mouth.

Michael scanned the sky for a second longer. A touch of concern hit his face as he asked,

"What are they up to?"

CHAPTER TWENTY
The ICE Train

The boys were travelling to the bus station in a cab with a driver whose English was good enough to sustain a bit of conversation.

"You don't want to take the bus, boys," said the grey haired taxi driver. His accent was strong, but the message was clear. "You need to go on the ICE train. It's a little more expensive, but a lot more exciting." His wrinkled face lit up with joy as he spoke of one of the true wonders of German transport.

After a bit more conversation, the boys were hooked. The cab driver had hit on all the right notions: speed, time, comfort. And it was not overly expensive, considering all the other wonderful benefits.

The boys gave it no further thought and instructed the cab driver to go to the nearest train station. The cab driver knew the boys would not be disappointed.

And thrilled they were!

They walked through the enormous station, which was grander and busier than anything the boys had experienced before. The young tourists dodged and weaved their way through the crowds, eventually reaching the ticket podium.

They soon held in their hot little hands first class bullet train tickets to Cologne. The price difference between ticket classes wasn't much and the boys decided they deserved a treat at the very last minute.

But while they were treating themselves, the state of Munich was in mourning.

The news of a horrific air disaster over Cologne was coming out on every TV and radio station. Additionally, unrelated to the air disaster were news stories about mysterious deaths.

The bodies of men that were necrosed. Human flesh that had artificially aged confused the German investigators. All the evidence did not add up.

The authorities were not only confused, they were concerned.

Of course, there was no coincidence here. No human investigator could possibly link the necrosis on the streets in Munich and an airline crash.

But unknown to any human being on Earth, Sebastian was the link that tied them all together, a link that stretched all the way to the depths of Hell.

As for Tony and Johnny, they were oblivious to the headlines. They were more interested in the information sheets about the ICE trains.

The taxi driver had done well in sparking their desire for knowledge.

Abbreviated from the words Intercity Express, these trains were shaped aerodynamically and travelled like a hurricane at speeds of approximately three hundred kilometers an hour. They were a fine testimony to German engineering.

Like any new technology, the trains had encountered problems from time to time, but considering their extensive use in Germany and beyond, this was the best kind of transport to get you where you were going—and fast!

The initial excitement of ICE train travel may have worn off for the people of Germany, but the boys were bursting with excitement. The trip was a first for them both.

The platform they waited anxiously on housed five ICE

trains with one entering the station about to drop off its passengers. What made this station even more impressive was the number of empty tracks. They could have tripled the amount of ICE trains in the station and still had room for a few strays.

The white train with a bullet-shaped nose looked the part. The first class section was immaculate. Their carriage was one back from the main driver's cabin. The extra comfy seats, nice trim and neat presentation gave the boys a little taste of class and that was fine by them.

Tony and Johnny boarded the carriage, eagerly awaiting its departure from the station. Others followed and boarded the train, entering first class or standard class carriages. The train left the station with a half load. For the boys, this meant more room to stretch and move about in.

Meanwhile, back in Cologne, Sebastian had taken refuge under one of the city's many bridges over the River Rhine. His dark, shadowy appearance meant he could easily blend into the shadows under a bridge.

If he lay perfectly still hard up against the bridge pillar wall, a person with perfect vision would have to look many times before they came to the conclusion of all was not right.

There were signs the sun was setting. The sky grew darker and duller with every passing minute and the city prepared for the approaching night time.

City street lamps turned on and so did the lights on the bridge under which Sebastian sheltered. It lit up and highlighted its beauty for all to see, but it did not give away Sebastian's presence. He continued to blend in with the shadows; camouflaged to perfection.

The night sky kept darkening and Sebastian remained sheltered and unnoticed until the dark truly set in.

It was still too early to venture out and besides, he wanted to use this time to rest up in preparation for the hunt for his next soul.

As a dark angel lurked in Cologne, the two young travelers headed into the same city on the express ICE train. They stood and held the arm straps on the train's indoor railing, rocking and rattling with the speed of the train. The boys watched the world go by at three hundred kilometers per hour.

The scenery was simply a moving blur of lights in the distance. It helped break up the night.

Tony could not look out of the window for extended periods. His stomach felt uneasy. Johnny, on the other hand was glued to the sight of the world going by in extra fast motion.

Tony left Johnny to his entertainment.

He walked the length of the cabin casually, strolling past the few passengers who had decided to join the boys in first class. Everyone in the carriage could see each other but they were all minding their own business.

A neatly dressed young German gentleman sat in his little section alone. Tony wandered by and noticed a crumpled up newspaper next to the man.

The young German saw Tony's observations and indicated with his eyes he had finished with the paper. Without a word being spoken, he gestured and gave permission that it was okay to take the news magazine.

In spite of the existence of an English and German language barrier, here was a language that was universal.

Tony thanked the man in return, once again, without a word being spoken, using the universal language of head gestures and facial expressions.

The young German gentleman politely returned a smile and then went back to looking out the window.

Tony couldn't bear to look outside. His tummy still felt uneasy. Keeping his eyes in the cabin helped Tony maintain an inner balance. He found himself a little corner and proceeded to interpret the stories of a German newspaper as best he could.

And as soon as Tony had straightened the paper out, there

it was.

It smacked him in the face harder than any punch he had experienced in his many years as a Karate practitioner.

The flight number was all too familiar and Cologne and Munich were mentioned.

He didn't need to understand German to interpret this story. The pictures gave Tony more than enough information to go by.

In a few seconds, the young traveler saw a flash as he witnessed his young life whiz by before him. In those seconds, Tony realized the innocent decision not to take a flight might have saved his life as well as that of his dear friend.

His stomach in twists and knots, his legs nervously lost their strength as they started to shake under the strain of his upper body weight. Tony dry retched, heaving his upper back as his body went into mild convulsions.

He restrained himself from vomiting, but the noises he made caught the attention of his friend.

Johnny rushed over. He was caring, but at the same time amused by what he saw before him. Tony closed his eyes and drew in his breath. The inhalation was slow and precise and he used the technique to calm his nerves and upset stomach. Tony isolated himself as he focused on getting his mind and body back to normal working order. His eyes shut and his breathing steadied.

Tony drew in a breath, two, three and exhaled, two, three. He repeated the process two times, three times and four.

Johnny stood there half smiling with amusement. His eyes met Tony's.

The smile was not well received and Tony was quick to indicate that he was not amused by his friend's attitude. He reached for the German newspaper and thrust it into Johnny's hands.

The shock was immediate.

CHAPTER TWENTY-ONE
Our Shadows

The night had settled over the skies of Cologne. Sebastian opened his eyes as the sounds of a nearby clock could be heard striking its chimes. It was another strange and foreign sound to Sebastian, but to anyone else, it meant something specific.

The sound echoed disturbingly, winding up and down the empty streets. With no other sound to compete with it, its vibrating deep tone resonated on, mingling with the lights and the shadows of the many lamps that lined the immediate streets and roads. The weird mix of sound and light came to the end of its cycle as the clock rang for the tenth and final time.

The silence that followed left the empty streets with an eerie feel.

The bitumen roads flowed onto the city squares and small parklands. The city buildings stretched to the river's edge where the boats had docked for the night on the calm of the Rhine. The human factor was much absent from this cold and bitter scene.

For Sebastian, it was dark enough to begin the quest for his next unsuspecting victim.

In the shadows and still crouched in an underneath bridge structure, he waited like a spider. The bitter cold kept most people indoors tonight.

All the dark angel had to work with now was time and patience.

~ * ~

In a residential home, not too far from the city center, Josef sat on the family couch watching TV while Anita and Günter were fast asleep. As grown up as the children were for their eleven years, they were still demanding.

And Josef had made the mistake of telling the children about a visit from a very special lady. A long-time family friend would be joining them for a leisurely lunch tomorrow. The children could not contain their excitement.

In turn, Josef had a terrible time trying to get them to bed.

As patient a man as he was, the children had pushed their limits with their father tonight. Josef's nerves were stretched and he was not pleased with the directness he had to take in putting his generally well behaved children to sleep.

His tired eyes now focused loosely on the TV.

The television flashed its lights around a dimly lit lounge room. Behind the dedicated father, the shadows of the furniture danced on the walls. But it was the TV lights in front of him that had his attention.

It had Josef mesmerized as he mindlessly flicked through the channels. He was not interested in any show in particular. He was looking for something that was semi-interesting to flicker in the background. And as time ticked by, Josef put less thought into his children and more into the events of tomorrow.

He continued to flick channels.

A few minutes here, another few minutes there. It was a nervous action as he jumped from station to station, never settling because boredom and mild agitation struck if he remained on the one channel for too long.

Change was the name of the game and, strangely enough, it helped him focus on his personal thoughts and matters.

And then his thoughts shifted to a luncheon scheduled for

tomorrow with a special and dear friend.

The chance meeting with the gypsy medium had started a friendship that had lasted most of the children's lives.

Madame Liz knew of the tragedies of this family, of Simone's death as she gave birth to her twin children. She knew Anita and Günter had never known the love of their mother. The tragedy was complicated even further by the interests of the spiritual world in the twins.

Madame Liz could see spirit guides around the children, standing out of them as if they were potato sacks. Unusually, these guides, the spirit entities of Charlie and Mary Gretsis, still refused to communicate with Madame Liz.

Both of these phenomena were strange to Liz. She would constantly tell Josef this.

Never had she encountered a spiritual guide who did not try and communicate. Never had she encountered a spiritual guide who occupied the exact space of a person. Generally, spiritual guides hung around. They could be overly protective at times, but never elsewhere did they extend out from the body of a child like an overgrown and close and personal shadow.

Whatever the reason, Madame Liz had been invited to become part of the children's lives.

That much Josef, and even Liz, knew for sure.

Coincidence? Madame Liz did not believe in coincidences and this had definitely rubbed off on the dedicated father.

There was a purpose to everything that happened in life. From the very first day that Liz had initially met the children and their spiritual guides, she had maintained her regular contact with the family.

Josef ended his thoughts with a smile. He was a little excited about tomorrow too.

It was very late and time for bed. A quick check to see if all was okay and then Josef would join his children in slumber.

~ * ~

Back on the riverside, Sebastian eagerly awaited. The chimes had started up again and they echoed in the silence.

One, two. The sounds were silenced as quickly as they began to ring out.

Sebastian had not moved for several hours except for the turning of his head.

He was keen for his next victim.

From the silence emerged a young male. He was walking alone on the river's edge, laughing and carrying on, clearly in a high-spirited mood.

Sebastian jumped at the opportunity. Swooping down from the bridge, like a hawk on a field mouse, Sebastian pulled up next to the unsuspecting young man who turned suddenly. He had no time to comprehend the vision before him as Sebastian began to vibrate his head fast, working on the youngster's soul.

The young man went silent and began to succumb to the invading terror of the dark angel.

Sebastian was now at the soul of this young man, rudely insisting that it move on and out of this shell of a body. Sebastian needed a host and there was not enough room in this young man's body for two conflicting spirits.

Several minutes passed.

"Where did you get to?" A commanding female voice yelled from a nearby distance, a girl looking for her boyfriend playing hide and seek in the early hours of the morning.

Sebastian's task was at risk.

He left the scene of the crime with unfinished business. The young man saw a blur of a shadow whisk by. This was followed instantly by a gush of wind. The young man was coming out of a shocking trance and the shadow and gush of wind were the least of his worries.

His soul had been violated.

Only the antics and sudden appearance of his girlfriend had stopped Sebastian's task from being completed.

Sebastian was quick. She had not witnessed anything out of the ordinary.

The young man could not respond to the playfulness of his approaching lover; instead he began to react in the same way Johnny did at the time of the Karate competition. The only difference here was that in the Karate competition, Sebastian purposely played with the soul of young Johnny without intent to vacate it.

However in this instance, Sebastian desperately wanted a host and had made every effort to vacate the soul of this young man.

The young man stood on the river's edge for a moment longer.

Suddenly, he collapsed.

Severe fever, fatigue, nausea all hit at once. The girlfriend instantly realized something was not right. Her jokes and antics quickly turned to worry as she rushed over to help her boyfriend.

"You're hot! I mean really hot! We got to get you to a hospital," she looked around, but they were alone. There was not a soul in sight. She had to get her boyfriend over the bridge and to the other side of town by herself.

She hoped help would not be too far away.

"C'mon, love, lean on me. Help me a little bit. We'll get there. It'll be alright, you'll see!" These words were more for her own self-assurance than anything else.

The young man was weak. He struggled to get on his feet, but with her support he eventually managed.

Sebastian took off for another part of the town. While it was still dark, he had to seek solitude and shelter. The last encounter was too close for comfort. As desperate as he was for a host, he could have no witnesses to his existence on Earth.

He had to be more careful next time.

He found himself perched high on the steeple of the nearby cathedral, an impressive landmark that had made the town famous. The dark and sharply featured church was almost as large as a football pitch and as high as a skyscraper.

Sitting high in the shadows of a dark and blackened steeple, Sebastian had a panoramic view of his immediate surrounds.

This holy landmark was lit up for display purposes and in the dark of the night, it shone like a beacon.

Still, Sebastian could blend in with the shadows of the great gothic steeples of Cologne's famous church.

As he scanned the grounds around and below, he could see no movement. Once again, human life was hard to come by. The night was colder than ever. The streets were silent except for the hourly chime of a nearby town clock.

His height made the street lamps below look like tiny bright ants. Any humans walking the streets did not look much larger. The bird's-eye views were second to none, but the number of potential victims was few and far between. And besides that, Sebastian had to pick his mark more carefully, making sure the next victim was isolated from prying eyes.

The night soon turned into day, and Sebastian was quickly tiring from his stalking efforts.

His plans had to wait.

It was more important he sought shelter for the next day. He was left with little choice but to try again for another night.

Out of sight and to not be disturbed was now his main objective as morning was approaching.

The massive cathedral with its darkened and many steeples provided many places in which to seek shelter. Even the sharpest of eyes would struggle to pick out the darkened body of this soldier from Hell. Even better was the fact Sebastian now rested several hundreds of feet above ground level.

There was nothing left to do so Sebastian lay perfectly still and blended in with the background.

This was an opportune time to meditate and rest.

CHAPTER TWENTY-TWO
A Lunch with Madame Liz

Traditional gypsy attire was Liz's trademark.

Her dangling jewelry rattled and clanged as she knocked on the door of her favourite German household.

The kids ran to the door with excitement in their stride. Josef was not far behind.

"Auntie Liz," shouted the kids as they embraced their adopted aunt and squeezed her tight. As tradition dictated, she brought chocolates and sweets from her travels. Treats of the highest quality for two very special children in her life.

Liz looked up above the heads of the children.

For a short time she focused on the spiritual shadows that extended out of their physical bodies. Josef could see the look in Liz's face and knew she was looking at something only she could see.

The two spiritual entities were deep in discussion with each other. Politely, they ignored the presence of Liz and chose to mute their discussion.

"I feel so bad, Mare," said Charlie. The pet name he had for his wife remained with her even in the spiritual world. His love and devotion for his wife was as strong in spiritual retreat as it was in Earthly marriage.

"We should tell her why we are here," he continued.

"We can't. You know we can't. We have this discussion every time."

"I know," said Charlie, with a slight remorse in his tone. "I can't help

myself."

"Our instructions are clear," replied Mary. "There will come a time where we offer protection. And we will know what to do. Until then we must let it be." Mary's diplomacy was mature. Conversely, Charlie's frustrations were not.

"I want to wave to her. It's not like us, Mare. I want to say hello. Maybe she knows something we don't. Maybe...," Mary cut off her husband.

"Charlie, I feel as close to these kids as I do to our own son. I have seen them grow into young adults. Günter shares so much with our Tony. The similarities are haunting at times. I know we will put their lives at jeopardy if we give away anything." Mary put her head down into the palms of her hand as if she was shielding herself from the rest of the world. She then looked her husband straight in the eye.

"I couldn't live with myself, Charlie, I couldn't. Knowing I went against very strict and direct angelic instructions. Knowing I may have endangered a life. Perhaps even altered what was meant to be. Not these children. Not this family. They've been through enough. Whatever they are destined to do, we are here to see them through it."

"How do you know? How do you know what we are doing is right?" asked Charlie.

"I don't! I just now trust they do." Mary looked up and pointed to the sky and Heavens above with her eyes, suggestively referring to the angelic hierarchy and their universal wisdom.

Charlie looked up and caught Madame Liz gazing in their direction. He politely smiled to her and she politely smiled back. It's about as intimate as it ever got between Charlie and the physical world. Mary had also only offered politeness and common courtesies, but right now she was more interested in the children than a nearby spiritual psychic.

Madame Liz, on the other hand, did not expect anything more. Not yet, anyway.

Josef, Madame Liz, Anita and Günter were only seconds from starting their lunch of gourmet sandwiches and cold snacks. Josef was creative with his cooking and made the simplest of snacks appear as special treats.

Liz looked up to notice the spiritual protectors of the children were back in discussion amongst themselves. Liz tried to eavesdrop, but once again, the sound of spiritual discussion was muted.

"Do you miss Heaven, Mare?" asked Charlie.

"Not really. I mean these kids are now my life."

"I know what you mean," added Charlie.

"I miss Tony and Mum and the family, though. That's the hard part for me," replied Mary.

"I wonder how our little man is going," said Charlie. "He's a fine boy, Mary. He's a hero to the Angels and he doesn't even know it. How could you be prouder?" Charlie's face lit up with the heartiest of expressions.

"He did things the Angels could not. I bet Lucifer is pissed off big time." Charlie then stopped for a moment. "Do you think that's it? Do you think it's got something to do with what our boys did in Hell?" asked Charlie.

"I don't know what to think, love. The possibilities are endless. The Heavens move in strange and mysterious ways and this is our part in it. I'm happy to go along for the ride with you by my side."

Charlie leant over and kissed his wife's lips.

Very soon after, the children finished with their lunches and walked out of the kitchen. With them went the spirits of Charlie and Mary.

Josef and Liz were left to have an adult talk.

Before Josef could ask, Liz intercepted the question. "Same old story, Josef. It's just a smile. They are still there. Nothing more. Nothing less. They know I am here. They talk, but I can't listen in." Liz paused.

"I am being instructed by another entity, Josef."

Josef went to interrupt, but Madame Liz held up her hand to tell him to stop. The palm of her hand shot straight up and stopped in front of Josef's face. The message to now be quiet was clear.

Josef knew the routine.

He knew how Madame Liz worked and continually marveled at the special gift she had been given to help people like himself. If ever he had been skeptical, now he was well and truly converted. He was a true believer of all things spiritual and beyond.

Madame Liz listened to her message from the beyond. She then turned to Josef.

"I need you to lie down, Josef."

Josef looked at Madame Liz with caution and concern.

"I won't bite," said Madame Liz with a hint of sarcasm.

Josef did not speak and followed the instructions. He lay down facing up on a nearby couch, making himself comfortable.

"All I want you to do is close your eyes. I want to read your spirit. Take a look at what is going on inside."

"Is everything okay?" asked a nervous Josef.

"It's all okay, Josef. This isn't a sickness thing. It's just a YOU thing."

Josef sort of got the gist of what Madame Liz was saying and followed her instructions. Taking in a deep breath, he exhaled slowly and simultaneously relaxed his eyes until they were completely shut.

"I want you to follow my instruction, Josef. Follow it to the letter. I am being talked through this and it is important you do as I have been told." Madame Liz then asked again, "Are you completely clear on this?"

Josef nodded his head in acceptance. "Good," said Madame Liz.

Madame Liz put her hands above Josef's face. Her hands hovered only a couple of inches above his face. She circled them around his face and top of head as if she were feeling for her answer.

Josef started to experience warmth. The sensation emanated from Liz's hands and travelled to just beneath his skin. Although his eyes may have been shut, Josef could feel where Madame Liz's hands were.

He felt the warmth travel with the circular movements of her hand. It left a trail behind that only lasted a second or two, mapping movement without the sensation of physical touch. It was another phenomenon to add to the list of things that impressed Josef about Liz.

"Yes, I see it," said Madame Liz.

"See what?" asked Josef.

"Shhh!" replied Liz. Clearly Liz was not speaking to him.

"Josef. You are all over the place. This is not you. Your spirit, your soul. It's going everywhere. Bouncing here, bouncing there. It's like you are living a dual life. Busy, busy, busy." Madame Liz then paused. "I see what you mean," she said, speaking again to the spirit guide.

"We need to do something about this," said Liz

"Do what?" asked Josef.

"Shhh!" replied Liz.

History and experience had taught Liz there were two types of approaches when dealing with messages from the other side. You could try and interpret them by putting your own slant on the message and, therefore, try and make them fit with what you thought was before your very eyes—the emphasis being on thought.

Or you could call it as you see it and leave the rest to personal interpretation.

The latter was how Liz preferred to work.

On the relationship front, the bond between Josef and Liz was unique. Josef loved Liz in a way a brother loves a sister. However, she had her moments and this was one of them.

Additionally, Josef respected that Liz told things as she saw them. He was convinced this character trait of hers had developed with her gift. As such, he was not offended, even though his patience was now being tried.

"Open your eyes, Josef," asked Madame Liz in the gentlest of voices.

"And one more thing. Your wife would like me to give you this." Madame Liz leaned over and kissed Josef on the cheek and gently stroked Josef's cheek with the palm of her hand.

"She drops in on you and the children regularly and she is so proud of how you have all coped. So proud of you."

"What about the children and the guides? Can Simone tell you anything of this?" asked Josef.

"It is not for her to say and not for her to get involved in. I cannot add any more than this. It is as much a mystery to her as it has been for me." Liz looked up into the eyes of the spirit Simone.

"But you mustn't worry about the unknown. Simone is more concerned about your wellbeing. You look calm and collected on the outside, but on the inside, you are bouncing off the walls."

"Well, yes. It's hard at times."

"I know, Josef. But ask for help. Take a holiday. Have some time to yourself."

"The kids are good, you know. They're Angels," said Josef. Liz was suddenly distracted by the spiritual face of Simone.

"Your wife. She's smiling. You lit up her face. I can't describe it, Josef. I wish you could see it. She is absolutely gorgeous."

Madame Liz turned to Josef.

A serious face set the mood for an important message. "No one is doubting you are a loving father. If it were up to me, I would nominate you for father of the century. Your dedication and passion for your children, your community, your work is beyond expectation. All we are saying is offload a little bit. Give a bit of your dedication to yourself."

"But—" Josef was cut off by Liz before he could speak another word.

"No buts. It's not a selfish act to give a little bit of time to yourself. Especially when you give out so much. Wait!" Madame Liz put up her hand. There was that stop signal again. It shot up a few inches away from Josef's face.

Madame Liz kept listening. She struggled with Simone's message.

It was garbled. She tried to listen, but it was hard to decipher any words. It was as if she was trying to whisper a message from a great distance.

It was draining for a spirit to appear. And Simone had tired. All she could do was put her hand up to her lips and blow back a big kiss.

Madame Liz moved her hand ever so slightly. Its movement was discreet and subtle as she waved goodbye to the spirit entity known as Simone.

Whatever the spiritual message, it had to wait.

CHAPTER TWENTY-THREE
In Dreams We Communicate

Pam was about to embark on her own personal mission.

I noticed the look on Archangel Michael's face as I walked by him. I guess it was the concentration on my face that gave away what I was about to do.

I noted the nod of acceptance from the great Archangel and continued to walk on by him.

I lowered my head to look at the heavenly floor to think about something other than the approaching task. It's amazing what I take for granted sometimes. I had to stop for a while to absorb it all.

I lifted my head a little and let my eyes wander. The rolling white mist that covered the grounds was simple in color and texture, yet so beautiful. The puffy white clouds rolled and turned; they were never stagnant, not even for a second.

To stop and absorb all this made me feel a lot better inside. It made me feel warm inside. In fact, I had never felt healthier in my life.

I also felt a sense of welcome, love, nurture and most importantly, a sense of being needed.

However, I had to find a place where I could concentrate in peace and quiet.

I looked up ahead and there was not a soul in sight. I could have stopped here, but I felt like walking a little longer.

I felt so anxious.

If I had a heartbeat, it would be racing at a million miles an hour.

A heart I did not have, but insight I did. I had lived the life of a human and that of the spirit.

And with a view to distracting myself from the task for a moment more, I thought about these two lives for a moment.

Having lived on both Earth and in Heaven, I wondered where our true place of existence was.

I would be inclined to say Heaven.

I'd bet everyone here would, too!

It felt more natural to me. I suppose it was because I felt as good as I had ever felt. But there was more to this place than feeling good and feeling comfortable.

There was also a sense of purpose to my existence in Heaven. A purpose that went beyond my immediate expectations. I couldn't see it then, but I can sure see it clearly now.

When I think about my existence on Earth, I have this to say.

Faith in God gives meaning and purpose to human life. When we believe in the existence of a good God, we see value in every life. We see purpose in living and seek to do what is right and good.

It is not enough to just believe in being a good person or in karma, what goes around comes around. That hollow view turns your life into a series of transactions and there is not much satisfaction in simply winning a few hands.

There is a Creator and he knew what he was doing when He created me.

The miracle of a human life is so complex and wonderful that there can be no other explanation of its creation.

We are not genetic accidents, we are intentional.

There is a reason why I was born when I was born and why I died when I died. There is much good that I could have done if I had had the time. But all and all, I lived a good life and made my own little effort to prove to my Creator that I was a good investment.

Everything comes back to a heavenly cause. Everything!

I could ponder this for an eternity—but that was enough for now.

I had avoided the inevitable for long enough and it was time to focus on the task at hand.

I needed to get comfortable and what better way than to lie flat on the heavenly grounds. I was surrounded by warmth as I watched the clouds of white mist dance over my body, covering me like a sort of blanket.

It made me feel at ease.

In a way, I didn't enjoy communicating with the living. It took up a lot of my concentration and energy. I know that some time back I startled my loving husband when I appeared before him. It was too soon, shortly after my death when my loss was still a fresh memory. The pain must have been too much for my loving Arthur. I am not sure how he will take this now, but we need to speak.

In dreams we will meet.

Here I go again. As energetic and as healthy as I am, I can feel things starting to change. The order of balance shifting as my energy drifts away. It's all draining and demanding. They're the sort of feelings you don't think about when you have been in Heaven for a while.

I feel lethargy is settling in. I hate this feeling. But I have to think of the greater good and concentrate, as I know this will be important. I know my Arthur will open his mind to me.

I can only hope my message gets through.

All I can visualize is my Arthur. I see him with every bit of my being.

I feel like a virus is taking over my body. It's a type of malaise you get when things aren't quite right. I've got to block this out of my head! The longer I concentrate on my energies, the less time I will get to spend with my Arthur.

Concentrate!

Arthur. I can see his face. Hear his voice. Feel his touch. In my spiritual mind I am being absorbed by everything that is Arthur. My thoughts are being stimulated by visual, sound and motion.

I see his weathered olive skin. His full set of grey hair as strong and as thick as the day I met him. Every wrinkle is a sign of us growing old together.

I hear his voice. It's a little coarser, roughened by the years, but still as sweet as honey to me.

I see how the years have worn him down. He's still a strong man, as fit as an ox despite the hardships of loss. If only he could see the other side, he wouldn't worry as much.

Death needn't be a sad thing.

I'm getting there. I can feel it. I see his soul and he sees me. He's getting closer. When the shell falls asleep, the soul is so inviting to those of the spiritual world. The soul roams like a wildcat on the prowl. And when two souls of both spirit and Earth meet, we communicate in dreams.

My Arthur isn't roaming anymore tonight. His soul has found me and I, him. I can't wait to hug him and it appears the feeling is mutual. To hug you is to love you for all eternity. I don't want to let him go. But this is not the reason I came.

"Walk with me, Arthur," I said.

I need to set the scene for Arthur. I know this church won't look familiar to him, but I will put it up.

It's a gigantic, gothic church so high, your head will tilt back as far as it can just to see the top. I need to blow out the proportions. Make this gigantic church even larger. It must leave an impression on my sweet, sweet Arthur.

I enjoy this bit.

As draining as it is, my creative side comes out. I couldn't even draw a stick figure when I was alive, but here I am putting up a masterpiece.

The gothic trimming has to be darker. It needs to be dark and eerie with an overcast cloud. Something dark and grey and looming.

That's it. Nearly there.

Now I need to push the scene forward. As if we are both looking at it through the lens of a camera.

Now for our grandson.

I'll have Tony walking into the church. That's good, love, take it all in. You need to watch this scene carefully. In your mind's eye, this will be the most vivid dream.

Please heed the message. It is important you keep an open mind to all this. I know you will, my love. It was always in your nature to do so.

You cannot see his face, but you know that's our Tony walking toward the steps of the gothic cathedral. Watch carefully. A predator lurks nearby. A winged demon whose nature is evil.

Take it in. Take it all in. Notice the demon and the evil creature that he is. Not an ounce of good is in his wretched soul.

His ugliness extends beyond his outwardly appearance. He is as monstrous on the inside as he is on the out. He lurks like a lioness on the hunt.

Our Tony is unsuspecting. I see the horror on your face, my love. Know that all will be okay. This has got to be timed perfectly.

That's it! Open the door. My dear grandson. Now go inside and leave the door ajar. Now leap, you demon from Hell! Leap like you have never leapt before.

In through the doors of the church, you beast!

Scene two, my love. Into the church we go. Stay with me. It will all make sense.

Walk inside with me and look around. Look at the beauty within. Isn't this church lovely? Look at the detail in here. The statues of key moments in Christian history.

Christ coming off the cross. Look at the expression on his face, the torture he endured. If only you knew what I can see. If only you could experience the wonders I have experienced. I have listened to Christ and worked closely with his Angels.

But not now, this is not for you. It is not your time, my love.

Let's take a walk, my love, hand in hand down the aisle. Look down the aisle. Tony is walking his path of righteousness. If only you knew what he had done for the Angels. How proud you would be of him, and of Johnny.

That's right, my love. The demon struggles to move forward. He looks like he is walking against a hurricane.

Our Tony will be okay.

He walks down the aisle with ease. He is welcome and safe in this church. He is protected by those you cannot see. He is loved and cherished by Angels and Heaven above. You need to know this. We are all looking out for him.

This is my message.

You needn't worry.

It will all be okay. I love you and I long to be with you. But your time is not near.

Be strong for the family. Send my love.

It hurts so much to leave you.

Our souls will speak again. Until then…

Arthur suddenly opened his eyes from his deep sleep.

His heart raced as he tried to make sense of the incomprehensible dream.

A flash of yellow light lit up the room before his eyes and was gone as quickly as it had appeared.

Arthur sat up in awe.

CHAPTER TWENTY-FOUR
A Worrying Message

After a restless night, Arthur woke to the world news.

A plane crash over Germany and the names of two major cities rang eerily familiar to Arthur's ears.

Immediately, Arthur rushed over to Tony's flight itinerary.

Arthur hadn't caught the number of the plane flight in question, but he linked the date, Munich and Cologne to the boys and their intended movements.

His hands trembling, Arthur rushed over to the telephone and called his son, Jack.

"Jack!" Arthur's voice rang out with a clear tone of concern and worry.

"Are you okay, Dad?"

Over the telephone, Arthur could hear Chris in the background enquiring as to what was wrong. All had quickly picked up on the tone of the phone conversation.

"I'm fine, but Tony, did you hear?" asked Arthur.

"Hear what, Dad? What about Tony?" Jack anxiously replied.

"There's been a plane crash. Somewhere between Munich and Cologne. On the day of Tony's flight. Have you heard from him?"

"No, we haven't." There was a little pause over the phone. "Just sit tight, Dad. I'll be right over." Arthur hung up the phone.

Arthur sat back not knowing what to think or do. Worry was expressed on every square inch of his olive skinned face.

And then it happened. As suddenly as it appeared, it disappeared.

A flash of yellow light lit up before his eyes.

Arthur didn't know it, but the message from above was being confirmed and in turn, processed in his unconscious mind.

As it did, Arthur relaxed. In the moments to come, the stress on his tired old face washed away. Arthur was relieved of his anxiety although he could not pinpoint the reason why.

It was as if every organic fiber in his body was telling him the same thing.

All was okay. No harm had come to his grandson or to Johnny.

Arthur could not explain the feeling. He couldn't begin to do so, but he believed wholeheartedly it was linked to a spiritual message from his wife. Arthur felt there was more to the message from above, but for now, the comfort of knowing his grandson was safe and sound was enough.

Arthur breathed a sigh of relief. His hands had steadied and the only thing that would bring him more joy was a nice cup of tea.

However, with all the anxiety, Arthur had forgotten his call to Jack. His sons were headed straight over to meet their father.

Jack focused on his driving as Chris concentrated on an entirely different matter.

Chris and Arthur had not spoken since the family barbeque, but the silliness of the argument between father and son was pushed aside.

At least it was pushed aside by Chris for now.

Another potential family emergency put all things into perspective for Chris.

It scared Chris to think if anything had happened to his dad then the argument would never be resolved. To think his father could go to the grave with them having spent their last moments on

Earth together in non-communication.

So Chris put aside his selfishness. The issue of Arthur giving Tony his savings so that Tony could travel abroad was something Chris could not answer. He'd never admit to being right or wrong. His selfish pride would never allow it nor would his, at times, inflated ego.

Both Chris and Jack were driving as quickly as they could, trying to piece together the pieces of this disturbing puzzle.

What had happened to their dear nephew?

Chris was still reliving the last few weeks. He was thrown back to a family argument over money and his jealousy about this nephew's trip. He tried to make sense of why he was jealous.

Chris had given in to what could only be described as childish behavior. His actions did not reflect his age —and not speaking to his elderly father was unacceptable. He realized the lesson in a fraction of a short moment.

Furthermore, the thought of anger and bitterness and taking these ill feelings to the grave gave Chris a long overdue reality check.

Jack parked the car and approached the front door. Chris held back a little.

"Don't be silly, Chris. This has gone on far too long." Jack spoke with an impatient sharpness. The current concerns of the day had put matters into perspective, and Chris quickly realized how tired his brother had grown of his silly antics.

Jack walked in the front door. He had his key and he knew his father was expecting him. Chris followed somewhat reluctantly because he knew with absolute certainty his father was not expecting him.

Arthur sat back in his chair, finishing his last bit of cup of tea. He looked very relaxed and comfortable with himself.

"Well, well, look what the cat dragged in." Arthur looked straight at Chris with a cheeky smile. Chris couldn't bring himself to return the look and moved his eyes away from his dad's friendly gaze.

"What's going on?" asked Jack. "We rushed over here as soon as we could. Is this some sort of silly prank?" Jack was confused by the relaxed nature of his father after the news he had only recently delivered.

"It's okay, son, Tony's all right," replied Arthur.

"So what's he got to say for himself? What happened?" Jack was still on a high from his recent rush of nervous adrenaline.

"Well, I, uh," Arthur didn't quite know what to say and Chris was determined to remain quietly inconspicuous until he felt more comfortable about taking part in the conversation.

"Well, I didn't actually speak with him, but I know all's okay."

"Okay, Dad, what's going on? You're not making any sense. Was there a plane crash or wasn't there?"

Arthur got out of his chair to place his tea cup on the kitchen sink. He walked steadily to the kitchen bench with his back to his sons. He was trying to comprehend how he might explain this without sounding ridiculous. He was not sure he could, so he just went ahead and said it.

"Look! There was a crash. It was a bad plane crash in Germany. No survivors and I still don't know for sure if it was Tony's flight. He was scheduled to fly out about now and this news is too close for comfort. I can't explain it, son, but I have this feeling deep down. I know all is right. That Tony's okay. That it couldn't be his flight or even if it was, then he wasn't on it."

"Just great!" Jack spoke out loud and sarcastically for all to hear.

"I know how this must all sound." The sympathy in Arthur's voice was evident, but it didn't matter for he could tell that Jack was torn between wanting to believe his dad and the logical facts before him.

"Can we call him? Do you know where he is or where he should be about now?" Despite the tension, Chris was concerned, too, and could not keep quiet any longer. He now had to get involved.

"I've only got flight details," answered Arthur.

"Dad, uh! Look, for what it's worth, I'm—," Chris was about to finish his drawn out sentence when Arthur interrupted.

"Let's put this one behind us."

Chris nodded his head in acceptance of a quick apology about a silly argument over money. Jack quickly returned to the mystery of his nephew.

"Dad! What about Tony?"

Arthur turned to face his boys. A gentle smile lit up his face as he tried to lighten the tension that was bouncing around.

"I could use another cup of tea. How about I make a pot."

CHAPTER TWENTY-FIVE
A Sinful Message

It was a routine that had gone on through the ages.

The long and draining trip was taken on too many occasions. So many, he had lost count of the number of times.

The Devil was on the march to the Transitional Border where dark met light. Here, one step could throw you from the darkness of an evil Hell into the glowing light of a loving Heaven.

Lucifer took extreme care. An accidental step into the Heavens could set off a pungent smell of charred flesh which would serve as a warning to all Angels that an intruder was in their midst.

The Angels rarely ventured into Hell. Lucifer, on the other hand, often allowed his soldiers to go on the attack.

His desire to take over the place he was once cast from was a personal goal he would never give up on.

But today he was on a different mission. He was not on the attack, even though his army of thousands followed. They were only there for added security and peace of mind.

If the Angels chose, at that point in time, to go into Hades, the surprise meet would render Lucifer vulnerable. Capturing Lucifer would have devastating consequences. It would put the kingdom he'd developed at great risk.

The Devil needed to focus on his evil task, as well as have his soldiers at the ready for self-preservation just in case.

For this reason, the Devil rarely ventured into battle and

certainly never went to the Transitional Border unaided and unprotected.

The Devil knew the landmarks of Hades extremely well and all he wanted to do on this occasion was to get as close to the border as possible without crossing the line of transition.

This journey had been exhausting, as it usually was.

When Lucifer arrived at his destination, his support soldiers took their positions around Lucifer and along the lengths of the border.

It had been some time since Lucifer was caught out by surprise as he staked out or crossed the Transitional Border.

The battle that followed back then was devastating to both sides.

One of the greatest battles in Heaven's history was a direct result of an invasion by both sides timed to unintentionally meet at the Transitional Border.

Both sides surprised by one another's appearance as the front lines of their invading forces simultaneously crossed over from their respective worlds onto the other side.

After surprise and shock came great loss from both sides.

As far as Heaven was concerned, converting a soul is a major win against the evil demonic forces.

The Devil, on the other hand, considers it a loss of a soul he has worked so hard on acquiring.

One loss equates to many hours' work on both sides.

Many Angels lost their souls on the great battle at the border. But of greater significance was this historic event taught both Lucifer and the Angels a valuable lesson on preparation and planning.

Since the battle of so long ago, the Devil had been better prepared. The strategic groupings around him allowed for quick support and swift action should the need for battle arise.

However, there was no pending expectation of battle.

With all that thought and preparation, it was time to start.

The Devil took his position as he prepared for his unholy task. He sat as close to the Transitional Border as possible without crossing over. Behind him were a little over nine thousand dedicated followers. Groups of soldiers stretched out along the border with a handful reserved for back up. Some troops surrounded Lucifer himself in a type of semicircle. He had soldiers stretched out to the left, to the right and behind him.

They stood in their groups like gangs of troubled youths; they positioned themselves at the ready.

As far as Lucifer was concerned, the protection was in prime position. There was no angle of attack not covered by able-bodied demonic warriors ready for the fight.

With peace of mind, Lucifer could now get on with his task.

He sat on the surface of small, rounded rocks. All around him was dark except for a yellowy light that burned far away. The source of this light was the great Ocean of Fire burning with great intensity.

From the Transitional Border, the Ocean of Fire gave the impression that it burnt with the intensity of a small campfire, however, it was much more impressive when you stood up close and personal to it.

But there was now another light that interfered with the glow of the Ocean of Fire. Lucifer still had to deal with the disturbing light that was placed there by two young humans. Heavenly lights which scanned the grounds of Hades like search beams scanning the night sky.

The distance made it hard to see the search beam-like lights with clarity, but they were there. The beams moved around randomly and erratically spreading God's light and annoying all creatures of fire and brimstone.

This was his one and only focus today. This was the reason Lucifer took this long and enduring journey to the Transitional Border.

The Devil made himself comfortable and took one last look

at the lights, the fiery glow that symbolized home and the heavenly lights that symbolized human interference.

It was a timely reminder. His anger must not only be directed at the Heavens but at man and Earth as well.

For the briefest of moments he let out a smirk, a smug reminder to himself of what could be with the success of Sebastian's special mission.

The Devil was trying to form a paranormal connection with the subconscious mind of man. Delivering messages of evil across the heavenly airways to establish a paranormal connection with the human population of planet Earth.

His evil message was carried on a wind of evil at a frequency that messed with man's being. He was communicating directly with the subconscious.

When it came to influencing the soul of a human being, Satan was on an even playing field with the Angels. His only disadvantage was his message had to be communicated through the lengths of Heaven before it finally reached the grounds of Earth.

The strength of the message was diminished by the length of travel, thus the need to remain as close to Heaven as possible. This ensured the evil message had as good a chance as any in reaching its destination.

Communications like these were becoming a regular part of hellish activity.

They were seen as an investment into the future of evil souls and demons.

Sending such messages was not a visible process; they weren't physical things. They could not be held in the palm of your hand or moved over to one side. They existed as a kind of wavelength that was either influenced positively or negatively depending on its source.

As Earth was connected to the spiritual realm through the Heavens, most of Earth's influence came directly from those who lived there. Heaven had the stronger influence, but Hell did its bit as well.

This was the sole reason Lucifer targeted souls already tarnished with thoughts and deeds of evil. He played a game of probability. There was little chance of him influencing a soul whose existence on Earth was genuinely filled with good and higher purpose.

But as the world turned and grew in population, people got busier. The niceties of life were forgotten and the likelihood of Satan making successful and influential communications to Earth increased significantly.

Lucifer digressed from his messages of evil intent, momentarily concentrating his efforts elsewhere. Sebastian needed some direction and Lucifer needed to invest a little time in Sebastian.

Lucifer sent out evil frequencies that carried across the Transitional Border, onwards through Heaven and eventually downward to Earth.

Message after subconscious message was sent. Lucifer paused for a second and messaged again, paused and messaged. The message was carried on a frequency which made perfect sense for the unconscious mind that chose to accept it.

Equally, Sebastian was given evil updates and instructions about what to do next to progress to the next stage of his master's plan. Sebastian's spiritual mind was well and truly tuned into the Devil's message. It was not a message of influence but rather a military style set of directions and orders.

Just as the enemy monitored communications in wartime, Heaven was onto this.

At the higher plane, the Virgin Mary sat with three of her more senior Angels. These were Angels of the highest choir whose skills and abilities were far greater than those of any other soul or spirit in Heaven.

Only one exceeded their collective ability and that was God himself.

But taking God away from the enormous task of managing all and one would neither be practical nor beneficial.

God influenced things on Earth in his own mystical way. This was not his battle to fight.

So, on a spiritual plane way above the Transitional Border, the Virgin Mary sat in the middle of an angelic triangle. At each point of this triangle sat three senior Angels.

Zophiel sat there with his dragon-like appearance. His many leathery wings made sitting look awkward. But as a dog sits upright and attentive, Zophiel was most comfortable and relaxed sitting like this.

At another point of the triangle was Oriphiel, like a rubber tire on a rim of a motor vehicle. Freestanding, he sat with his many eyes blinking away in their own and unique sequences.

Last but not least was Ezekiel who sat cross-legged as any human would naturally do. His enlarged head and many different colored eyes had him focus into the center of the triangle and onto the Virgin Mary. Unlike Oriphiel, his eyes all blinked in unison.

In the middle of the triangle, sitting like a sporting coach, was the Virgin Mary. "Now focus on my voice," said the Virgin Mother in the most angelic of tones.

"Focus your attention into the middle of the triangle. Focus with the love and affection of man. Focus for the sacrifice my son made. So he could bear the sins of all man and that man could live his existence in constant reminder of the Heavens and all of her love and glory."

The three Angels went into their respective meditative states, bringing between them a collective of superior harmony.

The emotional frequency with which it vibrated was extremely positive. The wavelength vibrated in order to negate negative emotion.

Energy built in strength and amplitude in the center of the triangle. And when the Virgin Mary was overwhelmed by its energetic presence, she sent it on its way.

"Man must follow the Heavens, be good to one another, and love one another brother to brother, sister to sister." Again the energy built up. The aura grew and grew as the Holy Mother's voice concentrated the efforts of the most powerful Angels.

She coaxed three Angels to share their spiritual energy so that she could forward a focused subliminal message of good down to Earth.

Like radio interference, her messages of good distorted Lucifer's messages. His evil message was constantly attacked and interfered with. Positive airways mingled with the negative wavelength. Sometimes good and bad cancelled each other out leaving a void of static. At other times evil triumphed over good and on other occasions it was the reverse.

Too many variables and not enough guarantees. All interlinked spiritually to impact on those who walked the Earth. These humans were none the wiser to the radio waves from the Angels and Satan.

Apart from all this and concealed from human eyes, Sebastian lay hidden high up on the steeple of a giant cathedral church. His meditative mind was tuned into Satan's message.

Under normal circumstances, Sebastian would receive messages with complete clarity. There was a little bit of heavenly static, but it did little to interfere with the content of the message of today.

This devilish instruction was loud and clear.

Tony and Johnny required a first class ticket to Hell and Sebastian was to be their personal tour guide.

CHAPTER TWENTY-SIX
The Ultimate Possession

Sebastian awoke from his slumber. He had become quite accustomed to the meditative state.

The beast of Hell was having his fair share of bad luck lately. It had to change and now was the time to take affirmative action.

Up until now, the progress was slow going. The pressure was now on to perform.

As directed, he had to locate the boys and soon. He did not know how much longer his presence could go unnoticed, but one thing was for certain: it was only a matter of time before he was caught out. He had left too much destruction behind, and the evidence was eventually bound to give him away.

As instructed, he had a clear directive from the one he referred to as Master.

Lucifer was king of a domain that went by many different names. Biblically, it had been depicted as a horrible tempest, a place of sorrows, a place of everlasting burnings and there were many other variations. It was ultimately and most commonly best known as Hell. And the Devil reigned as its King.

Sebastian knew the completion of his Master's mission was very difficult if he could not locate a shell to hunt in.

He looked into the dark sky of Cologne. Cradled in the church steeple, he noticed a moon whose shape was almost full circle. Its glow gave a natural soft light which stretched out through the night sky. Tonight's moonlight shone brightly as there was little cloud about.

All and all, a perfect light and night in which to hunt.

The darkness had only just replaced the light of day in Cologne. There was ample foot traffic in the streets below. The atmosphere was cold, but nowhere near as chilly as it had been. Many of the locals and tourists had chosen to take advantage of a generally pleasant, but cold night.

The pedestrians were none the wiser to what lurked above. Still, it was too risky for Sebastian to venture below. All he could do for now was sit and blend into the church steeple, to silently observe and wait for his moment.

Down below, there were activities of all sorts. Outside the cathedral there were those walking, talking, eating, playing, lovers strolling hand in hand and friends out and about.

Inside the cathedral, one of the pastors was preparing for his Sunday ceremony.

He was an invited clergyman who had visited the town of Cologne on several occasions. It was a privilege to be asked to give a sermon in one of Germany's greatest cathedrals and the pastor did not take this honor lightly.

The dedicated pastor utilized the week before him to come up with a sermon of significance. The visiting pastor wanted to use the time ahead to prepare for a speech that left a lasting impression with those who were open enough to listen.

The people of Cologne would hear someone new preach this weekend.

The priest, a man of dedicated faith, approached the front altar. Before him were religious statues. Two statues dominated the front stage: Christ on the cross and Mother Mary cradling her sacred baby child.

The clergyman knelt on the platform below and bowed his head in silent prayer. He looked for influence from above to inspire a speech worthy of this Sunday's congregation.

He searched his inner spirit as he prayed.

And then it hit him.

A discussion on inner demons was his topic.

The speech began to take form within his thoughts. In it, he warned against the inner voice that stops us from reaching our full potential, the voice that tells us we are not worthy and cannot grow or develop.

Through biblical references and years of counselling experience, he drew upon and would deliver a message about where we as individuals have choice. Where we can choose to not listen to our inner negativities and rise above expectations. In his mind, the sermon had begun to develop.

He had been in prayer for some time. The middle-aged priest had grown tired, but his Sunday speech had taken shape. The long day had turned into night. The plan that was in his mind had to wait another day to take form on paper.

Deciding to give into his tired body, the clergyman went about his duties of locking and securing the cathedral for the night. He decided to leave the comfort of the church and stroll into the moonlight-washed court yards surrounding the iconic cathedral.

Looking at his watch, the priest was taken aback by the fact he had lost track of the time. It was almost eleven o'clock.

Despite all this, the preacher was physically happy, emotionally satisfied and mentally at ease. But even dedicated priests have to sleep.

As he left through the rear doors of the cathedral, the foul demon way up above saw what he was looking for. Sebastian quickly scanned the front of the church, where there were still small crowds of people. They wandered about in the massive courtyard in front of the church's main entrance. Some were simply in awe from the view of the church before them. Others mingled with others in a fun, social sort of fashion. Sebastian then looked to the side rear of the church where one sacred soul was putting the final touches on securing the doors.

Sebastian had to hit hard and fast. Aware of all around him, he seized the moment, swooping down. The priest must not have a chance to raise the alarm and draw in the crowds from the front courtyard.

A gush of wind followed as Sebastian plummeted to the Earth. Sebastian pulled up and as quick as a flash, the priest turned to face an enemy of all that is unholy.

The priest had been a dedicated follower of his faith for his forty-six year life. The priesthood was his destiny, and as a young child he knew it.

As soon as he was able, he left school to join the priesthood and had known no other profession. He became a well-respected man of the cloth. His soul was good and his heart true. Still, he was mesmerized in a second or two.

Yet his soul remained strong and true to its cause.

Sebastian went straight into possessive mode. He would normally start off with a slow movement from side to side and build up to a speed that was simply a blur to the outside observer.

In this case, there was too much at risk and his plans had already been delayed enough. Sebastian went for the spiritual jugular and pulled no punches. His head vibrated instantly at full speed. His voice was clear and to the point. As he had always done, he was communicating with the soul in the most violent of fashions, demanding it vacate the shell it resided in.

Yet this holy man's soul was determined and demanded battle.

Sebastian was about to experience a first.

What was visible to the human eye was a priest face to face with a demonic beast whose head was vibrating with ferocity and intensity. Eye to eye and engaged.

On a spiritual plane, the beast was face to face with the soul of the holy man. The spiritual soul of the priest stood in defiance, arms folded and face determined. The spiritual face of the priest stared back at the demon with daggers in his eyes.

Even with the power of his spiritual essence, as hard as he tried, the beast could not spiritually violate the man of the cloth.

Sebastian was clawing away at his soul, ripping its spiritual existence, tearing the very fiber of its being.

In the physical world, the priest regained his own consciousness for only a handful of seconds. His eyelids fluttered open and shut several times over a second or two—and then they remained open for a few more seconds.

The priest wanted to scream for help, but he couldn't. His vocal chords were paralyzed with fear like the rest of him. His ability to remain in the conscious state was short lived and he quickly slipped back into unconsciousness.

Sebastian, more determined than ever, stopped vibrating his head. He quickly repositioned his face so the holy man and Sebastian were nose to nose.

Sebastian snarled and growled. The volume was kept low and once again, it was barely audible to anyone not in the immediate area. The ferocity and the snarls and growls were unquestionably hacking away at the holy man's soul.

On a spiritual plane, Sebastian had almost destroyed the safety barrier the priest once possessed. The priest's soul had not moved. His arms were still folded and he remained determined and defiant.

The priest's soul had at no point in time shown fear or submission, yet it realized it had very little to defend by once its spiritual protection had been destroyed.

Some fifteen minutes had passed and now Sebastian was nose to nose with the priest on both a physical and spiritual plane. The spiritual capsule had been violated and as exhausting as the task was, Sebastian had achieved his victory.

The clergyman's defenses had come to an end.

His determined look and defiant stance had turned into an emotionless stare. The priest had slipped into a hypnotic state on both a physical and spiritual level.

His folded arms had dropped, hanging lifeless by his side. His body was slightly slumped as if he was being dangled like a puppet on a string.

Sebastian stopped. In the physical realm there were no more growls or snarls and no more rapid head movements.

He just stopped.

And as quickly as he stopped, Sebastian took a few more seconds. Concentrating now only on the spiritual plane, he used this time to twist his head to an angle that was at a right angle to the priest's face. Nose to nose and eye to evil eye they stood.

Once in this position, Sebastian released his power. His jaws opened wide as he thrust forward, biting away at the spiritual face and skull that was before him. It was as ferocious as any carnivorous animal attack.

This all took place on the spiritual plane. The spiritual flesh was being ripped to shreds and torn apart.

Sebastian bit and ripped and crunched away.

He spat out the spiritual remains and went back for seconds and thirds. He kept going back, hacking away at every bit of this holy face and head. The bloodless face of the priest took a severe beating and Sebastian was not about to let up. The attack continued as ferociously as it had started.

The physical plane had not changed. By the rear door of the church stood a demonic being and a man of the cloth, both motionless.

On the spiritual plane, however, the scene was one of mauling. The shredding of spiritual flesh had begun to take its toll on this poor man's inner soul.

And then the crack was heard. Sebastian had achieved his goal. The shell of the man stood there ready to be possessed.

With one last look around, Sebastian ensured all of this had remained private and with that, quickly jumped in to occupy his new shell of a body.

The outer shell had not been touched, but the inner soul had been mauled beyond recognition.

The Angels above had borne witness to this atrocious attack. They were helpless and could not assist.

Inside the church all was silent. At the front altar stood the two religious statues.

The wounds of Christ opened up and the points on his hand and feet began to weep small trickles of blood. The blood flowed for a short while, dripping from the points where the nails had been inserted. Emanating from both hands and both feet, the trickles of blood stopped as quickly as they had started. The small streams of blood dripped to the floor and disappeared, leaving no signs of ever having hit the cathedral floor. All that was left was the smallest of trails on the hands and feet of the holy statue.

This was a sign of sorrow directly from the Heavens above. The angelic hierarchy had seen Sebastian's unholy act. It was a sad day in Heaven.

The Virgin Mary also sent her message of sorrow through the religious statue. Fitting to the unholy occasion, the statue of Mary shed a single blood tear. It trickled down the white marble face of the Holy mother, leaving a dry, red brown trail.

A tribute to a sad day for Heaven's community and all that bore witness to it.

CHAPTER TWENTY-SEVEN
In Düsseldorf

Madame Liz was on her travels.

On this occasion, she had concentrated her efforts in the middle and north of Germany.

Her colorful caravan and her genuine ability to reach into the other side had impressed many Germans as well as foreign visitors.

She visited villages as small as Dornheim in the nation's center and cities as large as the country's capital. No matter where she was and who sought her advice, her spiritual foresight was there for those who chose to utilize it.

Above all, this was linked to her one true belief in life: there are no coincidences and no chance meetings. She served a purpose to everyone and anyone who came to see her.

Madame Liz drove down the reputable Autobahn, towing her faithful trailer. The generously wide highways with their pristine roads generally gave faster access to the towns and cities of Germany.

It had been a long drive to Düsseldorf. There was nothing to do but reflect, something that was part of Liz's everyday activity. To take a step back and take note of one's significance in the journey of life.

Liz wound down her window a little. She heard the sweet whistle of the wind as it whizzed by her long blond hair.

Her hair caught the breeze and began to flutter. It was refreshing. The air had grown stale in the car and the breeze was pushing out the old.

"What of my special gift?" thought Madame Liz.

She was confident of her special talents which had given her a higher connection that few could claim. She had a connection with a higher order and a firm belief that God determined who walked into one's life.

Ultimately, it was all part of the master plan.

She spoke these words out loud. There was no one else to hear them but the passing wind.

Hands gripped tight on her steering wheel, she let it out.

"NO COINCIDENCES!

"We all have a choice and I made mine. No regrets," she thought.

"It's up to me and even up to the individual. God can connect the people. There is no issue there." That she was certain of. "It then remains the choice of the person. It remains my choice." She kept thinking.

"Free will as it were. God never tampered with free will but was always happy to help try and guide it, if he were invited to do so. In my own little way, I know I help God deliver his message."

The seriousness flowed out of her body. Her grip on the steering wheel loosened. Her shoulders dropped and tension flowed outwardly as she exhaled a deep breath of fresh air. The calmness in her posture starting to show.

For the first time in a long while, Madame Liz smiled, gently enjoying the pride she held for herself and her higher duty to mankind.

The feeling had finally surfaced. We all deserve a pat on the back every now and then, and this was her way of rewarding herself.

However, more thoughts kept coming. There was more to her life situation. More, because at the end of the day, it came down to judgments.

Simple choices. A decision of who you let walk away, who you let stay and who you refuse to let go.

Madame Liz held no prejudices and dedicated her life existence to this talent of hers. Either way, if Madame Liz was in a town on official business or otherwise and if someone wanted her time, she was only too happy to be there.

For a moderate fee that allowed her to continue to do her work, she gave an unbiased message of support with spiritual and angelic guidance.

However, there was a bittersweet concern. It lay deeper in the soul of this spiritual medium. It was a worrying perception. A thought of doing good in a time where the world was losing focus on God and his love for mankind.

The world was changing and not for the better. She felt it and deep down she knew it would get bad before it started to get better.

A worse time was approaching and it would be an anti-climax. She couldn't put her finger on it.

How did she know? What would this be?

And most importantly, where and when would this all come to a conclusion?

There was also a link to two children she had grown quite fond of. She was their adoptive aunt and they were like family. How would Günter and Anita be affected? How would their lives be affected? These were worrying questions to which she did not have the answers.

These thoughts brought on emotions and sometimes the emotions stirred up these worrying thoughts. Either way, long drives always gave time for reflecting.

~ * ~

An unexplainable shiver that slid up and down her spine occurred more frequently now than before.

It was a sign!

It was as if the frequency of the shivers increased as time drew closer to the mystery of an up and coming anti-climax.

The intense mental feeling slid and travelled predictably, with a smooth, steady rhythm. It was as if someone was running a finger up and down the inside of her spine, running it along her vertebrate like one runs a musical hammer across a xylophone.

She could feel every nerve tingling bump on the inside of her spine. In comparison, these were better than the other type of spine tingling sensation.

Given the choice, she preferred the xylophone. The other one hurt just a little more.

A pain of nerve endings that fired off sequentially. The feeling generated was quite different. The words in her head.

Ouch! Ouch! Ouch!

They were uneasy like: a type of slithering that moved up and down, starting from the tip of the neck right down to the tail end of the spine and then back up again.

This snake-like slithering moved rapidly, like a table tennis game.

Back and forth. Fast and quick.

This was but one part of the total experience.

The sensation wound up and down her spine for a little while waiting for its moment. And when it settled, it did so by randomly grabbing a spot and tightening.

The wrapping of its invisible coil around two or three specific sections of Madame Liz's vertebrate. This hurt just that little bit more.

OUCH!

The tightening was borderline painful and most uncomfortable. Liz knew this was no physical medical condition. Its message was uncomfortably spiritual in nature and only lasted a few moments.

Regardless of whether it was xylophone or slithering snake,

the unsettling feeling always ended in the same way.

The grand finale always finished in the depths of her gut, squeezing it like the wringing of a wet towel. These were stomach butterflies of the worst kind.

Thankfully, the feeling went as quickly as it came.

But all along, she felt the emotion was somehow linked to the fate of two young and talented children. Would it be good, bad or indifferent?

This she did not know.

She suspected it was also bound to something spiritually grand. It had something to do with a meeting of Heaven and Earth in Christian synchronicity. She felt this and somehow knew this with a confidence she had not experienced for some time. Something strange was about to happen. But what?

On Earth as it is in Heaven!

But what was the tie? What was the children's involvement? And her own? The answers would inevitably come when the time was right.

She had made her choices, and as per her life motto, she had no regrets and no coincidences. Whatever part she had to play in all this was yet to be determined.

The drive went on and on and on. There was nothing exciting to see but the modern roadway bordered by copious amounts of greenery. It was sort of pretty, but after many hours on the road, it became repetitive.

After a while her mindset quickly went back to her reflections. A silly, solitary statement popped into her head. "How lonely a life."

"NO REGRETS!" She spoke out loud, instantly dismissing and halting any further thoughts on the matter. This was her chosen life path and she was happy with what she did.

But the emotion festered on. It refused to be dismissed so easily and with that, tears trickled down her face.

Liz lifted her hand from the steering wheel, gently wiping

the trail of saltiness away with her forefinger.

Madame Liz was not one to wallow in self-pity. And this was not self-pity, but rather it was a case of being humbled to the special gift and foresight that she held. Of being humbled by the countless number of people she had helped.

Liz had lots of passing friendships, but no true sense that she belonged somewhere. This was the price she paid for her very special spiritual gift.

For many years, Madame Liz had not been able to truly call any one place home. Her life was always on the road.

However, since that fateful meeting with Josef many years ago, she longed to get back to a special place in her heart.

This family, that was now very dear and close to her, had invited her into their lives. They needed her as much as she needed them. The time was right for all of their lives to connect.

No coincidences!

The circumstances of Liz meeting Josef in her caravan may have been perceived to be innocent. But there was a spiritual link that initiated the meeting and the mutual invitation into each other's lives. The friendship from then on had been unconditional.

Liz was welcomed with a love and warmth she had never encountered before. And she had embraced the invitation like nothing else. For the first time in many, many years, she truly felt like she belonged. And it felt nice.

The thought of getting back to Cologne meant so much more than just another town to visit.

A widowed father and his children. A man who was like a big brother to her.

The thought of them brought a smile to her face as the lonely trip into Düsseldorf continued. It was her last stop before she returned to Cologne.

But she could not get the children out of her mind.

They were true saints. Anita and Günter were as adorable as any children could be. She had to set aside her thoughts of catching up with this special family for a few more days. She had business ahead in Düsseldorf, seventy odd kilometers north of Cologne.

Düsseldorf was an interesting place. It had a significant industrial zone, but it was mainly known for its reputation as a center of Germany's high end fashion. It also had a bit of a reputation for being a key German economic center. This status carried over to the people of the town.

Düsseldorf's residents were considered by their neighbors to be a little more smug than the average German. The people of Düsseldorf could argue that they were very proud of their beautiful city and fashion consciousness.

Madame Liz had been called to Düsseldorf.

She was guided by her gut impressions and disregarded her personal opinions. Smug or proud, people still looked for her help and assistance and she was only too happy to give it. She set up on the edge of the city's center and allowed her gift to be used for guidance and life enhancement.

But before she set up, she had to make a phone call. She longed to hear some familiar and loving voices.

Madame Liz looked for a public telephone box as she entered the early evening hustle and bustle of Düsseldorf.

Pulling up the car, she got out quick and eagerly approached the telephone with loose change in her hands.

She dialed the phone number with excitement. Her fingers could not contain the emotion trembling with every number button pressed.

"Hello," came a voice on the receiving end of her call. It was a mature and masculine sounding tone.

"Josef! How are the kids?" she blurted out.

"I'm very well," he said in a sarcastic voice. "Thank you for asking." Josef immediately recognized the caller.

"I'm sorry, Josef, I didn't mean to be so rude. It's just—"

Josef cut off Liz. "It's okay, Liz. I'm not offended. And how are you? Will you be visiting soon?"

"I'm a little tired, but I'm fine. I'm in Düsseldorf now. A few more days and then I will come by. May I speak with the children?"

Josef pulled the receiver away from his mouth. Liz could hear a loud voice calling out across the room. "Children! You have a special phone call."

Günter and Anita instantly knew who their father meant. Josef used the same terminology time and time again.

They ran to the phone, fighting to get there first. Liz heard Josef speak again.

"Young ladies before gentlemen." He spoke softly and with that came the sweet voice of Anita.

"Hello, Auntie Liz."

The children took their turns to speak with their adoptive Aunt, and Liz felt emotionally refreshed to hear two of the sweetest voices she knew.

Her hair was ruffled and windblown, and her eyes had grown tired and bloodshot.

Liz looked the better part of a mess, but the conversation was exactly what she needed to re-energize her.

It was these little things that motivated her enough to see her through the night and the next few days.

CHAPTER TWENTY-EIGHT
The Phone Call

It had only been a handful of years since Pam had passed away. The loss of one's life partner took an understandable toll on Arthur, but somehow life went on. Arthur coped by keeping himself busy.

The middle of an Australian autumn was as beautiful as any typical spring day. The temperature was in the high twenties with a light breeze kicking in from time to time that took the edge off the pleasant warmth.

It was just the day to be in the garden.

Arthur grew up in a time when the greengrocer wasn't exactly located conveniently around the corner. His was a time when people grew their own vegetables and used them for food or trade.

Things weren't so tough in the 1980s.

A convenience store was never too far away, but Arthur still enjoyed the pleasure of growing his own produce. The freshness could never be surpassed by anything bought from a grocery shop.

Arthur knelt by an empty patch of land in his garden. His capsicum seeds were close by. It was an excellent day to get the seedlings into the dirt.

Arthur had gotten himself organized. All he would need for his gardening was out and at the ready. He had just got himself comfortable and was about to give the earth its first strike.

Bearing his trusty old hand held hoe, he raised his hand but stopped his motion at the sound of the phone ringing.

Arthur was no spring chicken, and getting up took a little longer than it used to.

This was a time when phones were heading into a new age. Mobile pagers were still popular and the mobile phone had not quite made its mark on society. Even the home phone had only just made the transition to push button technology.

The old man had seen enough technological changes to last five lifetimes. Regardless, Arthur still liked his traditional phone with the metallic circular disc and a hole for every number. You could insert your finger and swing the metallic disc around until the other metallic end prevented your finger from going any further.

Phone technology might have been on the verge of a revolutionary change, but Arthur was not at all interested. He was in no hurry to change what he had owned for so many years.

He was, however, in a hurry to get to the phone before it rang out.

He approached his phone after quite a lengthy ring and picked it up, greeting the caller with a courteous, but somewhat puffed out voice.

"Hello," he said, trying to regain his breath. Arthur spoke over the beeps of an international call. Too busy catching his breath, he failed to notice the caller was from overseas.

"Are you okay, Grandpa?" asked Tony.

"I knew it. I just knew it," replied his grandfather, still a little huffy and puffy.

Tony had thought his grandfather had lost his marbles. He wasn't making any sense.

"Grandpa, is everything okay?" The huffing and puffing and confusing dialogue had Tony concerned about his grandfather's state of health.

"You needn't worry about me. I'm fine. But how are you? We've been worried sick."

"I would have called sooner, but we were on a train from Munich to Cologne, and then by the time we settled in and the time difference—"

Tony wanted to rattle off more excuses, but the reality of the matter was that he could have called sooner.

His grandfather interrupted the conversation before anymore could be said.

"I thought you were catching a plane. That's what your schedule said."

"We were supposed to, but we missed it. Johnny got sick and it all got a bit messed up."

"Well, thank God it did. Did you hear the news?"

"Yeah. It was a little scary. A bit too close for comfort. We would have been on that flight."

"Next time don't wait. You call me anytime. Don't let your grandfather worry like that." Arthur paused momentarily and then quickly added, "Johnny should ring his family. They're worried sick."

"It's okay. He's downstairs using the lobby phone." Tony paused for a moment. "We're perfectly okay. You needn't worry about anything."

Tony and his grandfather chatted for a little while longer. It was small talk and Tony was pleased with the conversation. He could sense his grandfather's anxiety had dissipated.

Johnny, on the other hand, copped a downright bollocking. His phone conversation was one sided and pretty aggressive. He listened to his mother give him a "What for?" and then, just in case he misunderstood his mother, his father repeated the message in the same aggressive and loving manner.

All he could do was agree and apologize.

Johnny walked back into the hotel room as Tony was hanging up the phone.

Johnny spoke. "Boy! That was heaps of fun." Johnny looked frustrated as he rolled his eyes in a sarcastic manner. His phone call was more like a battering than a conversation.

"And they wonder why we don't call more often," he added.

Tony walked up to his friend and patted him on the shoulder.

"Let's get out of here. We've got lots to see."

Johnny gathered his things and the boys ventured out for a day out on the town.

CHAPTER TWENTY-NINE
A Church-Evangelische Kirche Werden

Madame Liz was smiling to herself. A cheeky grin of sorts.

Her current happiness was deep and spiritual in nature. It was fitting for a psychic medium of her caliber.

It was and had been a pleasant trip.

It struck her as a little odd as it had been a couple of days since the last set of unsettling feelings. She last experienced them whilst she drove into Düsseldorf.

Her office, the caravan in which Madame Liz performed all of her readings, was decorated with a mix of gypsy and Christian objects. Colorful stones, drapes and lace along with ornaments, pictures and little statuettes of Angels and of all things holy. These were securely stowed when she traveled and were now set up, fitting to the tone of a traveling spiritual medium's room.

Each time she set up the back end of her caravan, it was similar, but different. It was like being given a blank canvas for your next artistic masterpiece. Setting up her office was one of the highlights for Madame Liz when on her travels. Each stop allowed Liz to creatively redecorate and rearrange.

Her surrounds were always tastefully decorative and pleasantly serene.

She sat in her caravan on the outskirts of Düsseldorf's city center. Regulars who had come to know Madame Liz knew her location and eagerly awaited her return.

Liz was in her caravan putting the finishing touches on the room for her Düsseldorf guests. To fill in the time in between her meetings, she sat reading her favorite books or losing her thoughts to the sounds of her music collection.

Today, she listened to one of her most cherished classical composers, a long deceased fellow German who went by the name of Mozart.

It was times like these that she often felt a deep spiritual emotion. One that would readily take over her caravan as if it were a living essence. It set the scene and the mood and put Madame Liz at complete harmony with all that was around her.

The emotion was always present, but the peacefulness and restfulness only ever lasted until the next knock at the door.

Liz didn't mind the interruptions. After all, this was what she was there for.

The signage outside hadn't changed. It was still the same two old separate pieces of off-cut wood written on with rough-looking black paint.

"COME AND HAVE YOUR FORTUNE READ," read the sign in big, black, bold letters. "ENTER SAYS MADAME LIZ," read the piece below it. She was now set up and ready to serve the people of the town.

She heard her first knock. "Come in. Come in," said Madame Liz from behind the curtain.

A familiar face walked up the short caravan stairway and in past the dividing lace curtain. Liz had seen this young lady before. She could not remember her name, but the face was definitely familiar.

"Sit down, my dear, and let's see what we can do for you today." Liz turned to silence the background music and then went on to make herself and her visiting guest comfortable.

~ * ~

The short days and long nights had come and gone. Madame Liz had reached the end of her stay in town. She had enjoyed a steady two days of helping those in need and those seeking spiritual guidance. She took the time to securely place all her things away.

"Another eventful short stay," she thought to herself.

Liz was pleased with her brief visit to Düsseldorf. There were plenty of people to help. This job of hers was very fulfilling.

For so many reasons, there was nothing more spiritually uplifting than helping a fellow human being.

At night, her caravan was transformed into a bedroom of sorts. The set up was quite basic with a simple fold out mattress for her night time slumber.

A quiet backstreet and a well deserved sleep.

In the morning she prepared for her trip to Cologne. But before she left, she had one more stop to make. Madame Liz headed for the outer suburbs of Düsseldorf on the other side of the city.

This particular suburb of Düsseldorf was a place where forest was dense and greenery was abundant. In amongst sparse housing grew tree after tree. And in amongst the sparse housing and dense forestation, a single and modestly sized church steeple penetrated, pointing up to the clear sky above.

There was a big church attached to this single steeple, but you would never know it if you were standing on a nearby hill top. The dense greenery did wonders in camouflaging not just the church, but the general area.

From the tree line above, the view of the church was limited. But what stood out was a perfectly squared, red tone brick column which supported a tall, white, pointed steeple. The clean, bright brick work was broken up by a large, single colored stained glass cathedral window, beautifully located about two-thirds up.

To finish it off, at the tip of the steeple was a plain and simple crucifix. There was nothing spectacular about this church and by comparison, it would have been dwarfed by the great cathedral of Cologne.

But not all churches can be grand in stature. This one was a typical, moderately sized house of prayer which served the local community. It was known as Evangelische Kirche Werden.

Simple in looks and tastefully decorative, Madame Liz had come to know the pastor of the church and regularly dropped in to say hello.

Mostly she enjoyed the warmth of the church and looked towards some downtime there before she kept travelling.

For whatever reason, she connected with this pastor and enjoyed his sermons. They rang true for her. She felt that in a way, this pastor gave to her what she was giving to many others. The only difference was usually Liz's messages were on a one to one basis, whereby the pastor's was typically delivered to the whole congregation.

That didn't faze Liz as she always found her truth in his sermons.

All was quiet. It was middle of the week and close to lunch time. In about thirty minutes, the pastor would give his late morning service to a congregation of young and old. No matter what time or day, this pastor had a gift for drawing in his flock.

Liz said hello to the priest and took her place in one of the aisle seats. The pastor left her there and continued with his office work, preparing for the service while people of all ages drifted in and took their places.

Madame Liz sat in silence, recharging and re-energizing. It was a special little treat for herself. A luxury she seldom got to enjoy, but on this occasion, she consciously made the time to seek and obtain it.

As she looked up and around, the few who had come to church early were simply sitting back and apparently doing the same. The sermon was not all that far off and the atmosphere in the church was most tranquil.

~ * ~

In the Heavens above, the Archangel Michael sought an audience with the Queen of Angels.

"Forgive me, Holy Mother, I have grave concerns about Sebastian and his wrongdoings."

"Yes, we all do. The higher order is working nonstop to bring justice to a big injustice." The Holy Mother then turned her back on Michael.

The situation worried her as much as it did the great Archangel. She had spent endless time orchestrating means in which to minimize the spiritual damage Lucifer or Sebastian could cause. She did what she could from up above to protect and serve all that is godly.

At this point, it had made little difference, which is why she turned away, not wanting Michael to see the distress on her face.

After what seemed like a lengthy and uncomfortable pause, the Virgin Mary kept her back to the great Angel and spoke.

"What of your concerns?" asked the Virgin Mary. There was another pause, this time, ever so brief and before Michael could reply, the Holy Mother turned around and faced him.

She added. "I can't tell you that God will answer all your 'Why?' questions. He may, but he may not. His purpose ultimately is beyond our knowing. Yes, even those around me can sometimes never fully comprehend God's ultimate plan, but I trust in his glorious wisdom."

"As do I, my Holy Mother," added Michael.

Mother Mary clenched her hands behind her back and slowly paced in a small circle. Her head facing slightly down, she lost herself in thought.

Archangel Michael stood by in silence and watched on. The Virgin Mary circled once, then slowly another time and then once more.

It was a very long silence, but Michael did not dare interrupt the thoughts of his Queen.

She stopped and looked up. Instantly, her eyes met with Michael's. "His timing is always unfolding for the righteous according to divine precision as Heaven is built on the principle that all things work together for good." The Virgin Mary continued, "And even if God reveals a great deal to us, we will never know as fully as he knows.

"We must believe that Sebastian and his movements were foreseen by our Lord. Even Sebastian's destiny has been mapped out and he, too, will face his moment of truth."

"I have no doubt of this Holy Mother, but...," Michael's reply drifted into nothingness.

"My sweet Angel. But what?" asked the Holy Mother.

"Your Holiness," Michael said.

The conversation then stopped. He knew what he was about to say might contradict what the angelic hierarchy stood for.

The Archangel could see where the Holy Mother was coming from. There was a plan in place, but he wasn't sure he could sit back and allow the plan to naturally evolve.

He wasn't even sure this was what the Holy Mother meant with her message of non-intervention.

And surely, she couldn't have meant it that way. Surely, she didn't expect for him to sit back and do nothing.

She had kept herself mighty busy trying to intercept the messages of evil that Lucifer himself was personally trying to communicate to Earth onto the dark angel, Sebastian.

The Virgin Mary used the higher order of Angels to achieve this. Michael now understood the purpose of gathering the immense powers of the senior Angels.

Zophiel, the right hand Angel of God.

Ezekiel, the Cherubim Angel.

And Oriphiel, the Throne Angel.

For Oriphiel to be involved initially had Michael a little

concerned. Oriphiel was the dispenser of God's judgment and Michael had witnessed many of his doings.

This Angel acted with what would look like no mercy. He executed plans with impartialness and humility to bring about the desires of the Lord. Sometimes these desires had devastating results.

The hierarchy of Angels were in symbiosis. The power combined of the three was much greater than the sum of the individuals.

Michael was suddenly hit with the sense of it all now.

There was nothing more to this gathering than the negation of everything evil.

As Lucifer delivered his evil wavelengths, the Virgin Mary and her band of Angels were there to negate, intercept and interrupt.

Good vs Bad.

Holy vs Evil.

This was her one and only intention. Yet the words she spoke to Michael indicated some shortcomings that the great Archangel was uncomfortable with. He couldn't sit back and just watch.

And so he wanted to speak his mind, but Michael was holding back, tentative about what he had to say.

Regardless of any impression the Archangel gave in either his actions or conversation, and whether or not these impressions were perceived positively or negatively, Michael would never rebel against anything that was godly. He knew he had the respect of the Heavens to discuss things openly and honestly, especially with his Queen.

She must have sensed his need to speak. She must have noticed the need to invite his discussion.

"Speak your mind," requested the Virgin Mary.

"My Holy Mother. I have lived my existence wholeheartedly believing in God's will, bathing in God's comforting love. And as I am amongst the Angels who link mankind with the Heavens, I have placed my entire trust in your son and his rising, so that mankind and all of his sins could be forgiven. So that all of human kind would be given the gift of eternal life in this place I call my home," said Michael.

"I cannot just think of Heaven, but of the wellbeing of all who live on Earth. All who worship the Holy Trinity. For all those who do wrong on Earth, there are many who do right and live with the belief and wisdom of the Father and the Son and the Holy Spirit. What we do in Heaven alone is not good enough. We are trying to fight a battle on Earth from the Heavens above. This will not work. I am confident of this. That is why I have a request, my Holy Mother."

He knew her. He could see it in her face. The worry. In some ways, she looked lost. Uncertain of what to do next.

She didn't have to speak. He knew what was needed. And as anxious as she looked, he was going to say it.

"We must deliver a miracle to Earth. Show them the way. Have them understand mankind has strayed from the divine intent of living a respectful and good life."

"And what would you suggest?" she replied.

"An appearance, my Queen. An appearance by you." The Holy Mother had made several appearances in man's history, but what Michael now spoke of was different. What Michael requested of his Queen was a special appearance before one specific individual.

CHAPTER THIRTY
A Very Special Sermon

Johnny and Tony's overseas adventure was drawing to a conclusion. The two friends realized the weekend was only a few short days away and early into the new week they would be catching their flight home.

Arrangements had to be made and the boys decided to get these tasks out of the way. It would make their last days in Germany so much more enjoyable.

So today was a day of organizing and running around. Not the most exciting of days, but things needed to be done.

Johnny and Tony had decided Cologne would remain their home base. It provided them with easy access to the final sights and pleasures they wanted to experience before departing.

The boys left their hotel room and walked down the street. High above the roofline of the houses and buildings, the massive steeples and crucifixes of the cathedral could be seen. They towered in the not so distant horizon. It was a landmark that could not be missed.

Simultaneously, the boys turned their eyes to the great steeple. Both of them stopped deadly still and looked up in a trance like state. They gazed at the massive gothic church, both unaware of the other's actions. It was as if they had been plucked out of time.

A few short minutes passed. The young Australians were unaware of their surroundings.

For everyone else, life continued as normal.

"Excuse me, are you lost?" A momentary pause and a few more seconds passed.

"Excuse me, ARE YOU LOST?" repeated the stranger. He must have picked up that the two young boys were foreign travellers.

The man was dressed neatly in business attire and with his stern German accent, he made his final point very pronounced.

The boys snapped out of their trances as suddenly as they had entered into them. A look of bewilderment washed over their young faces. The German businessman looking straight at them only added to the confusion.

"You appear a little lost. Can I help you?" he asked.

Tony, still a bit surprised by the sudden stare of a complete stranger, politely declined the offer and the businessman continued on his way.

"That was weird!" Johnny directed his comment about the German man.

They were both totally oblivious to what had happened. The moment was quickly forgotten as it was time to make their way into the city center.

~ * ~

Not so far away, in the neighboring town of Düsseldorf, Madame Liz sat at the aisle end of a church seat. The sermon had concluded. It was short and sweet, ideal for a weekday.

The silence gave the congregation the chance to enjoy a final moment of prayer. This was useful for the working man or woman who might want to find a little time to get some lunch before returning to his or her duties.

Madame Liz, on the other hand, was her own boss and was in no terrible hurry. Her duties in the town of Düsseldorf were now over, just like the sermon for the day.

The pastor was fiddling at the altar while the congregation gathered and scattered. All that was left to do was tidy up. He put things in place for the next sermon. He liked to keep it clean and neat so whatever the case, the church always looked presentable.

Liz sat back and watched the various personalities interact and get on their way. Young and old, some in a hurry to leave, others more interested in socializing. Every now and then the pastor stopped his tidying to acknowledge a brief greeting from one of his loyal churchgoers.

It looked like some were thanking him for another warm and meaningful message. Liz could not hear the conversation but she enjoyed watching people going up to briefly greet, thank or kiss the hand of their respected pastor.

His lessons hit the mark for many people.

Madame Liz was not alone when it came to this pastor and his special sermons. Liz also wanted to give her personal thanks, but she would have to wait for a little longer, until some of the crowd disappeared.

In next to no time, the congregation had dwindled down to a few people. Groups scattered around the inside of the church chatting with each other. Liz looked around and noticed things had become much quieter.

Now was as good a time as any. Liz got up off her chair and made her way to the front. "You're just the special little crowd pleaser today, aren't you?" said Liz in jest.

A modest man, the pastor returned a warm and thankful smile. He hadn't seen Liz for quite some time and was genuinely interested in her. "How long are you in town for?" he asked. His voice was as warm as his smile.

"I'm heading off this afternoon, Father. I wanted to thank you for another wonderful sermon."

"You are most welcome. As always, I wish you well with your onward journey." The Pastor, not meaning to be rude, believed the conversation was over and turned to continue with his tidying.

"Excuse me, Father."

He turned back around. "My apologies, Liz, how can I be of assistance?"

"I was wondering if it would be okay to sit here for a while. I promise not to get in the way." Liz looked around the church. "I just want a little quiet time to myself."

"That is quite alright, my child. I'll be shutting the doors soon. I'll be in my office for a little while longer yet so you can have all the quiet time you need."

"Thank you, Father." Liz made her way back to her seat. As she sat, she saw the priest disappear through the church office door. Soon after, the crowds were gone and he secured the large wooden doors of the church.

As the Father walked back to his office, he passed Liz. Their eyes met. She smiled her thanks and he replied with his gentleness.

Madame Liz had the church to herself. She sat in silence, gazing upon a large painting placed high in front of the church altar. It depicted Christ being let down from the cross. His body was limp and his mother held his lifeless hand as a handful of helpers lowered him to the white sheet that lay neatly spread out on the ground below.

The detail in the painting was phenomenal. From the expression on the people's faces through to the emotion of a mother who had lost her son, even down to the cuts and bruises and marks on Christ's lifeless body.

Nothing was overlooked in this Christian masterpiece.

Liz was mesmerized by the picture. She focused on its colorful details and got lost amongst the vivid colors. She found herself drifting away into her own meditative world.

The Holy Mother and Archangel Michael appeared in spirit at the back of the Evangelische Kirche Werden.

The spiritual entities hovered high in the air, looking at the back of Liz's head. Her head was still and her mind was pre-occupied with the painting.

The Holy Mother looked at Liz and then followed her gaze to the picture. It sent tragic shivers through her spiritual soul. Even to this day, the symbolism of the cross was firstly a reminder of the brutal torture of her son and secondly, of the forgiveness of mankind and all of his sins.

The Holy Mother looked back down at Liz.

"There she is, my Queen," said Michael. "This one is special. On account of her purity of heart, extraordinary spiritual foresight and her selfless and unconditional love for those she serves." Michael then withdrew himself, allowing the Holy Mother to do what she must do.

The Virgin Mother took her place within the painting. From a point in the painting where she was still and holding the hand of her deceased son, she now grew beyond the canvas, extending beyond the edge of the painting itself.

From there she grew even further out of the picture and became three dimensional in appearance. She floated before Liz's eyes as the gypsy woman remained in subconscious meditation.

The Holy Mother grew in size until she was quite life-like, hovering above the ground for only one spiritual medium to witness.

"Don't be frightened," said the Holy Mother.

Liz was far from frightened! She was ecstatic, but she held back from outwardly expressing it. She had never bore witness to anything holier than an Angel of the basic order and now she sat in awe in the presence of the Virgin Mother herself.

Liz knelt and bowed her head, but Mother Mary would not have it. Not this time.

"Raise your head, my child. I come to give a message. A message of grave importance."

Liz followed her instructions and looked up but remained on her knees.

The Holy Mother felt it necessary to build up her message. What she would ask at the end would be demanding for even the holiest of earthly souls. When the time was right, this message would make perfect sense to the recipient. This recipient had psychic insight, which was amongst the best the world had ever seen.

"What guidance can be given today for any man, woman or child as we all attempt to be true to the commandments of the Lord's Gospel? In this complex world of yours, how does one be pro-life in a consistent and meaningful way?"

The Holy mother turned her head around to once again gaze upon the picture of the torture and death of her beloved son. It was not the words but the gesture the Holy Mother made.

By looking at the painting in the way the Holy Mother did, Liz quickly realized what would follow would tie in closely to the sacrifice that Jesus made for all of mankind.

Liz was as still as a statue, remaining as attentive and alert as any soul could ever be. The Queen of Angels turned her gaze away from the picture to look into the very soul of Madame Liz. She continued with her special message, hovering above the ground, dressed in white. Her palms were held outwardly and open.

"There are some that will put their effort into overturning laws, policies, and rulings that jeopardize life. There are others who will put their efforts into protecting the sanctity of life in their more immediate environment. Some put their efforts into the care of children, the elderly, the infirm or the disabled. Others make larger self-sacrifices and others still serve with a passion and desire like you do. They do it without question or regret, without thought for their personal sacrifice."

As still and as attentive as Liz was, a solitary tear escaped her. She remained motionless as she allowed the tear to track down the side of her face. It quickly dried to nothingness at the base of her chin and very soon after, the sensation of its trail had disappeared.

"Not every one of us will be engaged in every one of these pursuits," said the Holy Mother. "But each of us is called by God to do something. Each of us has been given gifts by God to serve their fellow human beings from the womb to the tomb, and even beyond.

"Therefore, if we wish to teach the young people of today what they must do, we must be an example to the believers in word, in conduct, in spirit, in faith and in purity." The Holy Mother paused.

Madame Liz experienced an intense and familiar feeling.

The sensation had started. She had last felt it driving herself into Dusseldorf. The phenomenon had returned, but she sensed this one would be different.

But in what way?

Where, when and how would this all end?

She wasn't sure.

Was this going to be xylophone or slithering snake?

It didn't matter anymore.

She no longer had to wait for the finale. The tightening in the past had not been painful, but was, to say the least, uncomfortable.

But this time, the pain hit with much more intensity. It caused Liz to instantly crunch forward.

She clenched her eyelids shut and closed her teeth. As every muscle in her body tensed, trying to overcome the pain of it all, she did everything she could to avoid yelling out her agony. Any sound of pain would alert the office-bound pastor that all was not well.

This was an excruciating pain so immense, it fell only just shy of sending her body into shock. Madame Liz stabilized herself by grabbing the aisle seat in front of her. She gripped onto it so tightly, but it offered little in terms of pain relief.

Once again, the psychic medium knew this was no medical condition. Its message was most uncomfortably spiritual in nature.

Seconds had passed, but it felt like hours.

Unfortunately for her, this excruciating pain would last longer than it had ever done before.

As Liz tried to settle the pain with quick and repeated sharp breaths, a very clear and precise image entered into her subconscious vision. As it did, the pain subsided a little. It still hurt, but by comparison, the intense grips around her vertebrate were much more tolerable.

Together, the pain and the visual displays would make for a lasting impression.

A vision of six faces, grouped together as if in a family portrait. Still images of heads and faces only. As clear as the day, she recognized all the faces bar two.

There was no mistaking the faces of two very special children. Anita and Günter appeared as distinctly and as clearly as the last time she had seen them. The other two faces were their spiritual guides, the male and female entities known as Charlie and Mary who had spiritually shadowed the children since they could walk. The remaining two faces were not known to her yet, but Liz was certain they would provide the missing link to the mystery.

Her remaining pain completely disappeared. And after a moment, so did the portrait of the faces.

Just as Madame Liz was regaining her composure, another image entered her head. It was the beast known as Sebastian.

His enlarged eyes, burnt leathery skin and demonic wings were a dead giveaway. In his dark and natural form there was no mistaking this beast from the depths of Hell.

Madame Liz instantly recognized the origins of the beast, but had no idea Sebastian was so high up in the hierarchy of dark angels. That he was in fact, one of Lucifer's most trusted servants.

As a gifted psychic medium, Liz had seen it all. Seeing the dead and sometimes the unsightly was a downside to her gift, so it would take visions far more horrific to scare her away.

Yet this one very detailed image stood vividly before her subconscious mind, and caused hairs to rise on the back of her neck. Startled by the image, but not frightened by it, Madame Liz took in as much detail as possible.

The image sent shivers through her entire body. Her inner spirit was most uncomfortable with what it was viewing. Her soul uncomfortably bounced around inside her human shell, trying to hide from an image that was in no way, shape or form linked to the loving light of God or to the Heavens above.

It wasn't natural and under normal circumstances, no soul should ever bear witness to such a gruesome sight. The shivers continued, ceasing only when the image disappeared from her subconscious view.

There was nothing further revealed about Sebastian and his evil doings in Heaven and on Earth.

The medium had been distracted from the beautiful holy vision before her. She could not make sense of anything. One thing was for sure: every image she had witnessed was burnt into her subconscious forever, from Sebastian and the portrait of faces through to the Holy Mother herself.

Liz's vision returned to normal as she gazed upon the Holy Mother one last time. Standing next to her was another familiar vision. The Archangel Michael hovered next to the Holy Mother and before Madame Liz.

As per Archangel Michael's intentions, the message he wished the Holy Mother to deliver was now over.

As a parting message, Michael spoke the following words. These were the only words he spoke to her before he and the Holy Mother disappeared out of the psychic's view.

"Have the courage to stand up and refuse to be intimidated. Fight back to protect the innocent in a way that only you will know how. Protect the innocent from further death and destruction to say that THIS WILL NOT STAND! Beware! Be Warned! Protect!"

A brief pause and then Michael concluded. "We will be by your side in your moment of truth."

And as quickly as that, the spiritual miracle ended.

All this had been exhausting for Liz, both physically and mentally. She felt as though she had a mild case of the flu, even though her symptoms were not related to any human disease or illness. Malaise had set in and she was in no condition to drive.

She would spend another night sleeping in her caravan. She needed to rest up. There was a lot to think about.

CHAPTER THIRTY-ONE
Pam and the Preacher's Soul

The Archangels had personally entrusted Pam with a holy task which involved a man whose holiness began on Earth and ended in devilish tragedy.

~ * ~

Over the ages and since the beginning of time, man had made, had invented, had dared to venture out. And whether he knew it or whether he acknowledged it or not, it was all a tribute to the divine.

It made the Heavens proud when something of an earthly nature was constructed, achieved and developed, in the name of the Father, the Son and the Holy Spirit.

Heaven rejoiced at all of man's accomplishments, but now and then, something spectacularly different made Heaven really take notice.

One such marvel was the massive cathedral in the heart of Cologne. Its construction took decades and the finished work was nothing less than a masterpiece dedicated to all that is godly.

The sacrifices made to make this project reach fruition would not go unnoticed on Earth or in Heaven.

Priests from around Germany and even from the farthest stretches of Europe considered it a great privilege to be invited to deliver a sermon to the people and visitors of Cologne. It was a privilege to be at the front altar of one of Europe's finest cathedrals.

But on one such occasion, a German preacher whose dedication to his faith and people was nothing less than single minded devotion met his demise in the unholiest of fashions.

Now Sebastian resided in his Earth-bound shell of a body as Heaven dealt with the aftermath of his battered soul.

Pam had been given the task of nurturing this most giving of souls back to normality. It was not going to be easy.

Pam had dedicated so much time to the task and there was so much more that needed to be done.

In a quiet corner of Heaven, Pam and the preacher man sat several meters apart. It was important the distance give them the space to be on their own and yet together.

Like waves coming in towards the shore, the white clouds of Heaven's floor danced beside their bodies. It was warm and gentle, providing comfort when things were so disturbing.

The time had come in the healing process for Pam to leave the priest to his own devices, to let him sort through all that he had been taught so far. The progress was slow and demanding for both Pam and the tortured soul.

The last session was intense, but it would only get harder before it got easier.

Pam stood up.

I had to let him be. I had never in my time on Earth or in Heaven seen such horrific injuries. I could see he was healing. Heavenly light was good for that, but my God, what horrible injuries.

There's no blood up here. That's for down there. But he looks like he has been through a meat shredder. Bits of spiritual flesh hanging off his face like a torn and tattered piece of clothing.

I have no idea what this man looks like because he has no face, just a head with bits hanging off it.

What did Sebastian do to you?

I can't bear to look at him, but I can't stop staring either.

The poor soul.

He's sitting there with his head in his palms. I cannot imagine what he is going through. I hope the Archangels give that beast the beating he deserves.

How do you curse one who is already damned? He'll have to take it for what it's worth!

Damn you, Sebastian!

This poor preacher's soul. He's looking my way for help and I am struggling to give a reply. I can't even muster up a smile of support. This whole process of rehabilitation has been a struggle for me too.

But I wouldn't dare to imagine what he's feeling. I am here for him and I will see this through, no matter how long it takes. No matter how demanding it is.

I'm wondering what's going through his mind. He's staring at the sky now. I would say that he has lost all interest, all hope. He may feel lost, but I will work with him.

He may not be able to rejoice at the beauty of Heaven just now. I'll leave him to gaze upon the blue of the sky above. I'll let the heavenly light heal him. We both need a little more rest.

I needn't tell him the rage I feel over his attack.

Don't give in, I want to say.

You needn't drop your head in shame. You needn't hide your face in the palms of your hand.

Don't shed one tear.

Don't let Sebastian have the pleasure. Hold it up. Hold your head up high and don't let those hellish bastards win the battle over your inner spirit. You will survive and you will become stronger for it. You are now a valued member of this heavenly community and I would be proud to consider you my friend.

The long road to recovery has begun. But first, we need a very big rest.

The next session will be grueling for both of us. You sit there and I will be back.

I needed to get away from his presence. We both needed the time to ourselves and I couldn't remain too close. This area was open and large enough for me to walk through the misty grounds and take some time to myself.

My back was now to the preacher man. I purposely turned it this way for a little while. I wanted no reminder of what lay ahead. It all brought back so many memories of my own little journey.

So different was my journey and yet, in some ways, so similar.

I thought I had it bad. When my time came, I, too, found it difficult to accept Heaven —but that was under a different set of circumstances.

My reasons were nowhere near as dramatic. But each to their own. I know I had my own challenges to deal with.

It must be many years ago now. I've lost track of the time. But I can still remember it as if it was yesterday. The emotion, bitterness, the denial. It made the journey into Heaven hard for me and I had to do it alone.

Sort of, anyway!

Initially, it was hard for me to accept my new existence. I found it even more difficult to let go of my earthly duties.

After all, I held onto good old fashioned family values. I was proud of dedicating myself to my family. I was a devoted wife, mother and grandmother. How does one drop all that at a moment's notice?

The habits of my lifetime changed because my life on Earth had ceased.

My maternal instinct was buried deep within my soul. I carried this through life and into death. And I carried that responsibility with pride, devoting myself unconditionally to helping others. It might have been old fashioned, but it was the way I was brought up. It was the way I happily chose to live my existence on Earth.

It was time to move on and accept greater responsibility. This was the first of many challenges before me. I had so many unanswered questions. I needed to know everything. I had to understand it completely.

This was my mistake.

I should have let it all go. If I had my time again, maybe. But then again, hindsight is a wonderful thing.

How did I feel? Anxious? Uncomfortable? Sad? Lonely?

The second I realized I was dead, it hit me. The memories of those feelings will remain with me for as long as I exist up here.

I can't recall how long I had been in Heaven when it happened. Back then for me was different. I have learned so much now. I suppose the shock of it all had me lose track of time. All I can remember is that my chest hurt. I felt a sort of burning sensation around my sternum. I had to perform a self-diagnosis because there was no one else around to help.

I stopped and laid my hands on my upper chest. I had to feel all around. Down they went until I reached the base of my rib cage. Something wasn't right.

I had unanswered questions because I was refusing to acknowledge the facts. I was a loving mother and dedicated grandmother in complete denial. Confused and frustrated, but still, I continued on my pointless journey.

Unanswered questions. Where am I? Am I dead? These were the thoughts that crossed my mind.

I can assure you, these are difficult questions to answer about yourself.

I was not alone. I have counselled many since then and we all go through it. Some just find it harder than others. And I am not ashamed to say that back then, I was in a pretty bad sort of denial.

But the process made me a stronger contributor to the greater community of Heaven.

Highlights of my life story flashed before my very eyes. They played before me as if they were on an endless roll of movie film.

I had lived a good life.

Wonderful moments and some not so nice ones. Generally my life was filled with happy memories. The time spent witnessing my life's highlights proved to be calming and pleasant and yet I still resisted accepting that I had passed.

I walked the misty grounds of Heaven like I am right now. But back then I walked and I walked and I walked, unaccompanied by any other spirit or Angel.

Unlike the preacher man. He cannot be left alone. The damage to his soul is devastating. I understand that.

Silence. All around. Not a smell, not a sound. Most of my senses had been numbed by the experience of death. I felt a little and I thought I could see a lot.

I was given the time to come to grips with it all. I probably wasted most of that time. Not many use this time as productively as they could.

Ah, the power of hindsight!

In this numbing silence, I would stop again. This chest of mine was hurting. It was a burning sensation in a world where nothing else could be felt. I found it strange. My rib cage would be a constant reminder that all wasn't right.

Instead of looking down at myself, I should have looked up. Instead of rubbing my chest, I should have thrown my hands in the air and rejoiced.

I needed to accept my new surroundings.

How hard it was back then. Scanning the open grounds, wandering aimlessly, looking for something, searching for anything.

Heaven can be a little overwhelming at first.

A long time passed. It seemed like forever. And there was still nothing.

Nothing but the reminder in my chest and the curiosity in my mind.

And finally, the time came. Out of the blue I saw a shadow in the distance, the sign of another presence. I was no longer alone and I wasn't afraid.

A feeling of comfort offered by the heavenly light had taken over — mostly. Some anxiety still existed within me.

My first contact in Heaven remained a mystery for a little longer and then another shadow appeared behind the first one.

Even now I shudder at the thought of it all. How the truth hit me suddenly, crashing down on my inner soul like a building collapsing.

Brick upon brick tumbled down. Ruin and rubble fell. Unhindered and unstoppable. It seemed chaotic at first and then the building met the Earth and everything eventually settled. And as untidy as the mess was, the structure was cleaned up and rebuilt.

Heaven! When I finally settled, it stopped me in my tracks. I fell to my knees and put my head in my open hands. Back then my actions were much like those of the preacher man before me now.

I had come to realize the truth, the whole truth and nothing but MY truth.

My burden had been lifted, but the finale was emotionally overwhelming. My loving daughter and son-in-law stood before me.

It was like being slapped in the face.

It took my Mary and her Charlie to lovingly deliver the final blow.

I had my support. My Mary and her husband. She made me so proud. He did as well.

I learned a valuable lesson then. One I have carried with me ever since.

Even in Heaven, time is an excellent healer.

I use this concept to help me with my chosen task. It has proved to be invaluable in Heaven during my many years of providing counsel and guidance.

And of all the moments in my heavenly memory, I have to say that this was one of the most joyous. It was such a relief to finally get a hug from my daughter. The last time we had spoken was the weekend before her terrible car accident. Several years had since passed.

To hear the words come out of her mouth. "It's okay, Mum, I know it's hard to take, but it's all okay." To hug my daughter back and hold her in my arms after so many years of absence.

In many ways it was unbelievable, yet here I was. There was no denying it. It simply had to be. I had to ask the question but I only got two words out.

"Are we—?"

My daughter lovingly interrupted. "Yes, Mum, we are."

Charlie offered his kind words of support, too. "It takes time, Mum, don't fight it, go with it." It was the wisest thing I ever heard him say. It couldn't have been said at a more important time.

Accepting one's death is not easy!

Mary was right, too. The burning would get better. An after reminder of my earthly body subjected to countless attempts to resuscitate my life. The electrical discharges of a defibrillator.

Whoever would have guessed that this man made instrument would carry its after effects on through to the afterlife.

In amongst the comfort my daughter offered me, she also provided me with a very haunting gesture. I remember her words vividly.

"I wanted so much to take you early, but this was your chosen destiny. It wasn't pleasant, Mum. The paddles they use in the hospital. The ones they use to get people's hearts started? They gave them a real workout on you."

"It's not worth it, Mum. Sometimes we need to accept that things are the way they are. When you lay on the hospital bed, your body was subjected to endless attempts to resuscitate your life."

"That burning in your chest is the carryover pain of your Earthly existence. Your soul will heal, Mum. Heaven's light heals all with time. In next

to no time, you will feel the best you have ever felt. You'll see!"

Some words will stay with me forever. Her words are now my core values and I use them to counsel others.

And now I have only just become aware that they are on Earth babysitting two very important little children.

Mine is not to question the greater purpose and for whatever reason, the time to be told this news came to me parceled together with a tortured preacher's soul.

It is only now that I have come to know of my Mary and Charlie's whereabouts.

But it is time to refocus on events at hand. I can see him sitting there in the distance.

Be strong, my preacher friend.

I trust in my memories and my experience and in time, all will be healed.

Whatever purpose you will hold in Heaven, I will become your compass should you find yourself lost.

CHAPTER THIRTY-TWO
Simone's Reality Check

It was going to be a beautiful Thursday. The sun hovered in a clear blue sky. It had only left the horizon and floated just above the roofline of Cologne. It was not yet mid-morning and the sun had not risen high enough for the car's sun visor to offer total relief.

The bright sun rays pounced upon the eyes of Madame Liz during the final part of her journey into the suburbs of Cologne. Her eyelids were half shut as she made her way through the narrow, pristine streets.

She wasn't far away from her destination. One more turn and the house she sought would soon be in her squinting sights.

Josef and the children heard the distinctive clatter of Liz's trailer in the driveway. With all the chiming and jingling, one could have easily been tricked into believing Santa was in town.

Nevertheless, Liz had a way of letting everyone know she was around. Those who knew her and her gifted talents recognized the unique sounds of her chimes, jingling and ringing. Madame Liz had a way about her that brought joy, smiles and sometimes, tears. The tears, however, often lifted the burden of sorrow and misery.

This was Madame Liz.

Josef followed in the footsteps of his excited children as they burst out the front door. The door swung open fast and wide.

"Gently," shouted Josef as he tried to stop the door from

coming off its hinges.

Madame Liz turned off her car ignition. She was barely allowed the time to stand up before the children jumped into her arms. The greetings were lovingly sincere and always concluded with some special treats.

This time, Liz's treats had been left to the last minute. The children would have to settle for some candies from Düsseldorf.

To children, sweets are treats. The wrappers were torn off and in they went: sticky hands and dirty mouths.

Josef shook his head to himself. You would have been forgiven for thinking that the children hadn't been fed in a week. Either way, the kids were preoccupied with the sweets, which gave Josef the opportunity to hug and greet his old friend.

"C'mon inside. We'll unpack later. You look like you could use a nice hot cup of tea," said Josef.

"I missed you all. It has been so busy for me," replied Madame Liz.

Liz looked around at her adopted family. She was only observing the living right now. The spiritual entities had to wait their turn.

Her eyes looked lovingly at each and every member of this household. If her eyes could speak, they would tell of the joy of finally returning to the house she called home. They would tell of the incredible friendship and companionship she missed so immensely on her sometimes long and lonely journeys.

"Cup of tea? Absolutely! Would love one."

~ * ~

On the other side of town, the two young Australian travellers were in the lobby of their hotel leaving the reception area.

Dressed in matching tracksuits and running shoes, they limbered up for their jog.

Being the fitness fanatics they were, it was time to get in a good old-fashioned cardio workout. And what better way than a nice long run through the city of Cologne.

The hotel car park was a good place to stretch out their tight muscles in the cold, but pleasant morning.

Johnny was bent over, stretching out the back of his legs. As he stretched further and further, he grunted at the release of muscle tension lingering in and around his lower back and upper legs.

Tony was twisting left and right, releasing and stretching out his waist and hip area. He waited until Johnny stood upright and indicated a possible direction with a flick of his head.

There weren't too many places in Cologne that you would be able to stand without seeing the hovering steeples of the cathedral. The hotel driveway was no exception.

Johnny looked up yonder and agreed to his friend's suggestion.

The church was a fine destination for a morning jog.

The angelic, subconscious messages that were constantly being fed to the boys' subliminal and deeply connected spiritual minds surely had something to do with this. After all, it was not by chance the boys chose Cologne to be their place of residence during the final days of their trip overseas.

There was no logical reason to all this, but there was certainly some spiritual significance. The Angels had planted a message within the boys' minds. The boys didn't know it, but there was a need for them to be in this town. Cologne was very important to those in the kingdom of light, as was its gothic cathedral.

The boys limbered up a little more and got on their way. It was a good forty-five minutes to an hour before they reached their destination. The pace was moderate and the day was perfect for a run.

~ * ~

Madame Liz quietly observed the spiritual entities of Charlie and Mary as they shadowed over the physical bodies of Anita and Günter. As she observed them, she was well into her second cup of hot, black tea.

Josef was talking to his children and for the moment, Liz only needed to acknowledge the spiritual world.

As it had always been, the conversation between Charlie and Mary was muted, and Liz was purposely kept from hearing any spiritual discussion.

There was another presence in the room. A spiritual entity that Liz was only too familiar with: the deceased wife of Josef. The young and beautiful Simone was here today, but she had no interest in communicating with Liz or even through Liz with her family.

Instead, she was more intent on debating an issue with Charlie and Mary.

Madame Liz tried to listen in, but all she could do was observe the gestures and the body language. The discussion appeared to be argumentative on Simone's side and consultative on Mary and Charlie's.

"You cannot do it to them," stated Simone.

Simone was confronting and in some ways pleading with the other two entities. Her pleas were directed more to Mary than Charlie. Simone felt a little more comfortable with Mary. It might have been a woman to woman or a mother to mother thing.

And Mary, like her mother Pam, had inherited some very strong consultative tendencies. She was a natural counsellor employing diplomacy, active listening and empathy. Charlie also carried some of these skills; however, they were much more prevalent in Mary. This trait had carried on through the family line from Pam to Mary and from Mary to her only son, Tony.

"They're only children," added Simone.

Mary had to draw upon her many years' experience as a spiritual entity. It takes some longer than others, but Simone needed to understand that the grander plan is always eventually revealed and it usually (but not always) leads to a greater good.

"Heaven has foreseen this and for whatever reason, your children are to be a part of it."

"What? And put my family, put my children at risk!" questioned Simone.

"We don't know that. Heaven can foresee future events. But even to Heaven, the outcome is not always fully predictable and things don't always go to plan."

"And how is that supposed to make me feel more comfortable?" asked Simone. Her voice was still filled with anxiety. "Any way you look at it, you are placing my children in danger."

"I'm just trying to point out that steps have been taken. The children will not be alone. I, for one, will not leave them behind," said Mary.

"I'm here 'till the end too," added Charlie.

Simone turned her back on Charlie and Mary. Mary gently walked up and placed her hand on Simone's shoulder.

Her tone was soft and supportive. "I know they are your children. I am not their mother, but your kids are as dear to me as my own are. I have watched over them from birth, and I will continue to do so until Heaven has other plans for me."

It was a conversation made more meaningful because it took place between two mothers.

Simone, still faced with her back to Mary, raised her hand and affectionately rubbed Mary's hand on her shoulder. It was a gesture of warmth and understanding.

If she was given the choice, Simone would place her children in Mary's care in an instant. Mary possessed a loving and watchful eye as dedicated as any mother.

Simone did not mean for her words to come across as they had and Mary certainly understood the anxiety behind Simone's voice.

Mary stepped back a little, allowing Simone to turn around and face her and Charlie again.

"If it makes you feel any better," said Mary to Simone, "I truly understand what you are feeling. Trust me!" Mary added, "There's a bit of what you say that crosses my mind constantly. All I can say is preventative measures have been put in place."

With a dash of curiosity in her voice, Simone had to ask. "What do you mean?"

"Then please permit us to put this another way." Mary was now talking on behalf of her and her spiritual husband.

Mary lowered her head and looked at the ground. She hesitated a little and during that time Charlie approached her and put his arm around her in a comforting way.

Just for the moment, Mary did not want to look at Simone.

"When your children are in the thick of it all," Mary stopped for the briefest of moments,

"When Heaven's intention is underway and whatever part Anita and Günter and even Josef may have to play in it all. Well. It will be what it will be." She then looked up and made some soft eye contact with Simone.

"But in the physical world they will not stand alone." Mary then changed her posture completely.

She was now standing tall and upright, solid and strong like a colonel about to give his troops the ultimate command.

Deep inside, she held onto her concerns, but outwardly, she refused to show them.

"My son will be there, too."

CHAPTER THIRTY-THREE
Sebastian's Church

Sebastian's transition to earthly life had been, to say the least, uncomfortable. However, this transition was made a little easier thanks to the dedicated work of the many earthly souls that unknowingly became helpers of Hell.

This help started when Sebastian first arrived on Earth, living a lonely existence in the deep green foliage of Munich's English Gardens.

It extended to a taxi ride to the airport where everyone from the taxi driver to airport staff and air hostesses were there to assist—all without disclosing the true identity of this devilish soldier or his intent to undertake hellish activities on Earth.

And Sebastian himself proved even the best of plans don't go as expected.

His anger suddenly erupting at the cost of an airplane explosion which no earth bound soul or hellish helper survived. The only survivor was Sebastian and, to the disgust of all existence in Heaven, his terrible time on Earth continued.

It didn't stop there! This cathedral was now his realm and it was scary to think how far Lucifer's reach on Earth had extended.

A handful of regular church goers were even there to protect Sebastian while he made preparations in the last place you would expect to find a devilish soldier.

A Gothic cathedral was the ideal hiding place. A landmark

dedicated to the holy life was housing the one creature that should never have been allowed near it, let alone, in it.

Yet here he was, a wolf in sheep's clothing, a demon dressed as a servant of the faith. In the last few days, those who had sought the services of the priest —now a demon —were intercepted by churchgoers who had only one thing in mind: to keep the identity of this dark-spirited creature hidden from the rest of the world.

"He needs his rest as he desperately wants to be in good form for this coming Sunday," they would say.

"His throat has had an incredible infection. He has not been well this past week. You must respect this and leave him be. It is his wish."

The message would cleverly distract any church regular from making contact with a priest whose soul had long since left the shell of his body.

That shell now housed a demon who had very different plans. Plans that would come to life very, very soon.

They had to.

He could see that his flesh was beginning to necrose.

This shell of a body would only be good for a little while longer.

CHAPTER THIRTY-FOUR
Spiritual Intent

Josef recognized the look.

It was all too familiar to him. It was the look that said Madame Liz was now more interested in spiritual things.

And usually, if other physical entities were in the room, like he and the children, then something was about to be said that involved everyone in the immediate area.

Josef had learned a lot about the spiritual world and the way it strangely operated. He was a believer in its workings in spite of its sometimes mystical ways.

He had seen and experienced too much not to believe. Josef and the children stayed nearby and let Liz be.

Her second cup of tea had cooled.

For a little while, Josef stood there, not knowing what to do with the portion left in the cup. "Do I wash the cup? Do I reheat the tea or should I make her another fresh cup?" he asked himself.

Josef was a little nervous as he awaited his message from the other side. Some of the messages Josef had received over the years had left him a little worried.

Nervousness quickly turned into fidgeting.

He composed himself, sat down quietly and raised his finger to his lips to bid his children to be silent.

The children were behaving well. They looked up at their father and respectfully ignored the gesture. It was a message that didn't need to be conveyed in the first place.

Anyway, the children were happy enjoying the final tastes of their sweets and treats.

This spiritual routine was something the family had come to know well. They were happy to quietly and patiently sit and go along with the spiritual ride.

Volume and sound returned to Liz's ears. She could hear the spiritual world again, but clearly, the intimate discussion between the three ghostly entities was over.

Charlie and Mary stood there all quiet like, shadowing the two young children as they always did. The spiritual couple distanced themselves from any other direct communication with Liz.

"Nothing new here!" Liz thought to herself.

Simone, on the other hand, was experiencing some sort of internal dilemma.

She stood only a few meters away from Madame Liz. Her body was at a right angle to Liz. Simone would have to turn her head to intentionally look Liz's way, otherwise she could simply look straight ahead if she wanted, to avoid direct eye contact with the medium.

Liz knew better than to insist or to interfere with spiritual intention.

Whatever Simone was doing and however she was doing it, it all held a purpose.

As strange as it appeared to Liz, Simone repeated her patterns of movements. She stood at a right angle to Liz, turned her head and looked in her direction. She would contemplate and then turn her head back so she was facing straight ahead out of direct eye contact with Liz.

It was like Simone couldn't choose between coming forth or running away.

This happened again and again and again. Something was worrying Simone, that much was clear.

Madame Liz's spiritual intuition was extremely well refined. She sensed Simone's concern but she once again did not want to demand anything of her until Simone was ready to do whatever she had to do.

Liz was interrupted and for a brief time concentrated on Anita and Günter and their fight to get to the bathroom to wash off the evidence of left over chocolate and candy.

As they left the room, so did Charlie and Mary. They were doing what they had always done: keeping a close watch over the two youngsters.

Madame Liz quickly re-engaged herself with the spiritual activity around her.

As she did, Simone stared her right in the face. Liz, startled by the full look, jolted her head back slightly. All that Liz could see now was the spiritual face before her as if someone had outlined and sketched a drawing of a face and placed it so as to dominate one's peripheral and frontal vision.

She wasn't frightened by the sight, but all the same, she had been caught by surprise.

Simone cupped her ghost-like hands around Liz's face. Liz did not see the hands, but could feel the tingling of her gentle touch. The sensation transitioned over to the physical world with a beauty that Madame Liz seldom experienced.

It left her all warm and fuzzy inside.

"Tell him that all will be okay," said Simone to Madame Liz.

"He must maintain his faith. Trust in the higher purpose." As Simone spoke these words, Madame Liz repeated them. At this point, Josef stopped.

Attentive and alert, he listened to each word that came out of Liz's mesmerized mouth.

"There will be many by his side in his moment of truth," Simone continued.

"The children will be looked after," Simone then paused, allowing Liz to catch up with the message.

This was all taking its toll on Simone's energy reserves. Liz was in control. She knew exactly what she was doing and what she was being used for.

After all, this was her gift. But Liz could also feel her connection with Simone start to weaken.

For Simone, communicating with the living had its downside and Simone realized she would have to spend a long time resting and regaining her spiritual strength. As far as Simone was concerned, it was all worth the effort.

"Tell him how proud I am of him. How he so wonderfully dedicates himself to the upbringing of our children." With that, Simone disappeared out of view.

Madame Liz conveyed this message to Josef, who was trying to comprehend how he should best interpret it all.

Confused, Josef turned to Liz. Before he could speak, Liz put up her hand to gesture him to silence. Her hand was open and her palm was held outwardly to Josef: she needed to be acknowledged. "She is no longer here, Josef. I am no longer in connection with the spiritual world," said Liz.

"I have no idea what to think, Liz," said Josef. "I tell you, these messages can be quite confusing at times," he continued.

"My dear friend," replied Liz. "You know better than that."

Josef looked a little frustrated. A hint of embarrassment had also been dropped in to lighten up the mood.

"Yes. I know," said Josef. Sarcasm had suddenly been added to the mix.

In unison, Madame Liz and Josef spoke. It was timed to perfection.

"I will relay the message as I get it. Some of it may make perfect sense, some of it, you may come to recognize the importance at a later time."

Josef had learned the gifted medium's lesson only too well.

CHAPTER THIRTY-FIVE
Two Boys on the Run

The boys jogged with the grace of galloping gazelle s. Their pace was smooth and they moved in a synchronous rhythm. The journey had been lengthy, but well within the capabilities of these two young athletes.

They were near the cathedral. This area, like the immediate surrounds, was all too familiar to the young trav ellers by now. After all, they had spent plenty of time near this holy land mark.

A turn here and a turn there and they were soon jogging past the massive quadrangle that led up the front doors of the cathedral. The quadrangle was full of street shows being watched by a good mix of people.

Despite the foot traffic, Johnny and Tony were able to maintain their pace and work their way through the crowds and sideshows.

Tony gave a nod which Johnny understood perfectly. A park bench off to the back of the church looked like the ideal place to rest. It was unoccupied and still several meters away.

The endpoint was chosen without a single word being uttered by either of the two young gentlemen. The steady race now became a battle between the friends.

Each now to their own, they increased the pace, gradually working themselves up to a full sprint. Fifty. Forty meters and now it was on for the ultimate prize. Twenty, ten and it was Tony who reached out for the bench chair to secure his win.

Both boys walked around holding their sides. The finale had taken more of their energy than the whole run before it.

Tony waited to catch his breath and when he looked up to see Johnny looking back, he saw him give a little chuckle and winked his eye.

"Don't get too cocky," laughed Johnny. "One win out of how many?"

"Now who's being the cocky one?" Tony shot back.

With every second that passed, the boys breathed a little easier. Neither of them wanted to sit on the park bench, but it helped them to stretch out some achy leg muscles.

Tony and Johnny stood at right angles to each another. Tony faced away from the church and looked up to the large quadrangle. He put his foot on top of the park bench and stretched.

Johnny stretched out to the back of the bench, looking in the direction of the church. He did not quite have its full side in his peripheral vision. Johnny used the backrest of the park bench to get a greater and higher stretch.

No sooner had Johnny positioned himself and his foot, the side door of the church opened. It was on the edge of his direct vision and he did not notice what happened next.

Suddenly a face appeared. That of a devilish beast in priest's clothing.

The boys continued their stretches with minimal talk.

Sebastian walked out of the church. He was not enjoying the numerous tourists and visitors inside. He had done well in avoiding interactions with anyone, but now he needed a break.

He walked out of the side entrance to escape the crowds. He had no idea how much longer this would last or how much longer he would have to play the part of a God-fearing priest.

The thought sickened him to his devilish stomach.

He did a quick scan of the grounds to see how many people were out and about. There was no danger, just frustration.

Other than that, all appeared as normal as normal could be to Sebastian.

He noticed two young males near a park bench and went to scan the grounds ahead. Sebastian did not take the time to truly closely observe the young men.

The boys, busy with their stretches, did not even notice the priest walk out of a side entrance, hover around and walk back into the church.

The boys had finished their warm downs and walked around to the main entrance at the front of the church.

It was here that the large, wooden, highly decorative front doors faced the quadrangle. The boys positioned themselves with their backs to the large wooden church doors and gazed out at the many activities underway in the quadrangle.

Johnny turned to look at Tony. "What do we do now?" he asked.

Tony ignored what was in front of him and turned to face the massive doors of the cathedral. "I really want to see the inside this church again. It's just so appealing to me."

"A little respect," protested Johnny. "I know this church welcomes all sorts. They go in dressed in all sorts of ways, but still they look presentable."

Johnny then looked down upon his track clothes. Sweat marks were forming a "V" around his neck. Drips were running off his wet brow and hairline.

"You just don't walk into a cathedral looking like this."

"I guess you're right," replied Tony.

"Tell you what. We'll come here before we hit the town on Saturday night," stated Johnny. "A sort of farewell to the town and this church before we go back home."

Tony continued to stare at the church doors as Johnny walked away. It wasn't until Johnny got several meters into the middle of the quadrangle that he realized his friend was still at the foot of the stairs leading to the church doorway.

"Hey, sleepy head!" Johnny yelled. "Saturday night!"

CHAPTER THIRTY-SIX
Where the People Gather

The children rose at the crack of dawn. It was early morning and Anita and Günter eagerly tuned into the Saturday morning cartoons on television.

Soon after, their father stumbled out of his bedroom, stretching his arms as he wandered into the kitchen wearing his loosely fitted pajamas.

"Up with the birds?" he asked.

Madame Liz looked up from her book. She had settled into the kitchen about an hour earlier and was quite content reading in the peace and quiet.

"Cup of coffee?" Josef asked.

She nodded eagerly. "Did you sleep well, Josef?"

"Wonderful; thanks, Liz. And you?"

"So so. It's the habits of living on the road, I'm afraid. I can never get into a normal routine. That caravan bed is a bit average, if you know what I mean, but lying in a proper bed once in a while is a welcome relief."

Josef blurted his next words out. It had been a while since he had done this and he could no longer contain his excitement, which was now bubbling at the surface waiting to escape.

"Well, I tell you what," stated Josef, "I am going to break a routine right here, right now. I'm treating you and the children to a dinner and a night on the town."

"You needn't do that," replied Liz. She was a little shocked by Josef's generosity. It was more than enough that she had a house and proper bed to lie in once in a while. She was taken aback by a generosity few extend to their fellow human beings. And now this—a dinner! Liz felt like she had imposed enough.

Josef could see the modesty in her face.

"I will hear no more of this," Josef said. "I have made the reservations already. Be ready at six. I know we will," he continued with a cheeky little snort of a giggle.

Liz knew there was nothing more to be said. She didn't need the assistance of any spiritual guide to figure this one out. All she needed for now was to wait for that morning cup of coffee.

~ * ~

Six o'clock had come and gone. Josef, Liz and the children had finished a lovely meal and were headed out into the nearby quadrangle of the gothic church.

Street acts and festivities made the evening into something special.

It wasn't usual for Josef to go out at night, but he wanted to treat a special friend and his two very special children to something more than a home-cooked meal.

The group wandered around the street acts, stopping to take in the occasional musician, juggler or magician. There was plenty to see and do and Liz enjoyed the busyness.

Her distraction by the entertainment meant she could take her mind off the afterlife. Everyone needs to let go once in a while.

While Josef and the kids marveled at the magician before them, Liz looked up to admire the large open doors of the cathedral. People were still moving in and out, although at this time of the evening more were walking out of the church than in.

Then she saw them, the two faces that had been a mystery since her meeting with the Virgin Mary and Archangel Michael at the Evangelische Kirche Werden.

Those two young faces had appeared before her spiritual eyes in a vision in a little church. She didn't recognize them, she didn't know them, but there was no mistaking the faces from her vision.

The faces belonged to Tony and Johnny.

Two well-dressed young men walked into the church to have one final look at a monument that had kept their interest throughout their trip.

Once again, Madame Liz looked at the doors. More and more people were leaving the church, and none had entered since the boys had entered.

It was a bit unusual, but Liz was more infatuated with the mystery of the boys at this stage.

Even she was unaware of the subliminal messages Sebastian was sending to everyone except the two young men that he was so keen to meet.

There was nothing obviously sinister in Sebastian's message. It went something like, "You have overstayed your welcome, leave as soon as possible."

This subconscious, demonic suggestion would see the church vacated shortly.

Even the many people who were waiting outside found themselves choosing to come back at a later time. The crowds simply turned away from the church door and headed off to do something else.

It all looked (sort of) perfectly normal.

It was only then that Madame Liz saw what interested her the most. She was totally unaffected by these subconscious demonic suggestions. Liz had to know more.

She broke off from Josef and the children who were being entertained by a very talented magician.

"Don't leave now, Ma'am," said the magician. "My grand finale is about to come."

Madame Liz kept on walking. She ignored the magician's request, although others watching found his joking at Liz's expense mildly amusing.

Madame Liz drew closer to the church and as she did, more and more people left and still, no one else had entered.

This, however, was far from her thoughts. She had to find the two young men and work out why their faces had appeared in her spiritual vision.

Anita and Gunter turned to see their adopted aunt climb the few stairs that led to the church doorway. They had grown tired of the magician and went to follow Liz.

Josef signaled to his children to let them know he would follow shortly. He wanted to see the magician's grand finale.

The children caught up with Liz and grabbed her hand as she walked through the massive doors. Liz held their hands firmly, but not too tight.

She did not look down to acknowledge the children, but remained focused on locating these two boys.

As she walked in, the last members of the public had left the church walls. The church was eerily quiet and empty, except for the two boys, whom she could not find.

She knew they were still about. But where?

Liz and the children went a little further into the church, and then Liz caught sight of them. In the near distance, they were admiring some of the statues that depicted Christian saints.

As Liz approached the boys, the doors of the church quietly shut.

Outside, Josef grew concerned because he could not follow his children into the church. A commotion developed outside. The few left inside the church were unaware of the fuss.

Josef knew that the church rarely shut its doors until late evening, particularly on Saturdays. Josef and many immediately around him pushed frantically on the doors. And when they couldn't open them, they yelled to those inside.

The public assumed that someone could hear them, but no-one was on the other side of the doors.

The doors had been shut with a demonic force and the church was insulated from the sounds outside.

There were to be no interruptions.

Madame Liz, the children and the two boys remained unaware of the strange circumstances.

Even the spiritual entities of Mary and Charlie didn't pick up on the wrongdoings.

Everything appeared normal.

For now.

CHAPTER THIRTY-SEVEN
Sebastian's Sermon

This section of the church was below one of its massive steeples, in one of its corners.

A narrow stairway nearby curled all the way up for those ready to endure the long walk. And for those who did tackle the climb, the view above and across the skyline of Cologne was spectacular.

The boys had taken the stairs on a previous visit. For now, they were more interested in the statues and relics around the stairway on the ground floor.

The history of this part of the church was extraordinary. This room was filled with crucifixes made from human remains.

Not just one, but many different configurations of bone and wood came together. Where these artefacts came from and when was the mystery. There were crucifixes made from human rib bones and another formed from the bones of the spine and neck.

Another, and by far the most controversial and the most treasured was built on a wooden base forming a large cross that stood about five feet long and three feet wide with sharpened, pointed ends all bound in the middle with some heavy twine. At each corner hung a skull which had been pierced by the thick wooden stake and left to hang just below the sharp edge. Four corners of the cross, four human skulls, looking right back at you. This crucifix had come to be known as the "Four Children of

Christ" and was the only artefact in the church that was accurately traced back to the inception of Christianity itself.

How it came to be there still remained a mystery.

This section of the church carried the necessary warnings in many languages that the artefacts may offend and repulse some. However, they were part of the church's history.

Tony and Johnny looked upon all the human crucifixes with wonder. It was amazing to see the endless configurations creatively conjured out of human bone, and occasionally wood, to make a crucifix.

Her watch had just ticked past eight o'clock. Liz made her way towards the boys. She, like the other humans in the church, was unaware of the presence of the lurking demon, Sebastian.

The boys were pre-occupied with the art when Johnny felt a tap on his shoulder. Turning around, he saw Liz in her bright gypsy attire flanked by the two children.

"Excuse me for the interruption, but I seek an introduction with you both," Liz requested in formal German.

Tony and Johnny looked at each other. Johnny politely dismissed the request. "I'm sorry, we don't speak German." He thought this lady might be asking for directions.

Liz immediately understood, repeating her request in English, slightly accented with the sharpness of her native tongue.

Her request was understood this time around, but the boys were a little puzzled by this complete stranger.

The silence needed to be broken. "Please, let me explain," she continued. "I am well known in these parts. I possess a talent that not many have. I see things."

Johnny grew impatient. "We all see things, lady. I am not sure who you are after, but it's not us. You have us mixed up with someone else."

"On the contrary," replied Liz. "I am certain about you two."

As Liz tried to communicate with the two young men, the

children wandered off to look at the artefacts. They knew the church intimately. Their choir days had seen them spend copious time here, but not a lot of time was spent in this "human remains" section. Their father wouldn't allow it.

Anita and Günter took the opportunity to re-acquaint themselves with this part of the church.

As they did so, Liz momentarily focused on the spiritual side. The spirits of Charlie and Mary were unusually attentive to the physical world.

Mary, although she usually displayed no physical signs of breathing, was gasping. Both her hands were cupped around her mouth as if she had been given the surprise of her life, or rather, the surprise of her afterlife. Charlie stood by her spiritual side looking completely astonished.

This was a new experience for Liz and it deepened her curiosity about these two young men and their association with the spiritual entities.

Liz needed to confirm her observations, to confirm her assumptions. "Please be patient with me. I need to explain something to you both. Please wait here. Just a minute, please," Liz begged the boys to stay put.

"Okay," replied the boys.

This was when Liz heard her first words from the silent spiritual entities who accompanied Anita and Günter. Mary kept repeating the name of her son. Over and over again Liz heard the name "Tony!" It was repeated over and over again, "Tony!" She heard it so many times she blurted it out herself: "Tony!"

That caught the attention of the youngsters. The boys looked at each other and Tony asked, "How do you know my name?"

"As I was saying, I see things. The supernatural and the spiritual." Liz was all too familiar with how her unusual gift might sit with some, but Tony and Johnny appeared to take the strange developments with a hint of curiosity.

Liz was startled by the voices of the spiritual guides. They were now speaking continuously and lots of information was forthcoming.

Hearing their names and their intent, she turned to the boys and said, "Your parents, Tony, they are with me at the moment."

"That's a bad joke, lady," replied Johnny.

"I see a car crash, a terrible accident. Your mother and father were in an accident, a fatal accident. It happened long ago. You were only young, very young, but old enough to remember. Your mother's name. She shares it with our blessed Virgin. Mary, yes, Mary. Your father is also here and by her side." Liz then paused as she looked directly into Tony's eyes.

"Please! I have a need to speak with you both." Liz quickly told her story. She intended to capture the attention of the two young travelers and that she did.

Tony was taken back; Johnny was equally impressed. "I don't know why you know so much about my family history, but..." Tony was still recovering from what he had heard. It shook him to his core and he couldn't help but notice that Madame Liz appeared genuine and concerned. There was only one thing to say:

"Please. Continue."

"I have lived my life as a spiritual guide. I see and communicate with Angels and spirits and with those who have passed. Nothing much has amazed me in my life until I met these two children."

Anita and Günter were still intrigued by the artefacts. They were not aware they were being talked about and were certainly oblivious to the fact that Johnny, Tony and Liz were all looking at them.

Liz continued, "Spirits have come to me in all shapes and forms, but none like your parents. They seem to stick out of the children. Wherever the children go, they go too. They are always with the children, never leaving their side for a minute. Up until now, I had never heard your mother speak. All I ever got was acknowledgements. Smiles, waves but not a single word. This is unusual for me. Until I met your parents, spirits would always want to communicate to me, to communicate through me."

Liz focused her attention on Tony. "I can hear them now. It's like someone turned up the volume. I don't know why, but I feel there is something important to be said or something important that I need to communicate to you."

This was not an everyday conversation. Tony looked away and as he did, he raised his open hand to his forehead. He rubbed his forehead and stroked back his hair a couple of times.

All along, he was very meticulous about his strokes. It was his way of dealing with it all and in a way, it helped cover up his nervousness. Tony finished with a final brush, and as his hand came to rest at the base of the back of his head, he turned to face Madame Liz.

The boys had taken a few moments to process this unusual conversation. "That's one hell of an introduction," remarked Johnny.

Tony quickly cut into the conversation. "That's fine. What can I say? Your information is accurate, but why are you telling me this? Why here and now?" asked Tony.

"It was only recently, very recently that I saw a vision. It was in a church not all that far from here. In Düsseldorf."

"Yes, we know the town," said Johnny.

"I saw a vision of some faces. Some familiar faces and some not so familiar. The visions were as clear as day for me. And in amongst it all, were the faces of two strangers. Two young men." Liz then looked at the boys. It was clear who she was referring to by now.

"But I still don't understand," replied Johnny. "What's this got to do with us?"

Just then, a steady, continuous, evenly paced clap was heard from midway up the church. Sebastian, still in the form of a priest, approached with one of his helpers by his side. The helper was a mature lady of miniature stature who has unaware that she was playing the part of a servant to Hell.

The devilish aid continued to clap with every second step that she and her evil master took. Sebastian steadily walked towards the boys.

"Children!" called Liz in a firm tone. The children were quick to return to their aunt's side.

"It is pleasing to hear the introductions are over," said the assistant. Sebastian turned to her and quietly clattered, squeaked and growled. This dialect made sense to the assistant and she snickered away for all to see.

The sinister giggle had Liz concerned. She moved the children behind her. There was something not right about the priest and his lady assistant.

For the first time ever, Liz witnessed the separation of the children and their guardian spirits. Mary and Charlie were now standing in front of Liz.

They stood tall and proud in a protective fashion. This only made Liz more concerned.

Liz felt those familiar uneasy sensations, a spiritual shaking of the worrying kind. She felt trembling spiritual touches along the length of her entire spine and the vibrations gradually grew with intensity.

Simultaneously, the boys both raised their clenched hands to their mouths, blowing some warmth into their cupped hands. The air that left their mouths was misty, as were the breaths of Liz and the children.

"Did it just get cold in here or what?" Johnny asked.

The message being sent to Liz was very clear.

"RUN!" screamed Liz. "There is pure evil before us. Run for your lives." Liz took the children and ran towards the center of the church looking for pillars, confessional booths and anything big enough to hide her and the children.

Johnny and Tony stood firm. The priest continued his

approach while the mature female assistant headed off in search of Liz and the children.

Liz and the children ran fiercely. Hiding, stopping, running until Liz was certain that she had deceived the assistant. The safety of the little children was her prime concern.

The assistant walked with a steady pace. She knew there was no escape, that they were all confined within the walls of the massive church. Still, there were certainly enough obstacles in the church for them to play a good game of hide and seek.

The priest and the boys stayed in the same little section of the church in an uncomfortable face off.

"What's going on here?" demanded Johnny of the priest. The priest snarled back and as he did, a misty plume formed in front of his evil face, hovering there for a moment before disappearing out of sight, vanishing instantly. The evil reply was both visible and audible.

It was simply frightening.

Johnny looked at Tony. Tony shrugged his shoulders in concern. He had no advice for his friend. Johnny then did what he had been trained to do.

Putting up his fists, he went into guard mode. "Back off!" he yelled.

Tony stood by his side. He left his guard down, but positioned his front foot in a manner that had him ready to launch into fight.

With knees slightly bent, Tony waited for the next move.

The priest snarled again. Sebastian showed his human teeth as he growled with sinister intent. This was not natural.

All of a sudden, Sebastian burst out of his human host, abandoning the body of the priest like a piece of disposable rubbish.

The priest's body lay on the floor, motionless and lifeless.

The boys saw it, Liz saw it —but the young children did not. Liz was taken back immediately to her vision. Of all the faces she visualized that day, one had still remained a mystery for her: that of a devilish beast.

His enlarged eyes, leathery skin and demonic wings were a dead giveaway.

In his dark and natural form, there was no mistaking this beast from Hell. Her vision had now become a reality.

"RUN, boys, RUN!" yelled Liz, giving away her position.

Tony was at the ready and turned to climb the church stairwell. His friend followed, but didn't even have the chance to react before Sebastian pounced, sadistically demanding Johnny's soul vacate the shell of his body.

There were no games this time. Unlike back at the Karate competition in Germany where Sebastian was having a bit of innocent fun. That demonic "soul tease" resulted in Johnny becoming feverish in the most hellish of fashions. Back then, Sebastian had only wanted to play games with Johnny's soul.

They were now down to some serious hellish business.

Sebastian shook his head violently, communicating directly with the soul of a young Johnny. Tony continued to run up the stairs until he turned and saw no trace of his friend.

Instantly, Tony made his way back down the narrow stairwell.

As hard as Sebastian tried, he could not penetrate the soul of this young man.

Mary and Charlie would not allow it. They were at his spiritual side, keeping guard. On a spiritual plane, they were at a faceoff: two holy spirits against a servant of Hell.

Mary would sacrifice herself spiritually, as would Charlie, before they let Sebastian take over anything as sacred as the soul of this young man. Especially Johnny, who had unknowingly accomplished so much for the angelic cause.

Tony came down the stairs to see his friend in a deep trance, face to face with the demon. If Sebastian could not have the spiritual form, then he would attack the physical form.

As Sebastian drew back his lips, revealing his sharp teeth, Tony ran in and tackled his friend to save him from the oncoming onslaught. He wrestled Johnny to the ground and Johnny immediately snapped out of his trance.

With no time to spare, Tony and Johnny got back on their feet and ran. They staggered initially until they both regained balance and momentum. Splitting directions, Tony ran the length of the church, Johnny ran its width. Sebastian stood firm. This gave the young men the time to run to shelter from the direct vision of the beast.

Meanwhile, Liz and the children had moved through the center of the church, working their way in and around the pews.

Liz signaled them to be silent.

The children kept close to their aunt at all times, following and crawling, one after the other, like the carriages of a train. The assistant had lost sight of them. She was in their general vicinity but had no idea of their exact location.

Crawling on the ground, Liz had low level vision of what was going on. She would occasionally catch a glimpse of the assistant's legs and adjust her position if appropriate. Madame Liz continued to play this game of cat and mouse—only in this case, the mouse knew more than the cat did.

Running the width of the church, Johnny reached the base of the opposite steeple. Another stairwell curled its way up high. This section of the church was a bit different. Unlike the controversial corner opposite, this part of the church was filled with tastefully painted pictures and sculptures of symbolic Christian moments, angels and saints of all shapes and sizes.

But this was not a time to enjoy the displays of the church.

Johnny ran up the narrow stairwell and Sebastian followed. Steadily and methodically, Sebastian took one casual step at a time. Johnny, on the other hand, ran like the wind, sometimes taking two or three steps in a single leap.

But there was no escaping. The beast had come to know the

church and knew he would soon have his victim cornered.

Tony sat silently behind one of the church's center pillars. His heart was pounding with adrenalin.

He had seen Johnny dash up the stairwell with Sebastian following.

Tony centered himself. He looked straight at the outer wall of the church. *Think, Tony. Think,* he said to himself. He cautiously looked to the right of the pillar where he could see the assistant taunting her victims with a steady clap.

There was no sign of Liz or the children. He kept his eyes on the assistant for a little while longer, watching her walk the lengths of each church pew, steadily clapping as she methodically weaved in and out of each row. She was playing with her victims.

Tony looked the other way to realize Sebastian had disappeared up the narrow stairwell.

Enough was enough.

Tony stood up and rushed at the assistant.

The small lady did not stand a chance. Running to her with his arm extended, Tony used his forearm to strike the lady down. She may have been possessed, but she was still only a little middle aged lady. She went down hard and her skull cracked on the tiled floor. A small pool of blood formed.

The assistant lay with her eyes open, but she was knocked out. Her gaze was an unconscious stare. Her mind did not register any detail as she looked along the length of the floor straight into Liz's eyes.

Liz carefully raised her head, beyond one of the church pews.

Tony stood over his fallen victim and looked up. "Are you okay?" he asked. Liz nodded and helped the children up from the ground.

"What in God's name is that?" Tony asked.

"Not God but the other side," Liz replied.

"Excuse me?" Tony was confused.

"A demon. A servant to the Satanic Beast. This was my vision. Everything I have seen has all come together. Right here, right now." Liz looked around. There was no sign of Sebastian nor Johnny.

"Your friend is in grave danger." Liz looked at the children. "Find a place to hide. Do not come out until I say it is safe to do so." Liz was very direct with her instructions.

Anita was in tears. Reality had set in and it had all finally became too much. Günter was supporting his sister, but Anita held onto her aunt, not wanting to leave her side. "It will be okay. Go with your brother," Liz said in a more sympathetic tone of voice.

As they ran off, Liz reinforced her message. "Hide, children. Don't come out! No matter what!" She watched as the children ran, and for a moment she forgot her fears. She couldn't be prouder. Günter was being such a brave little man helping his teary sister out of harm's way.

The children stopped to look back at Liz and Tony. Liz had one final message for the young ones. "Take care of each other," she said. "Now HIDE!" she yelled.

Liz then held out her hand in a signal to stop.

She needed to check the spiritual plane and find a sign of Charlie and Mary. She could not see them. She looked towards the children as they ran off, but the spiritual guides were not with them.

Suddenly, Archangel Michael appeared before the medium. He repeated his important message. His delivery was quick and to the point.

"Have the courage to stand up and refuse to be intimidated. Fight back to protect the innocent in a way that only you know how. Protect the innocent from further death and destruction to say that THIS WILL NOT STAND! Beware! Be Warned! Protect!"

Liz had heard this once before in the church in Düsseldorf, the Evangelische Kirche Werden.

As Liz tried to understand the angelic message before her, she looked at the Archangel, who disappeared from spiritual view as quickly as he had appeared.

Tony could wait no longer. The young man was certain the assistant would not be waking any time soon.

He grew impatient with Liz's focus on the spiritual side of things, so he ran off towards the steeple stairwell.

And then it hit Liz like a smack in the face.

Her reason for being here was now angelically clear.

CHAPTER THIRTY-EIGHT
The Final Prayer

Sebastian had passed the half-way point. The massive spiral climb to the top of the gothic church steeple was exhausting, even for the beast.

Johnny was already at the top. His heart was thumping heavily. The pounding within his chest cavity was a combination of the big climb and anxiety about the impending danger.

Johnny looked out of the steeple top. As high up as he was, Johnny quickly came to the conclusion that the only way for him to escape was to go outside. He knew what approached from below.

The steeple's viewing platform was circular and gave a three hundred and sixty degree panoramic view of the city. As for size, well, if you could transform the circular open viewing ground into a square then this area was about the size of three standard boxing rings clumped together.

The view was spectacular from up here, but Johnny had no time to admire it. Rather, he was looking for a means of escape. He would take the risk if he could, but it seemed impossible as the area was well secured. Johnny would have no choice but to face the demon.

He looked around for help. There were no obstacles to hide behind nor were there any objects which could be used as weapons. Just one big, open, empty viewing platform.

The young man had to resort to his own defenses.

In anxious preparation, he stood at the farthest point from the stairwell. He needed all the time and space he could get.

Down below, Anita and Günter were as safe as safe could be, hidden away in a little section of the cathedral. Tony had reached the base of the stairwell. He was determined his friend would not face the demon alone.

Liz watched as Tony disappeared up the stairwell. She then looked for the children. She couldn't see them, which was a good sign.

She then knelt in the pew facing the front of the cathedral looking up at a large statue of Christ on the cross, her eyes fixed on his eyes.

She prayed.

"Father, I ask you to bless my friends, relatives and those I care deeply for. Show them a new revelation of your love and power. Holy Spirit, I ask you to minister to their spirit at this very moment. Where there is pain, give them your peace and mercy. Where there is self-doubt, release a renewed confidence through your grace. Where there is need, I ask you to fulfil them. I ask for your divine protection in my time of times. Amen!"

Liz then got up, crossed herself and bowed to the holy statue in front of her. She then made her way to the controversial corner of the church.

The Angels were watching from their spiritual plane. By their angelic sides stood Mary and Charlie. They heard her plea for protection, but right now they could only offer their spiritual support and guidance.

Tony kept climbing the stairwell. It was so tight it was hard for him to go any faster. Up above on the viewing platform, Sebastian and Johnny were in a standoff.

Johnny took guard as Sebastian approached with clear intent to attack.

Johnny was backed into a tricky position. He dodged to the left but the beast slapped him back into the center of the platform.

Johnny boxed out, one, two, one, two, occasionally connecting with the head of the beast. The beast recovered quickly from the heavy punches.

Johnny went to dodge right, but the beast, once again, slapped him back into central position. Sebastian was determined to keep his young opponent in the one spot. Johnny was going nowhere and had to rely heavily on his defenses and less on his attacks.

Whatever he gave out, the beast gave back three times as much, slapping and scratching with its demonic paws. Johnny kept on boxing. At the very least he would keep the demon's teeth at bay by hitting out at his jaw line whenever the opportunity arose.

The payoff wasn't great. For every attack Johnny delivered, he received blow after demonic blow. The beast's hook slaps painfully shook his defenses—and occasionally his head.

Johnny's legs wobbled, a clear sign he was losing the upper hand. He knew he couldn't take too much more, but he was determined and wouldn't go down without a fight.

The demon swung hard and Johnny took a devastating blow milliseconds after he had delivered a powerful right cross to the jaw of the demon. The creature staggered back and Johnny stumbled to the ground. They both took a little time to recover from their respective blows and rose to resume the battle.

Johnny had half stood up when suddenly an old memory flashed before him.

It was a spiritual present from Charlie. This memory might do him some good.

He remembered an important qualifier competition in Australia. The fight he fought with a young, cocky Western Australian who did nothing exactly wrong, but who did exploit the rules of a fair competition. This opponent took an unorthodox defensive position in order to see out the time of a competition fight. Johnny retaliated back with a powerful kick to the young cocky fighter's jaw and got disqualified.

There was only one reason why the Western Australian fighter went down. He simply put up his defenses half-heartedly, not expecting Johnny to attack with such ferocity.

The thought of a strong defense gave the young fighter new hope. Johnny took a lesson from the cocky Western Australian; in particular, his unsportsmanlike defense. Johnny's energy levels were being depleted by the second so he quickly switched his fighting tactics, going on the defensive to get some much needed recovery time.

He lowered his body, crouched and put up his guard. Much like his Western Australian opponent, he covered himself to the best of his ability, making himself as small a target as possible, covering all vital points of attack.

Unlike his Western Australian opponent, Johnny made his defense tight and strong. Every ounce of strength went into holding the integrity of this tightly closed defense. He offered the attacking beast nothing more than he had to.

Charlie was frustrated. All he could do was watch from the spiritual plane, but he applauded the change in Johnny's fighting strategy. Charlie had achieved his objective of subconscious suggestion and was pleased with the result. He hoped it would buy Johnny some time.

The beast clawed away. He was ripping through Johnny's clothing, clawing away at his flesh, and blood appeared. As painful as it was, Johnny endured one demonic attack after another.

Tony got to the top of the stairwell and momentarily froze at the sight of the fight. He felt mixed emotions, but primarily he felt loyalty and love for his friend.

Down below, Liz was dislodging the "Four children of Christ" from its resting place. This was what she had to do. She carried the cross on her back as she began to climb the windy staircase.

Tony went on the attack. He took out the beast in the same way he had taken out the assistant. He ran towards the beast with forearm extended, ramming his head with a solid strike, causing his skull to snap back. This sent Sebastian staggering back in a haze.

Sebastian had not braced himself. The attack was entirely unexpected. The devilish soldier was stunned only for a moment. Tony's running momentum and strength had delivered a righteous strike.

As Sebastian struggled to regain his composure, so did Johnny.

Weakened and bleeding heavily from his right arm, Johnny stood up. He braced himself against the back wall of the tower. He was giddy and uncoordinated but becoming more aware of his surroundings by the second. Tony had bought him the recovery time he so desperately needed.

His left arm had been well protected, but his right was damaged and in need of medical attention. His legs had not been attacked, but they needed a bit more time to muster the strength to hold his body up. Slowly, he began to regain his composure, even though he still needed to steady himself.

The boys didn't know it, but the spirits of Mary and Charlie were by their side.

Should the spirits of the boys be freed, they would be given a first class ride to the safety and comfort of Heaven. Mary and Charlie could protect the boys from spiritual demonic influence, but they could offer little in the way of physical protection.

The demonic beast had tried his luck with a spiritual attack and had grown impatient. He gave up on the idea of destroying their souls and was now intent on doing only physical damage.

"I'm hurting," said Johnny as he tried to stand true and proud. All he could manage to do was stand without being supported, but he was hardly in a strong state.

Tony took a step in front of his friend. Johnny kept his position to the back of him, protecting his damaged limb. It was an effort to keep his boxing guard up, but that he did: left arm up and at the ready, right arm down, bloodied and bruised.

Tony put his guard up, too. He shared Johnny's attitude. If he was to be defeated, he would go down with a fight.

"I'll take him. You go," said Tony.

"What? And miss all the fun! Never!" Johnny made his feelings about this ridiculous request clear.

There was nothing more to be said. The boys stood at the ready. Sebastian made his way in to attack the already wounded Johnny. He would have to walk through Tony to do so, and Tony definitely had some thoughts on the matter. He jumped into action, intercepting the attack, stepping forward and kicking the beast.

Sebastian may have intended to finish off the wounded Johnny, but Tony would not allow it. Stepping forward, he delivered a crashing, front thrust kick to the beast's jaw.

Tony then delivered a flurry of kicks and punches. It was a serious counter attack.

Johnny maintained his stance behind Tony. His energy levels were recovering slowly. Tony had a little more luck with his techniques than Johnny did. More blows were finding their target, but the demonic beast was very resilient.

The beast staggered back only to recover quickly. Each blow Tony delivered made his demonic enemy stagger back just a little further —and it took just that little longer to recover.

Still, progress was slow.

The beast gave back as much as he took. Tony was now defending as much as he attacked. Tony's defense tactics stopped the beast from hitting with full force, but his opponent was strong. Tony deflected the attacks to the best of his abilities, parrying and dodging, but still, the demon's attacks were beginning to get the better of this young and competent martial artist.

Tony danced around the open area. He needed the time to recover and footwork was his only way of doing so. Quick on his feet, he dodged the oncoming attacks. The beast charged, recovered, repositioned and charged again as Tony danced around like Mohammed Ali at his finest.

Johnny moved along the edge of the open platform. He was trying to keep close to his friend. Despite his injuries, he was now alert and on the ready. He would jump in with every last bit of energy if he was needed.

Tony dodged and Johnny followed to the best of his ability, staying close behind his friend. Sebastian lunged and then there was a momentary lull.

The boys were at one end of the viewing platform and the beast at the other. The boys kept their composure, glaring angrily at the beast.

Sebastian snarled, allowing a misty bloom of demonic air to hover before it disappeared completely.

Sebastian had grown weary of Tony's footwork.

Outclassed, the demonic warrior looked for another tactic. He refocused on Johnny, knowing Johnny couldn't move as swiftly. The beast walked steadily towards the wounded fighter, anticipating Tony would be ready to jump in.

Instinctively, Tony and Johnny both waited and then when the distance was right, they both went on the attack. Johnny grabbed the beast in a headlock with his good arm, trying to wrestle him to the ground. Tony took on the beast at his midsection, helping wrestle down the body. Sebastian's great strength did not make this an easy task. Together, the boys struggled to ground the beast.

At this moment, Liz reached the top of the stairwell with the crucifix over her back and right shoulder. She hauled the cross over her shoulder in the same way Christ had hauled the cross up the hill to his crucifixion.

Madame Liz was furious with the beast when she saw the boys wrestling him down with difficulty. His singed, blackened, leathery wings were anything but appealing.

"Protect the innocent," she said to herself.

Very quickly, she mustered up her courage and screamed as she charged the beast. She still carried the cross on her back with the top stake protruding from above her right shoulder.

The screaming sound was enough to grab the attention of the boys. They let go of the beast and gave Liz room to do what she had to do.

Sebastian turned to face the oncoming onslaught of Liz as she ran at him. Her intent was to ram or indeed, to spear the beast.

Sebastian took the full brunt of the attack, rolling back as he was pierced by the wooden stake. The sharpness of the stake and the holiness of the relic combined to inflict the damage necessary to bring this beast to his end.

As Sebastian rolled backward, Liz tumbled forward. The upper end of the cross had lodged itself in the rib cage of the beast.

As he fell, the bottom of the cross rotated up like a fulcrum. And as the cross rotated, it flicked Liz up into a rolling tumble. She landed at the other end of the cross.

The beast was now pierced by the top of the cross and Liz's ribcage was pierced by its side arm.

Liz and Sebastian lay only the length of the cross apart.

Liz faced the beast, who had died instantly. She stared at his closed eyes and looked up to see Archangel Michael, who was standing in the spiritual plane before her. He had restrained the demonic soldier as a policeman would a common criminal.

The demonic beast was no match for the Archangel Michael. She smiled and the Archangel smiled back. A second later he was gone—and so was the evil spirit of Sebastian.

Left in the spiritual plane was Mary and Charlie. They half smiled at Liz. Their look said it all: they were waiting for her.

Tony ran over to Liz with Johnny not far behind. They didn't know what to do.

Suddenly and unexpectedly, the church doors opened below. Josef and the crowd rushed inside. The children saw their father and ran to the safety of his arms.

All those downstairs were oblivious to the goings on in the steeple tower.

Liz turned to the boys in her weakened state. "You must swear to me. Two things I ask of you."

"Anything," said Tony sympathetically.

"I do not want the children to see me like this."

"Of course," replied Tony.

"Secondly," Liz said as she gulped for another breath of air. She looked at Mary and Charlie, who nodded their heads in acknowledgement. She reached out for the hands of the two young men.

They were keen to offer her whatever comfort they possibly could.

"This is not to be discussed. You must never speak a word of this to anyone." Liz then paused as the pain from the stake suddenly became unbearable. After a small moment that seemed like an eternity for her, she turned back to the boys.

"Promise me," she kindly demanded.

"It will remain with us," replied Johnny. As he made this promise to Liz, the gypsy Madame shut her eyes forever.

At that moment, a misty cloud formation appeared before the boys. Tony's parents and Liz stood side by side in ghostly, but recognizable forms.

Charlie had his arm around Mary as he stood by her side. Mary delivered one final gesture to the boys. She clasped her hands together and placed them on her heart, signifying the love she wished to share with Tony and his loyal friend.

Charlie stood by her side as proud as any father could be. Madame Liz looked like she was at peace with her passing, as she looked at the boys for one final time from beyond the other side. The three ghostly entities walked towards the two young men, stepping right through their physical beings.

The boys felt a sudden warmth and then simultaneously, they gasped for air, as if they had surfaced from a deep ocean dive.

The ghostly vision was gone. Mary and Charlie had left

them with one last gift: the ability to remember, but to not be mentally anguished by their experiences on the tower. Despite their grueling ordeal, the boys were now at inner peace.

CHAPTER THIRTY-NINE
For All, a Homeward Journey

Pam stood in Heaven in awe of the sight before her.

There stood her daughter and son-in-law, whom she had not seen for some time. The unexpected vision kept her staring in disbelief for the longest time. Next to her daughter were two female entities, unknown to Pam.

Simone and Madame Liz had already met—but in different states of existences.

One was of the spiritual plane and the other, the physical. Now they all stood on common ground, heavenly ground, re-acquainting themselves as if they were old friends.

Madame Liz had taken to her heavenly transition exceptionally well.

Beside them all stood the Archangel Michael with the restrained beast, Sebastian. Michael did not even stay to talk to Pam. He said a few words to Mary, Charlie and the immediate spiritual entities and then he was off to take Sebastian to face a higher order of Angels.

There would be much to gain by converting him to the heavenly ways.

If this daunting task could be achieved, Sebastian would be a prized trophy for Heaven—and a substantial loss to Lucifer. The conversion of the devil's soldier would take much work and even more patience, but this was too good an opportunity to miss.

The task required the work of the higher order Angel Zophiel, better known as the right hand Angel to God. Off went Michael to deliver his prized package.

Pam looked on, and after Archangel Michael had left, she made her way towards her daughter.

Mary ran towards her mother and was received in her extended arms. They embraced for the longest time.

During the loving hug, Pam was confronted by an old and bittersweet memory: the fear she would never see her daughter again. She recalled Mary and Charlie's sudden departure from Heaven; the memory still held some anxiety for her. "Where? Why the mystery?" Pam asked, while her daughter lay embraced in her mother's arms.

"Honestly, Mum, I didn't know. And it didn't make sense to me. Not at first, but I came to realize by protecting two of the sweetest children...her children, Mum," Mary said as she pointed to Simone who was nearby talking with the spiritual entity of Madame Liz.

"Through her children, I would eventually come to offer protection to my son. And, Mum ...," Mary paused as the emotion stirred within her and she sobbed for a moment, "...I got to pass on my love and say a final goodbye to Tony. He's grown into such a fine young man. He and Johnny. It was worth the wait."

Mary was emotional whilst Pam was churning all the information before her.

Two and two was just not adding up to make four. All this talk about spiritual protection and the sight of the Archangel with a demon from Hell. Pam knew the history of the boys. She was well aware of the angelic mission they carried out in Hell and she was even more aware of Lucifer and his sinister attempts to seek revenge on the boys and the Heavens.

Pam gasped with sudden fright. "Is Tony okay? What did that beast do to him?"

"Mum, he's fine. Johnny got cut up a bit, but he'll be okay.

They look after each other. There is absolutely nothing to worry about."

Pam was still puzzled by it all. Her mind was still trying to piece together the puzzle of Mary and Charlie's sudden departure from Heaven. The spiritual entities gathered around Pam. She was surrounded by Charlie, who embraced her after many years of absence, as well as Madame Liz and Simone.

"But why her children? Why protect two young children who lived on the other side of the world to our family?"

"It would have been too obvious, Mum," replied Charlie. "Lucifer needed to believe his plans to seek revenge on the boys would not be hindered. If we hung around the boys, he would have worked around it and come up with a plan to hurt the boys and us at the same time.

"This way, the element of surprise allowed me to step in. I got to stand side by side with Mary before Sebastian and we stopped him from inflicting irreparable damage to their souls."

"You got to hand it to God. Always one step ahead of the competition," remarked Simone.

"It brings true meaning to the phrase, 'God works in mysterious ways'," said Madame Liz. The group exchanged some light hearted laughs.

Pam joined in, even though her laughter hid her relief. She was so relieved that those that she cared for in the physical world were finally safe from harm.

Meanwhile, Johnny and Tony had remained true to their promise to Madame Liz.

They didn't say a word about their experience. Instead, they left it to the authorities to decipher what stood before them.

The boys spent the next few days dealing with officials.

Some of Europe's highest church representatives had flown to Germany to witness the sight sealed off to public viewing. They had not removed or moved the remains of Sebastian, whose flesh deteriorated into nothingness over the next few days.

Its form lay rotting on the cross for all to see only for a short while.

The sight of the hellish beast on the cross remained a church secret. Beyond senior church officials, only a handful of Germany's detective investigators were allowed to get involved.

In one final meeting seated in an isolated conference room, all those who had seen the hellish sight discussed their views. Church officials, detectives and two young Australian travellers listened to theories and drew conclusions. The boys kept their promise and maintained their silence.

Unanimously, the meeting room agreed as the chief detective in charge uttered these final words to close their very secretive meeting.

"The individual is smart, but the general public is not. If this was to get out, then there would be a mass panic."

Everyone in the meeting room understood and all signed an oath of honor.

Everyone who left the meeting that day never ever spoke another word about the unearthly vision and the tragic death of a fine human being.

Madame Liz had respectfully been removed from the cross and Josef was left to deal with her death. The funeral was private and simple.

Josef, the children, a small gathering and the boys held a closed and intimate sermon at the cathedral.

She would have been proud of the service her long time friend had arranged for her, but she would never see or hear about the event.

The priest from the Evangelische Kirche Werden delivered the funeral sermon. He was one of the select few invited to the funeral. The service he delivered for his old friend was one of his finest.

When everyone had left the service, the priest climbed the stairs of the tower and kissed the "Four children of Christ" at its center point. It lay there with no remaining signs of hellish flesh.

Taking his time, the priest hauled it down the stairs and placed it back in position. A little adjustment here and there and it soon appeared as though it had never been moved.

The boys had stayed on a little longer than they had expected. The last few days of their time in Germany had been, to say the least, full on.

In return for extending their time in Germany, the boys had been offered a first class flight back home, all expenses paid.

The last few days were busy and the time passed quickly. Tony and Johnny got up as their flight was being announced over the speakers in Frankfurt's airport.

Josef shook the hands of the young men.

"It was an honor to meet you both," said Josef.

The boys smiled back with warmth and affection.

"You are welcome in my home anytime," Josef added.

Anita and Günter embraced the two young men as if they were saying goodbye to old friends.

Tony kneeled down to face the children. He reached into his backpack and pulled out some fine German chocolates. Remaining on his knees, he embraced the children one last time.

With Günter on his right and Anita on his left, Tony cuddled them while Johnny stood tall by his friend's side.

Johnny affectionately ruffled the tops of their heads. It was his own little quirky way of saying goodbye.

The final call came over the intercom speaker.

"FINAL CALL FOR PASSENGERS BOARDING LUFTHANSA INTERNATIONAL FLIGHT TO AUSTRALIA"

THE END

About the Author

Eddie Georgonicas' passion for writing started probably a little later than most but when it came…the story needed to be told. With keen interests in the paranormal, after-life, horror and sci-fi genres, he hopes to entertain audiences for years to come. The launch of *Spiritual Dreams of a Heavenly War* is part of a trilogy ANARCHY OF ANGELS. He wishes you a safe journey (in book one) as you join two young friends as they venture deep into the land of Hades. You are now reading book two, *A Heavenly Interception* and in book three, *The Angelic Intent,* where Heaven finally succumbs to the demonic invasion. How will two young men on Earth help their efforts? Please reference www.eddiegeorgonicas.com for launch details of book three.

————————————

Spiritual Dreams of a Heavenly War
Book One in the Anarchy of Angels Trilogy

Tony's life has had its challenges and Johnny has always been there for him. Two young men, inseparable and as close as any two best friends could be. The Angels have been observing them for a long time. There is a plan in the making and they need their help. Every rule in Heaven will be broken in order to achieve this ultimate objective. And as a result, two young friends will die well before their intended times in order to help the Angelic intent. Selfish? Maybe but then again... Heaven gets more than what it bargained for. And Heaven is in more trouble that it lets on. The boys will come to see this as they go deep into the land of "fire and brimstone." They will come to venture where no Angel dare.

Coming Soon

The Angelic Intent
Book Three in the Anarchy of Angels Trilogy

Heaven finally succumbs to the demonic invasion. What part will Tony and Johnny play on Earth to help those in the spiritual dimension?

Please reference www.eddiegeorgonicas.com for further updates.

VISIT OUR WEBSITE
FOR THE FULL INVENTORY
OF QUALITY BOOKS:

http://www.roguephoenixpress.com

Representing Excellence in Publishing

Quality trade paperbacks and downloads

in multiple formats,

in genres ranging from historical to contemporary romance, mystery and science fiction.

Visit the website then bookmark it.

We add new titles each month!